THE PRODIGAL ONES

The One Who Wrote Away

JOANNA ALONZO

Published by: Hineni Publishing
Cover Designer: Joanna Alonzo

CONTENTS

THE ONE WHO NEEDS TO THANK SOME PEOPLE

To Anna, if not for your encouragement and prayers, this book wouldn't be here now. With all my heart, thank you.

Thanks to my family for bearing with me throughout this process.

Thanks to this book's beta readers — all 18 of you — for their invaluable feedback!

Thanks to the Author of Life for enabling me to write. May each word be incense, a sweet aroma rising to Your throne.

Δ . F . T . L .

To anyone who has ever
dreamed of writing a book.

The pen is your
superpower.

Find your noble theme,
and become the ready
writer.

THE ONE WHO WROTE AWAY

This is a story
About the outcasts
Who don't know how to blend.
About the lonely
Longing for a friend.
About the desperate
Who are trying to stay on trend.
About the creatives
Who are searching for an end.

This is the story
Of extrovert and introvert,
Caleb and Nova,
Who walked through life as strangers,
Until they discovered something deeper,
And ended up saving each other.

part one

PRESENT DAY
CIRCA 2000'S

one

THE ONE WHO LOST A BET

Shaken by an unexpected superpower reveal and a gut-wrenching murder, Caleb Grant dropped the thick, loosely bound manuscript from his hands to his lap. He took a deep breath to recover from the harrowing scene written in such a poignant way, he doubted he could ever shake it from his soul. Despite the hankering to find out what's next, Caleb's gut was still roiling from the betrayal a fictional character in the book had suffered. So, Caleb took pause, shifted on the dark-wood-and-black-metal bench, and re-calibrated his senses to focus on the park pulsing with life around him.

Suddenly, as if he had stepped out of another realm back to reality, his awareness of his earthly surroundings increased. The leaves of an evergreen tree rustled above him. A pop song played from a stereo nearby. Dog-walkers, cyclists, and random strangers went about their early morning routines, whizzing past the round water fountain facing Caleb. Hotdogs grilling nearby teased his nostrils. His stomach grumbled. A reminder of the breakfast he hadn't yet eaten. Caleb sighed. It could wait. To him, finishing this novel ranked much higher in his hierarchy of priorities.

Caleb took a few more seconds to absorb energy from all the activity going on around him. He needed to replenish his soul's strength if he was to finish this manuscript before he would need to rush off to work. He checked his watch. Eight o'clock. He still had an hour left. Eager to return to the gripping story that had somehow appeared out of thin air and fallen into his hands, Caleb was about to pick up the manuscript and delve back into the fictional world this mysterious author had created. However, a glimpse of something strange and curious jolted Caleb's attention away from one of the most riveting reads he had encountered in a long while.

Amid the hustle and bustle of strangers minding their own lives, a bunch of colorful helium balloons flailed in the air as whoever was carrying it zoomed forward with lightning speed.

Caleb dropped the manuscript to his side on the park bench — his favorite reading retreat whenever he wanted to get away from the stuffy office atmosphere. He angled his head forward, facing slightly to the right, and blinked his eyes to make sure he wasn't just seeing things.

No, definitely not a figment of his active imagination. There it was, a scene out of the ordinary unfolding before him.

On the path circling the water fountain, a little boy was running at a speed unnatural for a kid his size. The balloons were trying to keep up with him as they hung on strings clutched by his small hand. Quite a distance behind him was a masked woman with long, dark curls. Her pure white catsuit, silver utility belt, and blue knee-high leather boots made it seem like she had somehow escaped a graphic novel.

The boy was fast approaching Caleb when the woman — closing in on the kid — leaped over a running dog to the edge of the water fountain. She ran several steps at an almost 45-degree angle on the edge of the fountain and propelled herself forward by jumping from the fountain edge to the ground, then leaping up to step on the arm of the park bench Caleb was sitting on. Astounded, Caleb leaned back to avoid being swiped by her boot as she flew from one arm of the bench to the other and landed on the solid pavement, blocking the path of the balloon-carrying boy still running full-speed ahead.

Caleb's jaw dropped as he perused the stunning figure before him. Until that moment, Caleb had never understood all the Bible verses referring to beautiful women being like gazelles. Now it all made sense to him. *Heavenly Father above, she's magnificent.* He narrowed his eyes when he noticed the royal blue cape draped behind her back. She was like a character right out of the comic books he used to devour as a teenager.

With one hand planted on her waist and the other stretched in front of her in a gesture for the runaway kid to stop in his tracks, Caleb expected the boy to slow down to a full halt. But no. This kid would stop at nothing, and it seemed like the small unstoppable force was about to crash into this life-sized immovable superwoman. And Caleb was sitting there, holding his breath, privileged to witness every moment of this glorious scenario.

Sweet and spicy parkour. I must have done something right this morning if God is blessing me with a vision like this.

The boy rushed to ram his head into the woman's stomach as he yelled, "It's my birthday! These are mine!" Before his head could punch her in the gut, however, she gripped his shoulders and held him back.

"Kid, I bought these balloons. If you wanted them, you should have asked me for them. You shouldn't have stolen them and ran away."

"I didn't steal them! It's my birthday! The balloons belong to me!"

Both of them panting, the kid slumped himself on the ground, exhausted. Along with the sudden motion, he seemed to have forgotten about the balloons he was fighting for when he let go of the strings keeping them within his reach. The super woman gasped. Acting on reflex, Caleb grabbed as many of the strings as he could. Some of the balloons got away, although most stayed intact, clumped and tangled in his grip.

That's when the woman noticed him. Behind the plastic white mask covering the upper half of her face, her brown eyes flickered and widened at the sight of him. "You!" she exclaimed.

"Me?" Caleb asked. Did this stunning stranger know him?

Her mouth parted to say something, but the boy suddenly started wailing. "Those are mine!"

The woman's attention shifted back to the little thief. Her shoulders slumped. "Come on, kid. Where are your parents, anyway? Why are you in a park all alone?"

Caleb cleared his throat and pointed to an exhausted-looking couple jogging toward them. Both were panting for breath as they approached.

"We're so sorry," the man managed to say in between gasps for air. "We tried to stop him. He's too fast."

At this point, the kid was already having a meltdown on the ground, yelling, kicking, and crying to get his balloons back. Meanwhile, Caleb sat on the edge of his seat, clutching a bunch of balloons, wondering who this woman was and what she needed all these balloons for. Also, why did she yell "you!" upon seeing him? He still couldn't quite make sense of what was happening, but one thing Caleb Grant knew for sure was this: that day couldn't end without him finding out the name of this beautiful strangeness God had somehow saved for him to meet that day.

Just like that, Nova Stone watched a decade of deliberate and strategic avoidance circle down the proverbial drain. Caleb Grant was looking — no, staring — at her like she was a shocking mutation produced out of a lab experiment.

This wasn't how she had imagined their first meeting would be; then again, she hadn't quite predicted them ever meeting — not when she had been dead set on making sure that would never happen.

Yet, here she was, in full costume, standing in front of her childhood crush. All because of that stupid bet! She should have listened to her mother who, since they were young, had cautioned her and her brothers never to gamble. "Gambling ruins families," Clara Stone had always said before explaining how their grandfather had lost their family fortune to casinos.

The bet Nova had gotten herself into was now rewarding her — as well as this kid's family — a disastrous morning. She assumed the couple catching their breaths were the parents of the boy who had stolen her balloons — the boy who was now rolling on the ground, yelling for justice, because she had bought the balloons a few minutes before they could.

With her ultimate crush holding the balloons and the strangers trying to console their child, nonplussed, Nova made a mental note to kill Vienna and Miles later. If only this skintight costume came with actual superpowers!

Caleb cleared his throat. "Hi. Hey. So—" he extended his arm forward to bring the balloons closer to her "—these are yours?"

Nova bit her lip and nodded.

"No!" the boy objected. "They're mine! Those are mine!"

The mother cast an apologetic glance at her.

Nova gulped. "Your kid sure can run," she mumbled.

"He can." The mother sighed. "He's part of his school's track team. His therapist advised that he join because he's so hyperactive. It's a means to release all that energy."

"Mom, I want the balloons!"

Nova had never seen a kid cry, kick, scream, and make this much of a ruckus before. As a kid, her younger brother, Nolan, had mostly been precocious and well-behaved. Nova tilted her head to the side. She made another mental note to send him a text message to ask how his college applications were going. Her heart sank upon recalling that Nolan would leave home soon.

"Hey, kid." Caleb's voice yanked thoughts of her brother's impending departure away from Nova. He handed her the balloons and crouched on the ground to talk to the child. "It's your birthday, huh? Happy birthday!" He patted the boy on the head. "How old are you?"

"Seven." The child whimpered.

"That's awesome! It's amazing how fast you run at that age! Super woman here was barely able to catch you. I'm so much older than you are, but I probably can't run as fast as you can."

A flicker of wonder in a morning that was turning out to be one of Nova's strangest, the boy blinked his eyes, looked at Caleb, and sat up. He nodded slowly. "I'm the fastest one in my whooooole—" he made a big circle with his arms "—world."

Caleb chuckled. "Your whole world, huh?"

The huge beam that formed on the kid's face showed two missing teeth. "I get in trouble because of it a lot of times, but sometimes, if I run really really fast, the trouble doesn't catch up with me." He squinted his eyes and sent Nova a death glare. "She did, though."

Nova debated within whether to be offended or amused. Did this child just refer to her as trouble? After he made her chase him all over the park on a day when she needed to be early for work? Nova facepalmed. Work! She wouldn't be able to show her face in that office again if she walked in late for work dressed the way she was.

"I have to go," she said. "Are we okay here?"

The parents nodded, but Caleb didn't even bother to acknowledge her, his focus fully on the boy.

"Do you want all the balloons?" he asked.

The boy nodded.

"Well, Miss Trouble here seems to have already paid for these. We're not sure what she needs them for, but can she give you one balloon instead of all to wish you happy birthday?"

The kid scrunched his nose. "I can't fly with only one balloon."

Caleb shrugged. "You can't fly with all of them either, but what does that matter? When you run, it's almost like you're flying already."

That statement animated the boy's face. "You think so?"

"Sure. It's rather impressive." Caleb turned to her. "Hi again. Do you mind giving him one balloon?"

Nova shrugged. "Sure." She pulled out a balloon and handed it over to Caleb.

The moment Caleb took it and turned his back to her, Nova waved goodbye to the parents, whose quizzical glances at her were starting to make her antsy. Of course, she couldn't quite blame them, could she? Not when she was walking around in public, dressed like a deranged superhero.

Without bothering to even give Caleb a second glance, she ran off. After all, upon reaching the office, she could still look forward to a full day of figuring out how to survive the office without again bumping into Caleb Grant.

two

THE **O**NE WHO **C**AN'T **S**TOP LOOKING

From a distance, the shimmer of the sun's reflection on its glass panels and the geometric architecture of the skyscraper made Caine Tower look like a futuristic fortress straight out of a science fiction novel. One could almost imagine both the alter egos of a superhero and a super villain working there, their hidden identities waiting to be exposed.

Nova huffed. Perhaps her imagination was trying to calm her down as she stood at the foot of the fifty-five-floor building. She tried to ignore the curious stares passersby were shooting at her wacky ensemble. A breeze was making the balloons bounce against each other, and the sound of plastic bumping plastic was irritating her eardrums.

Nova wrinkled her nose and took a deep breath to gain courage for what was ahead. Not too long ago, building security had kicked a clown out of Caine Tower. Rumors flew across Caine Corp headquarters that the Caine family had forbidden clowns from ever entering any of their premises. Why, Nova could only guess, but the growing odds they would classify her as a clown — balloons and all — and kick her out of her workplace niggled at her.

How had she gotten roped into this?

"What are you waiting for, Super Nova?" Vienna Boulevard's arm brushed against hers.

"Super Nova would make a great superhero name." Miles Bailey stepped to her other side, squeezing Nova between her two coworkers, as he tried to bat the flailing balloons away from his face. "Super Nova already sounds so brilliantly explosive, and Nova, baby, that costume is fire on you!"

Nova groaned. "Don't call me that."

"Call you what?" Vienna linked arms with her. "Super Nova or Nova baby?"

"Both." They began walking toward the entrance.

"I should have brought my camera." Miles rushed ahead of them and walked backwards to face Nova and get a good look at her. He shook his head slowly. "Amazing. Also, stunning work on the costume, Vienna. I can't wait to see the looks on their faces."

"Thank you!" Vienna bowed her head in acknowledgment. "I wasn't sure Nova would wear it, but I'm glad she did."

"Do I have to wear this the whole day?" Nova made a face.

"Bet's a bet, Nova!" Miles shrugged.

"I need this job, you know." Nova's nervousness grew as they neared the entrance. "They won't let me in, Miles, or worse, Steve will fire me, and it will be all your fault."

"Are you kidding?" Miles laughed. "Steve will lose his mind when he sees you. You probably won't just get a permanent job at Frontier Press after this. You'll get a promotion." He winked at her before turning his back on them to walk ahead into the building. "You'll thank me for this someday, Nova Stone!" he said as he walked ahead.

Nova slowed down. Promotion? What was the man going on about? Was he delusional?

"Hey." Vienna nudged Nova on the shoulder. "It'll be fine. We already told Steve you lost a bet, so we made you wear a costume today. He knows what you have to do and already warned all the people on the list that a surprise will come through their door today. Trust me, Nova. This will be good for you.

If you want to go from temp to a regular employee, you need to be memorable. This stunt will put you on the map. I think Miles did you a favor when he convinced you to do this."

"I want to be remembered — and hired — for the quality of my work, Vienna. Showing up to work like this makes me feel like a side show attraction."

"A gorgeous one. Believe it or not, Nova, no one will soon forget the way you look right now."

Nova winced. She was hoping people would forget. After all, she had never worn anything as daring as the jumpsuit Vienna had gotten her to wear. Her choice of clothes had always been a lot less flashy — frumpier, according to Vienna — compared to this.

But, she was here now. She had gotten herself into this. She might as well push through with it. So, Nova inhaled, squared her shoulders, and exhaled. Maybe Vienna and Miles were right. It was time to pitch her novel to the agents of Frontier Press, and the costume would probably give her the confidence she needed to do it. Her superhero alter ego might have the power to turn her life around and take her from temp at the publishing arm of Caine Corp to one of its published authors.

Thus, Nova conjured up every last shred of confidence she could muster and strode into Caine Tower, determined to push through with the challenge Miles and Vienna had given her.

At worst, this could be the most humiliating day of her life; Nova didn't mind a little embarrassment. At best, it could give her some visibility and create a path toward the career she had always dreamed of.

Either way, Miles Bailey would never again have the right to accuse her of lacking the courage to go after her dreams. She might have lost their bet, but she intended to come out of this challenge victorious.

The only problem was the last name on the list of people she needed to visit that day.

Caleb Grant.

How she intended to avoid him and still give him a pitch to her novel, Nova wasn't sure, but she had avoided him for the past twelve years. Surely she could get through this for the next few hours.

So, off she went.

Half an hour later, Nova knocked on the office door of the first agent on the list — upon seeing her, the assistant had smiled and waved for her to go ahead. Vienna must have been right. Their manager, Steve, had already given out warnings that a costumed woman would show up to some of the offices.

The agent's eyes widened at the sight of her.

"Interesting," she said.

Nova tried to push back the urge to throw up. "Hello, Miss Hall," she said before proceeding with the script Miles had written out for her. "I'm Nova Stone. I'm a temp working for Mr. Steve Chen in Marketing, and it would be an honor if you would consider representing a novel I wrote. It's a superhero retelling of The Count of Monte Cristo."

The agent's brow quirked up. "Sounds fascinating, hon, but I represent clean romance novels. I doubt I'll be the best agent for a story like that."

Nova sighed. Miles's stipulation that she had to do this with every agent and editor in the company — regardless of what types of books and genres they represented — had to be the most ridiculous and humiliating part of this task. "I completely understand. Here's a balloon anyway — something to brighten up your day! My number is on the balloon, in case you change your mind."

The agent glanced at the balloon and nodded upon seeing a piece of paper taped to it. By the expression on her face, Nova wouldn't be surprised if, by the end of day, more than a handful of employee complaints would be filed against her for wasting everybody's time.

Miles and Vienna had been convinced this would grab attention, and it surely did. Another agent and two editors later, it became obvious to Nova that her years of steering clear of Caleb Grant's path was about to come to a screeching halt. She would have to pitch her novel to him and risk the possibility of him finally seeing her, finally realizing that she had always been in his life, existing, inspired by him.

Caleb's forehead creased as he re-read a line in a page he had mostly skimmed through, because his thoughts kept meandering back to a parkour-powered superhero. Who was that woman? How did she know him and he not know her? Surely, he would remember meeting a woman like that.

He rocked his head to get back to the manuscript, because he still had at least half an hour before he needed to show up at work.

He paused. Was it possible for him to read through the rest of the story at the park? He had nothing scheduled that day except to find a book and an author to present at their next monthly pitch meeting. All of his other clients were either writing their books or waiting to go through yet another stage on the road to their book being published. Technically, this was his work, and he would be able to do it so much better outdoors, at the park, instead of inside a stuffy office.

Caleb took out his phone and typed a message for his assistant, informing her that if anyone looked for him, he was at the park outside their office building, reading what he thought had the potential to be their next bestseller.

Satisfied, Caleb returned to his reading bench under a tree and dove back into the story. As the tension escalated and everything began closing in on the main protagonist, Caleb found himself holding his breath multiple times.

Right when the book was about to reach its climax, just before a huge character reveal, it ended. Mid-sentence.

Stunned, Caleb checked and re-checked the perfectly bound manuscript if some pages had somehow been misplaced. No. There was no mistake about it. He was holding approximately ninety percent of an unfinished manuscript — one containing a story he desperately wanted a conclusion to.

Caleb flipped back to the front page of the manuscript. *Edge of Darkness* by Alex Orwell, it said. No address. No contact information. Just the sticky note that came with the spiral-bound manuscript some anonymous person had left on his desk weeks ago. *You won't regret reading this*, the note said. Caleb gritted his teeth. How could a writer stop the story at a point like this? He flipped to the next page and smiled at the epigraph before the first chapter.

"It's necessary to have wished for death in order to know how good it is to live."
- Alexandre Dumas, *The Count of Monte Cristo*

It had been years since he had first read *The Count of Monte Cristo*. This very quote was what had gripped him from the beginning and caused him to keep reading *Edge of Darkness*. The sharp wit and scalpel of Dr. Edge as he rose out of the ruins of injustice and built a medical empire designed to decimate his enemies had lured Caleb into a fascinating world of this author's making, and now, all Caleb had was a cliffhanger that would eat him up for days. Who was this Alex Orwell?! How on earth was Caleb going to find him?

Flustered, Caleb rushed back to the office, on a mission to discover the identity of this author. His first instinct was to go to HR to find out if he could ask around about the owner of the manuscript. It was a long shot, but it was worth a try.

When he reached the office, however, as he waited for the elevator to reach his floor, his determination grew. Whoever this Orwell fellow was, Caleb wanted to be his agent, so instead of going to HR, he ended up a few more floors up — right to the office of his boss, Ethan Caine.

"He's not present at the moment, but I can leave a message for him, if you wish," Mr. Caine's executive assistant explained.

Caleb shook his head. "It's fine. I'm sure I'll catch him once he's around. Thank you."

It was probably for the better. After all, how could he pitch a novel to his boss without knowing who the author was?

Still shaken by the events in the novel leading up to the missing pages, Caleb drifted back to his office. He groaned inside as he neared the private room. He missed being in a cubicle surrounded by other people and couldn't understand what was great about having a corner office with a view. Dreading the solitude, it was to Caleb's delight when he reached his office and discovered he wouldn't be alone. His delight fused with surprise, because he never would've expected to find the balloon-wielding park superhero in his office, looking just as stunning as she had earlier that morning.

She stood in the middle of his office, holding a single red balloon. She shuffled on her feet, as if unsure whether to stay or leave. The red tint on her cheeks — only half-hidden by the mask covering her brown eyes — triggered his curiosity.

"You!" he said, mimicking the way she had said it at the park.

"H-hello, Mr. G-Grant. I—" She bit her lip.

Why she was stuttering was beyond him. Was she nervous? Why? But wait. She called him Mr. Grant. She did know him!

"I don't believe we've ever met," he said when she didn't continue talking. "At least not before we saw each other at the park this morning."

She gulped.

He smiled at the way her jaw slightly tilted upwards as she did. "May I know your name?"

"Uhm, yes! Sure. Nova!" she exclaimed. "I'm Nova Stone."

Caleb took a step forward as his mind raced to process why the name was familiar. "Are you related to Nolan Stone?"

"I'm his sister."

"He goes to our church."

"Right." Nova's shoulders straightened as she handed him the balloon. "I'm so sorry to disturb you, Mr. Grant. I was just— Perhaps I should go." She brushed past him and rushed toward the elevators.

"Miss Stone, wait!"

Still, off she went.

Caleb stepped out of his office to watch her rush into the elevator, running faster than she had earlier while chasing after speedster boy at the park.

Across the hallway from his office, his elderly assistant, Molly, peered at him from her cubicle. "Was her pitch any good?"

"Pitch?"

"Her boss at Marketing explained how she lost a bet, so they dared her to pitch her novel to all the agents in the office. Something about getting her out of her shell."

Caleb shrugged. "Well, she gave me this red balloon and her name. She didn't pitch me anything."

"Ah well, she's lovely, isn't she?"

To that, Caleb could only agree. If she was Nolan Stone's sister, had she ever gone to their church before? How had he never noticed her?

He would have to ask Hannah after work. Right now, he had to somehow put aside thoughts of Nova Stone and clear a way for him to commence his quest to find an author named Alex Orwell.

three

THE ONE
WHO WROTE
THE NOVEL

As he neared the end of his workday, the image of Nova Stone running away was still lingering on Caleb's mind. He had half the mind to go to the Marketing Department to ask her about her novel pitch, so she could fill him in on whatever he had missed. However, for one thing, based on how fast she had run from him, she wasn't in the proper state of mind to pitch a novel to him; for another, it was still his work hours, and he still had work to do.

Caleb stared at the incomplete manuscript on top of his desk. Who was this Alex Orwell? What author in their right mind would give a literary agent an unfinished manuscript? Even if it was one as great as this! Caleb rubbed his palm against his forehead. This cliffhanger was going to kill him. Who was helping Dr. Edge all along? Was it who Caleb thought it was?

"I need to find this guy." Caleb leaned back in his black leather swivel chair. Upon thinking of Alex Orwell, it drew a huge blank in his mind, and amid that space, an image of Nova from that morning at the park emerged. Caleb smiled at the recollection of her standing in the speeding boy's way, her hand raised to stop him from barreling into her. Who was Nova Stone, why had she run, and why had Caleb never encountered her before?

A knock on his door pushed Nova to the back of his mind. Caleb was about to rise from his seat, but it swung open before he could even budge. Into his office strode his boss, Ethan Caine, part-owner of Caine Corp, and CEO of Frontier Press. He sat on the cushioned chair next to Caleb's desk.

"Mr. Grant, I heard you were looking for me." Ethan checked his watch. "I have half an hour. How can I help you?"

Surprised his boss would go to his office and not call him up to the CEO's office instead, Caleb scrambled for words to say before clearing his throat and tapping on the manuscript in front of him. "I think I found an incredible manuscript that I believe in and would love to represent. It's a superhero novel that is a loose retelling of *The Count of Monte Cristo* by Alexandre Dumas..." Caleb spent the next ten minutes gushing over what he had just read. By the end of his pitch, Caleb was so fired up, he had almost forgotten why he had wanted to go see Ethan in the first place. Caleb sighed when he remembered the main issue. "The only problem is the manuscript isn't finished, and I have no idea who Alex Orwell is."

Ethan smiled as he tapped his palms over the arms of his chair. "It's good to see you so passionate about this, Caleb, and from what you've told me, it sounds like a piece of work we can all get behind. There's definitely a market for it, and if it's as well-written and as well-told as you make it seem — enough for you to gush about it the way you do — then we might be sitting on a gold mine here, but—" Ethan sighed.

"But?"

"There's not much we can do until you find the author of the novel, so why exactly did you want to see me, Mr. Grant? What can I do for you?"

Caleb sat up straight, so he could level with his boss. "Someone left the manuscript on my table with a note. It wasn't mailed in — definitely unsolicited. I'm hoping the writer is working for Frontier Press. Can I have permission to use office resources to look for the author?"

"Office resources?"

"Nothing out of the ordinary. I just want to ask around and make sure you're aware before I do anything."

"I appreciate being given notice." Ethan's expression dimmed. "It's more than some have the courtesy to give. Can you believe one of the temps went around the entire company in a superhero costume passing out balloons to pitch her novel? Some sort of lost bet. Their department head gave the go ahead for it, but no one bothered to inform me."

Caleb bristled. How could he help get Nova out of this mess? "Is she in trouble for that?"

"You know about it? Did you come across her today?"

Caleb nodded slowly. "Yes, I did." He couldn't lie, no matter how much he wished he could protect her.

"Was her novel pitch any good at least?"

"We didn't get to that part." Caleb scratched his head. "She ran out of my office without telling me anything. I'm guessing she's embarrassed by the whole thing if the only reason she's doing it is to square a lost bet."

Ethan shrugged. "I plan to talk with the head of marketing about it. While I'm happy to encourage creativity in the workplace, I would also like to receive a heads up regarding stunts like these. Let one get away with it, and before we know it, we have temps running around in costume, pitching their random ideas to everyone."

Caleb flinched. Was Nova in trouble? Should he find a way to warn her? Maybe that was a good excuse for him to visit the marketing department to see her. He caught himself. Why did he care so much about Nova? The image of her at the park leaping from the fountain to his bench crossed his mind. Beautiful like a gazelle. That was why. Caleb cleared his throat and shifted in his seat to snap his brain out of the park with superhero-clad Nova and back to the office with his boss. "Would you have given permission had she asked for it?"

Ethan rubbed his clean-shaven jaw with his thumb and forefinger. "I don't know. It's always a case-by-case basis. It's a good thing the office wasn't too busy when she chose to do it. From what I heard, they've been planning for her to do this for weeks now, but they made sure to pull it off on a calm day at the office. That's a point for their team, at least. Well, anyway, you have my permission to find whomever this Alex Orwell is. Hopefully, the person is in this office, though there's no one here by that name."

"Most likely a pen name," Caleb said.

"I gathered." Ethan straightened up on his seat and waved a hand dismissively at Caleb. "Do what you must, Mr. Grant. I trust your instincts. Your father has always had a knack for discovering great literature that appeals to the masses. I'm sure you will do everything in your power to preserve his legacy here at Frontier Press."

Caleb tried not to cringe. Marcus Grant represented such a great part of the kind of man he wanted to become, and he was never certain if he could ever get there. "I'll do my best, Mr. Caine."

"I'm sure you will." Ethan stood up, and Caleb quickly followed suit. "If you need anything else, Mr. Grant, feel free to approach me. I have such a deep respect for your father, and I would like to make sure you feel comfortable and valued here at Frontier Press."

"Thank you. I'm honored and grateful to have your support." Caleb shook his boss's hand before heading to the door to open it for Ethan. A quick look around revealed that the office was already half-empty. He checked the time on his watch. It was past six. Caleb frowned. He could worry about Alex Orwell and Nova Stone later. His sister would chew him out if he showed up late for dinner that evening — especially with guests coming over.

Half an hour later, he arrived at the apartment he shared with his sister. Thuds and clinks in the kitchen preceded Hannah's voice calling out to him. "Caleb! You're finally here!"

"Sorry, I'm late. I had a last-minute meeting with my boss." Caleb removed his jacket and hung it on the coat and hat rack.

"Isaac and Kelly are already on their way here."

Caleb made his way from the entryway to the kitchen. "How can I help?"

"You can mince the onion and garlic for my stir fry."

"I'm on it."

"Everything is already on the counter," she said.

No sooner had Caleb finished when a buzz sounded from the door. He rushed to open it and found his older brother and sister-in-law waiting in the hallway.

"Where are the kids?" Caleb asked. He had assumed they would bring his nephew and niece with them.

"One of the ladies at church volunteered to babysit tonight. Thank God!" Kelly gave Caleb a hug. "Hi, Caleb." She walked right in and made her way to the kitchen. "Hannah!"

While the ladies chatted away, Caleb clapped his brother's shoulders. "Bro. How's everything going? I have to say I'm disappointed my nephew and niece aren't here."

"I'm not." Isaac shook his head as he walked into the small entryway. "Kelly and I could both use a break. Especially her. It's amazing Mrs. P. volunteered to babysit."

"Miss Rhoda?" Caleb threw his head back in surprise. "Who's taking care of her daughter?" He closed the door behind him.

"Rachel's at our place with the kids. I figured maybe Mrs. P. also wanted Rachel to have some playmates."

Caleb shrugged. "Anyway, I'm glad you're here."

Isaac laughed. "So am I. Hannah, what are you cooking? I'm starving!"

In the hour that followed, Kelly helped Hannah get everything ready while Caleb caught his brother up on updates from Josh and his missionary adventures with their father and mother. Isaac updated him on how the younger twins, Sam and Deb, were faring at university.

Only after they said grace and started eating did the events at work earlier catch up with Caleb. So, as everyone dug into their food, Caleb asked what he presumed was a random question. "Did you guys know Nolan Stone has a sister?"

Hannah and Kelly exchanged glances before shooting Caleb a funny look.

Isaac creased his brows as his forkful of vegetables froze midair from the plate to his mouth. "You mean Nova?"

Caleb swallowed his mashed potatoes. "You know her?"

"You don't?" Hannah tilted her head to the side. "She's been to several of our summer camps, and she started attending church regularly again not long after Nolan came back."

"You mean after Clara's husband died?"

"Right," Kelly said. "Nova helps with Sunday School sometimes. She's one of the children's favorite teachers. She's amazing with kids. I've seen her silence a roomful of children just by telling a story."

"So you know her pretty well then?" Caleb asked Hannah.

"We're not super close, but we're friends, for sure," Hannah said. "She tends to be quiet, so she kind of fades into the background. Especially when her brother is around."

"Makes sense." Caleb grinned. "Nolan can definitely catch and hold people's attention for as long as he wants."

"That kid is a star-in-the-making," Kelly said. "I don't think Nova minds him outshining her, but she's great to talk to once she gets more comfortable around you."

Caleb frowned. "How come I don't remember ever meeting her or even seeing her?"

"Where have you been?" Hannah smirked. "Don't you remember seeing her at her father's wake? The funeral?"

"The only thing I remember about their father's wake was Nolan's performance, and I wasn't at the funeral."

Hannah frowned. "Where were you then?"

"Where else?" Isaac shrugged a shoulder. "He was probably with Olivia."

The women laughed.

Caleb rolled his eyes, but the mere mention of his ex-girlfriend's name made him grit his teeth. He had to make a conscious effort to push away the jadedness that came with Olivia's memory. He needed to forget about her. A glimpse of Nova in his office handing him a balloon flickered across his mind. He smiled. Forgetting Olivia might be much more doable now that Nova was in his life. If only he could get her to stop running away.

"Nova Stone, you can run but you can't hide."

"I'm not running from anything." Nova's fingers flew across her computer keyboard to encode the letter her boss had handed over earlier.

"You owe me one then," Miles said.

Nova typed the last character of the letter, clicked on the save button, and peered past her computer screen to find Miles leaning his elbow on her cubicle's partition, a wolfish grin on his face. "I owe you nothing," she said.

"Oh, but you do." He winked.

"We kind of did something." Vienna's head popped up from the cubicle next to Nova's. "Please don't get angry."

"Why would she be angry?" Miles scoffed. "She should be thanking us!"

"Vienna." Nova gave her friend a glare. "What did you guys do this time?"

"We helped you become a star author, that's what!" Miles threw his arms in the air before making a whooshing sound with his lips to mimic the sound of wild applause. "Thank you! Thank you!"

"What do you mean a star—" Nova's jaw dropped. "Vienna! What did you do?"

"Remember when Caleb got transferred from his position at Caine Corp, so he can become an agent at Frontier Press?" Vienna scrunched one side of her face up.

"How can I not?" Nova wrinkled her nose. "It's how I lost our bet."

"Well, yeah." Vienna cringed. "You know how you keep a copy of your novel in your personal folder? Miles and I found that when you were still pretty new. We've been reading it."

Nova's cheeks burned — whether out of anger or shame, she wasn't sure. "That's private property! I can't believe you were snooping around in my computer!"

"We tried to respect that, Nova! We did, but we caught you checking the manuscript during one of our lunch breaks, so we kind of took a peek, and the moment we read the first line, Dr. Edge had us wrapped around his surgically skilled fingers."

Nova tried to search for words to say but came up blank.

"Now that you're aware we've been reading it—" Miles nodded his head like he had done nothing wrong "—can you please tell us how it ends? Have you finished it?"

"Are you kidding me, Miles? You weren't supposed to—" She stopped. "Wait. What did you do? What does any of this have to do with Caleb's new position?"

"Well, on his first day as agent, Miles printed out a copy of your manuscript and left it on his desk."

The news numbed Nova — like it was her worst nightmare and grandest dream coming true all at the same time, and those two extremes balanced out her emotions. "You left my manuscript on Caleb's desk? Miles, why would you do that? You had no right! Also, why him of all people?"

"Why not him?" Miles shrugged. "He's the one who would most likely be interested in your novel's genre, which is why I don't understand why he didn't connect the dots when you pitched the novel to him yesterday."

"I can't believe you would do that, Miles. That's overstepping." Nova buried her face in her palms. "I would die of embarrassment, but I can't. I have to punish you first. You're unbelievable!"

"Sure. We can do all that punishing later." Miles huffed. "Don't change the subject, though. How did your pitch to Agent Grant go yesterday?"

Nova lowered her hands to clear her vision, but even uncovered, it was as if everything around her had gone blurry. Her mind was a carousel spinning so out of control, all its bits and bobs were about to get dismantled and thrown into the air. If Nova could control the carousel, she would make one horse fly right at Miles. She shot him a glare before shaking her head. "I didn't pitch the novel to him." She bit her lip. "But, I gave him the balloon, so that's pretty much a pitch already!"

"Nova, nooooo..." A mix of concern and amusement laced Vienna's voice. "You didn't just give him a balloon and run, did you?"

Nova blushed at the recollection of Caleb's face when he had found her in his office. She was on his radar now, and she would give anything to hide herself from him once again. "I couldn't do it. You don't understand how hard it was for me to face him."

"Don't worry about it," Miles said. "It doesn't matter now, because, as I said earlier, you should thank us, Nova, my sweet."

She scowled at him. "The last thing I want to do right now is thank you, Miles."

"You will when you find out the good news — so good that I bothered to stop by your cubicle during my coffee break." Miles wagged a finger at her. "I deserve to be in the acknowledgments page of your book, authoress."

"Just tell her, Miles."

"Word around the office is that Caleb Grant is hunting down Alex Orwell. He — like Vienna and I — can't wait to find out how the novel ends."

Try as hard as she could to process everything Miles had said, Nova couldn't quite catch up. Caleb read her novel? Did he like it? Should she resign now? Because the last thing she wanted to do was reveal to him she was Alex Orwell.

"You have to go tell him you're Alex Orwell, Nova," Vienna said. "Honestly, he's new as an agent, and he has such big shoes to fill with his father being Marcus Grant and all, so we didn't even think he would give an unsolicited manuscript by an unknown author a chance."

"Apparently, he did. Now, here we are, and you, Nova Stone, owe me." The smuggest smile appeared on Miles's face. "Especially now that I know you didn't even fulfill your end of the bet."

"Hey! I did everything you asked me to!" Nova frowned. "I was tired. He was the last person on the list. I couldn't go through with it."

"Well, now is your chance to reveal yourself to him, not only as the girl behind yesterday's mask but also as his new favorite author." Miles grabbed the back rest of her swivel chair and started pulling it.

"Miles! Stop!"

"Come on, Nova. It's the right thing to do."

"I'll pitch it to him, okay? Just give me time to recover."

"If you're scared he won't like you—" Miles sighed "—trust me on this. He will. I would like you if I wasn't already in a relationship with Vienna."

"Ha!" Vienna rolled her eyes. "You wish, Miles."

"Fine, fine. I get it. We're all chummy friends." Miles shook his head. "I'll go get my coffee. Don't forget to secure your agent, Nova. A lot of authors would do anything to be in the position you're in, so you're welcome."

Nova watched him go. "I don't understand why almost half of the women in this office have a crush on him."

"And yet, he chose to hang out with the two women here who refuse to have anything romantic to do with him." Vienna smirked.

"I'll give it to him. He handles rejection well."

"Only guy I know who turns rejection into friendship — the most annoying kind."

Nova sighed. As much as Miles got on her nerves, she felt safe around him. She liked that he didn't hold it against her when she rejected a date with him her first week at Frontier Press. She appreciated how they had remained friends; she couldn't say the same of other men in her life. Was Caleb more like him or those other men? What if Caleb turned out to be just like her father? Or maybe like her high school best friend — someone she had once leaned on and trusted, only to have him prove himself a wolf in sheep's clothing. Nova shuddered. Both faces left a bitter taste in her mouth. Caleb couldn't possibly be like either one of them. Of course, there was only one way to find out. She had to get to know Caleb, but Nova wasn't sure she was ready to meet the real Caleb Grant — not just the idealized version of him she had invented in her head since she had first laid eyes on him.

"Nova, you are going to see Caleb about the novel, right?" Vienna leaned her chin over her arm, which she had laid flat on the cubicle partition. "We did overstep, and for that, I apologize, but still. It's an amazing opportunity, and who better to work on that novel with you than someone you already respect and admire?"

"You're right." Nova conceded. "I'll face him, eventually. I just need to gather the courage. We didn't meet under ideal circumstances yesterday."

"You know Miles and I mean well, right? We believe in your work and in you."

"I know." Nova forced a smile. "Thank you, Vienna."

Nova returned to her work, and despite her heart pounding against her chest from anxiety over the predicament her friends had yanked her into, Nova thanked God for them. She had prayed for Him to give her friends in her new workplace, and it took but one week for her to hit it off with Miles and Vienna. Still, she couldn't believe they had done something like this!

Nova took a deep breath. Maybe she should just get this over with and march into Caleb's office. But what if he wasn't there? Should she schedule a meet-up?

She looked at the spreadsheet on the screen of her computer. She could barely make out the numbers all clustered together as she tried to decide what to do.

Hours whiled away, and Nova remained undecided and unproductive. Before she knew it, the day had ended, and she still had zero courage to go see Caleb.

"Tomorrow," Nova told herself. "It can wait until tomorrow. I won't let Miles and Vienna pressure me into this. It'll have to be on my own time."

"Are you talking to yourself?"

Nova froze. She raised her gaze from the computer screen — now shutting down. She swallowed hard.

There in front of her was Caleb Grant.

He smiled to show off a set of perfect teeth. "I'm not sure what to call you. Is it Nova Stone? Or is it Alex Orwell?"

four

THE ONE
WHO SAW HER
SMILE

Nova Stone was staring at him like he had caught her committing a crime. Whatever heinous thing she had done, Caleb was now complicit, because he couldn't bear the thought of turning her over to concerned authorities. Caleb gritted his teeth. This was the revenge plot of Dr. Edge messing with his head. He needed to know how Dr. Edge's story ended! It had been a long time since he had been so invested in a fictional character, a character whom the beautiful young woman in front of him created under the name of Alex Orwell — assuming Caleb's guess was correct, that is. Was Nova Stone the author he was looking for? Was she Alex Orwell?

From the guilty look on her face, Caleb's confidence grew. He had found his author. If only he would snap out of perusing her lovely face now that it was no longer hidden by the mask she had worn yesterday. Big brown eyes framed by delicate angles of an oval face with a firm jawline matched her long nose and full lips. His pulse doubled at the idea of seeing her smile. She must have a lovely smile. If only he could say or do something to deserve to see it. His gaze fell between her collarbones. He furrowed his brows at how her chest remained steady. Had she breathed at all since he had asked her if she was Alex Orwell?

"Mr. G-Grant?" Her voice cracked when she spoke out his surname.

Caleb's breath hitched before he raised his gaze to meet hers. Heat rushed to his cheeks. How long had he been standing there staring at her? "I would prefer it if you call me Caleb."

"Of course. Caleb." Her jaw tightened when she swallowed. She shifted in her chair and fidgeted with her fingers.

Bothered by how uncomfortable she seemed, Caleb handed her a piece of paper his assistant had found inside the balloon Nova had given him the day before. "The balloon popped," he said. "Molly found this when I asked her to throw it out."

Nova took the note from him and read what was on it. A deep shade of red brushed her cheekbones.

"Did all the balloons from the park have that note inside?"

Nova nodded. "I already talked to the guy selling them the day before." The corners of her lips lifted ever so slightly, hinting at a dimple on her left cheek.

"I see. That's why you were so intent on getting them back from the boy." Caleb leaned his arm on the cubicle partition standing between them. "We wouldn't have wanted all your novel's blurbs to go to him, would we?" He narrowed his eyes at her. "Which then makes me wonder why you didn't pitch your novel to me yesterday. It would have saved me an entire day of trying to figure out who Alex Orwell is. The only reason I found out is because one of my fellow agents told me what you pitched to her, and it sounded strangely similar to this amazing — *unfinished* — manuscript I'm reading. It clicked in my head even more when Molly gave me this note from your balloon. Did you write this blurb? I hate to say it, but it doesn't quite do the novel justice."

"You've read it?" Nova gulped. "The manuscript, I mean."

"I have, and I would like to read the rest, if you would let me. Have you finished writing it?"

She nodded slowly, her eyes still wide open, conveying how stunned she was.

The full realization that Nova Stone — park superhero — was Alex Orwell hit Caleb right then. It had only been a growing hope earlier, but now it was real. As a response, all he could do was stare at her, his gaze going over her long black curls, the shape of her inquisitive eyes, and the line of her jaw.

She cleared her throat. "Mr. Grant?"

She had caught him staring. Again. Where were his manners? "I apologize, Miss Stone. I find myself fascinated. Your work is enthralling, and if you can find time to step into my office, I would love to discuss the possibility of signing you as one of the authors I represent."

Her mouth parted for a split second before she regained composure. "I—" She shook her head. "I can't."

"What do you mean you can't?" The woman at the cubicle beside Nova's stood up. "Nova!" She smiled at Caleb as she tucked a strand of her straight brown hair behind her ear. "Mr. Grant. I'm her friend, Vienna."

"Hello, Vienna." Caleb returned her smile.

As if morphing into someone else, her smile disappeared as she shot a glare at Nova, who reached for her bag, placing it over her lap.

"I need to get home soon." Nova lowered her eyes, the red blush on her cheeks still there.

"Can I walk you to your car then?" Caleb stood to his full height. "I'm already on my way home anyway."

Nova glanced at her friend, almost as if to ask for permission. Vienna tilted her head to the side and mouthed, "Come on." Nova then dragged her gaze to meet Caleb's before she inhaled and said a breathless "Okay."

She made it sound like being with him was a chore she had to bear with, but Caleb let it slide. He could only guess at why everything about her was so tense, so guarded, but he chalked it up to her nervousness over him discovering her identity as Alex Orwell.

"So," Caleb began the conversation as they waited for the elevator, "why Alex Orwell?"

Nova didn't immediately respond. Instead, she took a deep breath, checked what floor the elevator was in, and said, "I just finished reading *The Count of Monte Cristo* by Alexandre Dumas and 1984 by George Orwell when I picked my pen name."

Caleb quirked his brows. "Tough reads."

She glanced at him and a hint of a smile appeared on her face, but it quickly disappeared when the elevator dinged and its doors slid open.

Caleb gestured toward the elevator, which already had several people inside. He wished he could get them all to get off the elevator, so he could have a chat with Nova in private.

She stepped in, and Caleb followed after. It took only two more floors before more people entered and squished them into opposite ends of the elevator. Caleb glanced at Nova and cocked his head back when he found her with her eyes closed, her lips moving. Was she praying?

Finally, the elevator reached the ground floor and everyone milled out of the enclosed metal box. Caleb and Nova were the last to go. Caleb deliberately slowed down his pace, because he wanted this walk to the parking lot to be as long as he could possibly make it.

"I found the quote you picked interesting," Caleb said.

"Quote?"

"At the beginning of the novel. The quote from *The Count of Monte Cristo*."

Nova recited it from memory. "It's necessary to have wished for death in order to know how good it is to live."

"Yes. That one! It's appropriate for the plot of your novel, especially since it's a loose retelling of the Dumas classic, but it gave me food for thought, as well," Caleb said. "Do you agree with the quote?"

Nova narrowed her eyes. "Don't you?"

"I think we can be thankful for how good life is without reaching the point of so much suffering, we wish we would die."

Her expression grew pensive as they neared Caine Tower's exit. "Have you ever gotten to a point in your life where you asked God to just let you die?"

Caleb gulped. "I have to admit I haven't."

"I have," Nova said.

Her confession was a reminder to him of everything her family had been through. The Stone family's background was no secret to people at their church.

Nova continued. "Whenever I compare where I am and where I was before, I have a much deeper appreciation of the life I'm experiencing now. I understand your point though, and I agree. If you look at it that way, I can see why you would disagree, but I chose the quote from the context of being a Christian and needing to die to one's self to truly appreciate what it means to have an abundant life in Christ. Also—" her eyes rolled upwards as if she was recalling something "—in the novel, I think that's the very core of Dr. Edge's story. He did everything he could to survive, to live, so he could exact revenge on his enemies, but ultimately, it wasn't until he was willing to die for someone he loved that he understood the fullness of what it means to live, to really live."

"Interesting." Caleb grinned. "And what do you think it means, Nova? To live, to really live."

Nova shrugged. "Greater love hath no man than this, that a man lay down his life for his friends."

Caleb slipped his hands inside his pockets. They were now in the parking lot, so he tried to walk slower. "How do you figure?"

"Jesus loved us so much, He died for us. For us to enjoy the life He gave us, we need to learn to love that way, as well. To have people we love so much, we're willing to lay down our lives, to sacrifice, to die to self, for them. I think until we've reached that point, we haven't really lived the fullness of life."

What would it be like to love her that way? Caleb's breath hitched as he caught the thought, glanced at her, and stopped walking. When he did, so did she. He turned to his side to face her before allowing himself the liberty of appreciating her lovely features once again.

She shifted her weight from one foot to the other as she met his stare, looked away, then met his stare once again. She winced. "Was I talking too much?"

He laughed. "Not at all. I love hearing what you have to say. I'm more than a little dumbfounded, that's all."

She swallowed hard. "Okay?"

"Nova, everyone in my family knows you, except me. Hannah, Isaac, Kelly, even my nephew and niece. After seeing you at the park yesterday, discovering that you are Alex Orwell, and now, hearing you talk like this, I—" Caleb shook his head "—can't believe I haven't met you before yesterday. Where have I been all this time?"

She didn't respond. How would she? It wasn't up to her to know where he had been.

"What I'm trying to say, Nova, is that it would be an honor for me to work with you. I love the story you wrote, and I'm almost desperate enough to beg you to send me the rest of the manuscript, because that cliffhanger is killing me." He flashed her a sheepish smile.

And then there it was. The smile he had been so longing to see. It lit her face up even as that adorable little dimple caved into her cheek. "Okay," she said. "Your phone?"

Caleb pulled the phone out of his pocket, unlocked it, and handed it to her.

"I'll give you my number." Her fingers moved quickly across his keypad. "Text me your email address. I'll send the ending of the novel to you tonight." She handed his phone back to him. "Thank you, Caleb."

"For what?"

Nova's smile grew in response. "My car is over there." She pointed at a subcompact silver Sentra just two cars away from where they were standing. "Thanks for walking me here." She headed for her vehicle.

Caleb sped up his steps to keep up with her. "Please tell me you'll consider signing me on as your agent."

"Finish reading the manuscript first. If you're still interested, then we can talk." She brought her keys out of her bag. "I'll see you tomorrow?"

It took a couple of seconds for Caleb to process what she had just said. They were going to see other tomorrow? "Right. At work. Sure. I'll see you." Same church. Same office. Most likely the same school. How had her existence not registered in his brain all these years? Had he been that obsessed with Olivia?

Again, Nova smiled at him, her eyes glistening even as she opened her car, and for a moment, though it baffled him, he feared she was about to cry. To his relief, she didn't.

Caleb waved her away, and he stood there for quite a few minutes, wanting nothing more than to unravel the rest of the mystery that was Nova Stone.

Nova licked her lips as she stepped into the entryway of their home to be welcomed by the garlicky aroma of her favorite Filipino dish. There was no mystery about it. They were having *adobo*[1] for dinner. Nova made her way to the kitchen and placed her bag on the counter before peering over her mother's shoulder. Her mouth watered at the sight of the dish. It had been a while since Ma cooked adobo for them.

"That smells good, Ma." Nova kissed her mother on the cheek.

---

1 a·do·bo /ah-dōbō/ noun; a Filipino dish of chicken or pork stewed in vinegar, garlic, soy sauce, bay leaves, and peppercorns.

"Prepare the table *na²*, *iha³*. We'll eat soon."

"We'll set the table." Nolan walked into the kitchen with Serene, their hands intertwined. "I'm so hungry."

"Great!" Nova grabbed her bag and hugged her brother. "Thank you, Nolan." She then embraced Serene. "Hey, Serene. Lovely as usual."

"Not as lovely as you, Nova!" Serene exclaimed. "You're blooming! Is anyone inspiring you lately?"

Nolan coughed. "Probably someone at the office. She's never been this motivated about work before."

Nova widened her eyes at her brother to get him to stop talking. "It's nothing like that." She bit her lower lip. Was that a lie? Was she more motivated by her work at Frontier Press, because Caleb was there? The memory of him staring at her in the parking lot made her blush. "I'm just super excited about something huge happening in my life right now. I'll tell you guys all about it when it all pans out. Right now, I need to do the work. I'll be back to join you guys for dinner."

Nolan narrowed his eyes at her, making her feel exposed. No one knew her as well as her little brother did. When he smiled, she tried not to breathe a palpable sigh of relief. "I'm on your side," Nolan said. "Whatever you're up to, Serene and I are in your corner all the way through."

"Hundred percent," Serene agreed.

Nova rushed out of the kitchen with the sound of Nolan drumming against the island counter, while Serene sang a tune to his beat. "God, give Nolan his musical break," Nova whispered her prayer as she ascended the stairs. "He is so talented — probably even more than Dad and Nate were, combined." The grief that gripped her heart at the memory of Nate and her father just as she reached the top step made her grip the railing and change the tone of her prayer. "Protect my brother, God. Don't let him fall into the same patterns Dad and Nate fell into.

---

2 na / nah / adverb; already

3 i·ha /ee-hah/ noun; daughter; appellation by elder to young girl.

Lead him Your way and preserve both him and Serene in their relationship."

Satisfied, she claimed what Christ did at the cross, said her amen, and proceeded to her room. The moment she got in front of her computer, she winced at the thought of emailing Caleb. Somehow, it was easier to pray over her brother's heart than her own. As she booted up her computer, she blushed at the recollection of the short walk to the parking lot with Caleb. She surprised herself at the degree of comfort she had around him. What could he be thinking of her after gushing about her book like that? Then again, he seemed to be as passionate about her work as she was.

He had said such kind words about her novel and about her, and the fact that he wanted to represent her written work as an agent blew her mind. Despite all her attempts to avoid him, Nova had wanted nothing more than for Caleb to notice her back in high school, but he never had. How could he? He had Olivia.

The computer's operating system loaded, and she connected to the internet. She spent the next five minutes thinking and re-thinking how she would write the email to Caleb, only to end up with a succinct note telling him that the novel was attached, as promised. The moment she clicked the send button, an email popped up in her inbox.

The name of the sender made her freeze.

Knox Cartier.

No.

This couldn't be happening.

How had he gotten hold of her email?

Nova deleted the email before even opening it. She disconnected from the internet and suddenly couldn't stand being alone. She shut down the computer and rushed out of her room.

It had been so long since his last attempt to connect with her. Not since their graduation. She entered the kitchen, trembling.

"What happened to you?" Nolan asked upon seeing her. "You look like you just witnessed a murder."

Nova shook her head. "I'm fine. I got a message from an old friend. It's no big deal." She took her seat between Serene and her mother. Nolan's stare made her shift in her seat. "Stop staring, Nolan. Everything is okay."

"You sure, iha?" Ma asked.

Nova nodded yes.

"Go have your dinner then. Your food will grow cold."

Nova swallowed hard and glanced at Nolan. His jaw tightened before he shrugged and proceeded to finish his dinner. Nova said a quick prayer, only to realize her appetite was gone. Why was he trying to connect with her again? She transferred food to her plate and tried to eat only because she wanted to avoid Nolan's questions.

The rest of dinner whooshed by her. She was too wrapped up in her thoughts flitting from Knox to Caleb, and then back. She was grateful when Nolan and Serene excused themselves to go to the living room to work on their school project. Ma would be far less inquisitive than her brother.

Nova helped Ma load the dishwasher. Once they were done, she was about to leave the kitchen when Ma took hold of her hand.

Laughter resounded from the living room, across the entryway, and into the kitchen.

Nova tried to force a smile. "Doesn't sound like they're studying."

"They're a good match. I'm glad they're trying to go about their relationship in a more Godly way this time around." Ma smiled as she turned on the dishwasher. She squeezed Nova's hand. "What's going on in your mind, Nova?"

"What do you mean?"

"I don't always say anything, but I pay attention, and something is clearly bothering you, iha. Tell me about it." Ma pointed to the table.

The idea of being alone in her room kick-started the inner debate within her: should she tell her mother about Knox or not? They took their seats beside each other in the now-clean dining table.

Nova sat sideways in her chair to face her mother while talking. What she would say, however, she didn't know. She could either tell her mother that her former stalker had emailed her, and it was freaking her out, or she could talk about Caleb.

The latter would give her mother more peace than the former, so she told Ma what had happened earlier, with Caleb finding out about her book and walking her to her car.

"I didn't know you had a crush on Marcus and Naomi's son," Ma said after Nova finished recounting her story. "Why didn't you tell me?"

"He never noticed me before, so what was there to talk about?"

"Well—" Ma smiled "—he has noticed you now, hasn't he?"

"I don't know what to do, Ma. I've always placed him on a pedestal. He was the image of my ideal man, my standard. What if I get to know him and find out he's just like every other man I've ever met? Just like Dad and Nate?" Nova bit her lip. Regret at the mention of her father and brother rushed over her the moment their names came out of her lips.

Her mother's face crumpled.

"I'm so sorry, Ma."

The apology didn't help, because upon hearing it, a gasp escaped Ma's lips before a sob came out. "Oh, Nova—"

"You don't like to talk about them, I know." Nova lowered her eyes.

Ma grabbed her wrist. "Iha, look at me."

When Nova did as she was told, the intensity Ma exuded took her aback. "Ma?"

"Nova, since you were small, whenever things got rough here at home, you had a way of retreating." A bittersweet smile traced itself on Ma's face as she wiped away a tear. "I've always wondered at your ability to do that. I even envied it sometimes, but Nova, in your ability to do that, there were many times when it was almost like you were invisible. You faded into the background, hidden by your older brother's anger, eclipsed by your younger brother's personality. All these years, not once did you complain. You were so steady, Nova." Ma's grip tightened around Nova's wrist.

"I didn't want to be more of a burden to you. That's all. Also, growing up, I wanted to shield Nolan from everything going on."

"I know, iha, and I am so proud of you for that, but Nova, you have to realize you deserve to be seen, too." Ma brushed her fingers against Nova's cheekbone. "I am so grateful for you, my daughter, and between the two of us, I am the one who should apologize for all the times I have neglected you and failed to fight for you and your brothers. I'm sorry, Nova."

Despite her attempts to hold back her tears, a sob broke out of Nova. She hadn't even known how much she needed to hear those words, to have her own mother acknowledge the role she had played in their family all these years. As she sobbed, Ma drew closer and hugged her, and in doing so, it felt as if Nova experienced the words written in the book of Jeremiah: Like a mother comforts a child, so I will comfort you...

As the embrace lingered, Nova's awareness of God's presence with them at that moment increased.

Once Nova was able to get a hold of herself, she sought to assure her mother. "Ma, you don't have to say sorry. You did the best you could. Nolan and I know that, and we love you."

"Whenever I look back, I recognize all the ways I could have done better, but I'm thankful to God for the many ways He has restored us. He has made up for all my failures and has given you and Nolan to me. I can only be thankful for that." Ma took a deep breath as she once again wiped a tear away — this time more out of gratefulness to God than sadness.

Nova leaned her head against her mother's shoulder. "Me too, Ma. I'm thankful to God. He has healed me in so many ways since Dad died, and I think he has done the same for you."

Her mother nodded. "He has."

"Thank you for saying all those kind words, Ma. It means a lot to me. I hope we can talk more about the past. About Dad and Nate. We need to, if we want to walk out the healing that God has already begun in us."

"There's nothing I would like more, Nova." Ma combed her fingers against Nova's hair. "I've been praying for this moment between us, and it's amazing to me how God answers our prayers! My door is open to you, my daughter. Don't ever feel like you can't mention your father and brother to me. It hurts us all to remember how we lost them, but you're right. We need to be able to talk about the things God has brought us through."

Their hands clasped together. "Maybe in doing so, we can help each other move closer to God's purposes for us," Nova suggested.

"Yes. Especially your brother," Ma said.

"Nolan?" Nova straightened up in her seat to give her mother a look. "Why? Everyone raves about how amazing he is as a worship leader at church. He's probably closer to God than either of us."

Ma sighed and shrugged. "Don't mind me too much. Call it a mother's instinct, but I sometimes wonder if Nolan goes to church for God or for Serene."

Nova was about to come to her brother's defense but paused when it hit her that she often wondered the same. "Let's keep praying for him then," she agreed. After all, what harm could it do to Nolan?

"Now—" Ma squeezed Nova's hand "—about this Caleb Grant."

Nova winced. She had hoped Ma had already forgotten. "It's fine, Ma. We have a professional relationship at work. He wants to work with me on my book. I'm probably just overthinking this, because I like him."

"Or maybe, God has opened his eyes, so he can see you now. Whatever the case, stop hiding, iha. Let yourself be seen. Someday, the right man will come along for you. He will treat you right, and he'll be nothing like your father was. If Caleb can be that man for you, then I praise God for it, because that is my prayer for you, my beautiful Nova. That's what you deserve."

Nova smiled at her mother, but the idea of coming out of hiding was one she wasn't sure she wanted to entertain. Not with that email coming from someone she once held dear, but now dreaded. Not when just being around Caleb made her feel the most vulnerable she had ever felt in her entire life.

What was wrong with being unseen? It was so much safer that way. As if to solidify this conviction within Nova, the next morning, she walked out of the parking lot to head to Caine Tower to find someone leaning against a motorcycle, arms crossed over his chest.

She swallowed hard as her mind raced to process the sudden appearance of the only person she had ever regretted allowing into her life.

Knox Cartier smirked at her. "Hello, Nova. Did you miss me?"

five

THE ONE
WHO WOULD
RATHER HIDE

With dark hair, aviator sunglasses, a leather jacket, and short stubble lining his jaw, Knox Cartier easily caught the attention of women passing by. His focus, however, was solely on Nova, and she would have done anything to make him look elsewhere.

Not wanting to engage with him, Nova spun to her right and sped up her strides, heading toward Caine Tower's main entrance.

"Hey, hey, hey!" Knox caught up with her. "Come on, Nova. Won't you even talk to me? For old time's sake?"

Nova bit her lip and tried to ignore him.

"Nova." His tone — much lighter earlier — grew grim as he grabbed her arm.

Out of pure instinct triggered by his unwanted touch, Nova swept her bent arm upward in a diagonal motion. "Don't touch me!" Her elbow connected with his jaw.

Knox yelped when his face snapped to the side, a bruise sure to form on his face. "What is wrong with you?" His voice raised as he slightly lifted his arm, his fist clenched.

Nova didn't even flinch. There was no way Knox would hurt her with this crowd around them and building security just a couple hundred yards away of them. "Go ahead. I dare you to try."

Knox figured the same thing she did, because as he rubbed his assaulted jaw, he lowered both his arm and his voice. "I'm just trying to reconnect with you. Why are you being such a—"

Nova recoiled at his choice of word.

"Nova, I don't understand why you're so mad at me. Have you forgotten everything we survived? Don't you remember how much I loved you?"

The question derailed her thinking. Love? Was that what it was called? How did he not understand after everything he had put her through? "Leave me alone." She couldn't even say his name. It tasted far too bitter in her mouth. She walked forward, but he was relentless.

"Nova, please."

"Is everything okay here?"

The soothing baritone voice asking the question brought Nova to a full stop. *Lord, please. Not him, not here, not now.* She turned around to find Caleb eyeing her with concern.

"You all right, Nova?" he asked.

"Who's this guy?" Knox's face darkened as he shot an accusatory glare at Nova. "Are you with him?"

Nova wanted to disappear. She crossed her arms against her chest and brushed her palms up and down from elbows to shoulders, then back. She faced Knox. "Please leave me alone."

"Nova, don't do this." He stepped forward and reached out to touch her.

"You heard her." Caleb blocked his way, taking a protective stance between her and Knox.

"Hey." Knox shoved Caleb's shoulder back. "Whoever you are, stay out of this. Nova and I go a long way back, and I'm just here to talk to her."

"You may have a past with her, but right now, she clearly doesn't want to have a future — or a present — with you, so go."

Knox narrowed his eyes at Caleb. "Wait a minute. I recognize you. You're—"

Panic shot through Nova's system. "Knox, please. Don't make a scene here. Just go."

A muscle in Knox's jaw twitched as his glare shifted from Caleb to Nova. He moved his fingers over his chin in a V motion before smirking and shaking his head at Nova. "Tsk, tsk, tsk."

The sound sent shivers up Nova's spine, but she exhaled when Knox relented, twisted on his heel, and walked away.

Caleb laid a hand on her shoulder. "You all right?"

She nodded at him, barely able to look him in the eye. What was going through his mind? How would he possibly interpret the things Knox had said?

"Did you know that guy?"

Nova hated how shaken she was. Even after years of self-defense lessons to get more confident in a situation like this, how could Knox still make her feel so helpless? She opened her mouth to answer Caleb, but she didn't know what to say. Did she know Knox? She certainly hadn't known him well enough to recognize he had been bad news through and through.

"Never mind him," Caleb said. "Let's go in."

They walked through the main entrance, up the elevator, and right to the office pantry, where Caleb handed her a glass of water.

Nova drank from it. Was Caleb expecting an explanation from her? Did she owe him one? She felt like she did.

"You don't have to tell me anything if you don't want to," he said, as if he just read her mind.

"What did you see earlier?" she asked.

Caleb shrugged. "I saw you elbow his jaw, if that's what you're asking me." He smirked before peering at her through long dark lashes. "Hero move, in my opinion."

Nova blushed, despite how shaken she still was. "He's someone from high school. We weren't together, but—" she caught herself. Why was she telling Caleb all this? He didn't need to take part in her life's drama — especially when it came to Knox, who shouldn't even be in her life anymore.

When she didn't continue, Caleb must have gotten the cue, because he sighed and brushed his thumb against Nova's shoulder blade. "As I said, you don't need to tell me. I just want to make sure you're okay. You are, aren't you?"

She nodded. "Thank you."

"Tell me, though. How long has that guy been bothering you? Is this a regular thing?"

Nova shook her head. "No. He just showed up out of nowhere today. I'll keep ignoring him. He'll get the hint and go away. It's not a big deal. I'm okay." Truth was, she wasn't sure she was okay, because the presence of both Caleb and Knox in her life was short-circuiting her entire nervous system. She flashed Caleb the best smile she had to convince him she was telling the truth. "I appreciate your kindness."

Caleb's smile widened as his gaze lingered on her.

His stare made her wish for the power to be invisible. "What?" she asked.

"If you need anything at all, let me know, okay? I can walk you to and from the parking lot every day if you need me to."

Nova grinned. "That's unnecessary, but I won't complain about your company should you choose to give it to me."

His shoulders lost tension at those words, almost like it relieved him to hear she actually liked him being around. "That's great to know. Now, sorry for the shift in tone and subject, but—" He pressed his palms together in a praying motion and squinted one eye. "I read the rest of your novel."

Nova drew a quick intake of breath. "And?"

"Let's just say I'll be busy the whole day, because I want to make sure I have a proposal ready for you to review by Monday. It would be such an honor to represent you as an agent, Nova, so I hope you take this weekend to pray about it."

Nova couldn't believe her ears. Her mouth slowly dropped open as she tried to process the information he was giving her.

"In case it wasn't clear, I loved it," he said to address her speechlessness. He raised a forefinger in the air. "We may need to work together to make a few changes to perfect the manuscript. At the very least, we'll need to get an editor to go through the entire thing before we shop around for publishers, but Nova, I think we can get an incredible publishing deal out of this book. I do."

His enthusiasm was intoxicating to her. If only he knew how much she had dreamed of a moment like this since eleven-year-old Nova had developed a crush on him. Nova pressed her palms against her cheeks. "I don't know what to say, Caleb. Thank you." Her lips curled up at the sound of his name spoken through her voice, but she had to get a hold of herself. Caleb wanted to be her agent, not her boyfriend.

"No, Nova. Thank you," he said. "I hope to talk with you more next week."

"I'll look forward to it." Nova nodded. That was only partially true. Even if Nova refused to admit it to herself, she looked forward to every encounter she had with Caleb, but the more she opened up to him, the fear within her increased. After all, she once would have trusted Knox with anything, but that had proved to be a huge mistake. Still, could Caleb be anything like Knox? Nova couldn't tell for sure.

She made her way to her cubicle and booted up her computer. When she checked her emails to find out if Steve had any work for her, she found instead another email from Knox. Whatever lighthearted anticipation her time with Caleb brought earlier, it disappeared in an instant. Nova's heartbeat sped up out of anxiety. She didn't want to go through all of this again. How was Knox even figuring out her contact information?

Nova deleted the email and blocked his email address. This time, she prayed to God to get her through the day. That's when Vienna arrived to tell her about an assignment requiring her to leave the office, and she could get permission to have Nova assist her. Grateful for the distraction, Nova thanked God for answering her prayer.

By the end of the day, however, Nova was just grateful to go home and rest for the weekend, hopefully with no more encounters with Knox.

As Nova laid her head to sleep that night, two conflicting memories intersected in her mind: Caleb's delight at the office pantry and the back of

Knox's hand painfully connecting with her cheek once when she was younger, her resolve weaker.

If only she could hide from both men.

Maybe then, she would once again feel safe, but while Knox threatened danger against her physical well-being, he held no power over her heart and soul, but somehow, Caleb did. Her life had begun to intertwine with theirs, and all Nova could do was pray for God to protect her from the one she wanted to shun and the one a deep part of her had always been hoping would see her and stay.

part two

THE PAST

FOURTEEN YEARS AGO

six

THE ONE
WHO NEEDED
A HERO

- NOVA, 9 -

At an early age, Nova discovered that all it took was one misplaced word for a nice family get-together to explode into life-shattering smithereens.

In that night's case, the word was "has-been".

Her older brother, Nate, had rolled his eyes and called their father a "has-been" under his breath. Unfortunately, Damien Stone had heard, and the term was enough to turn his ego into dynamite and blow any chance of having a good time on the first night their family had been complete in years.

Dad bolted forward to his eldest son and pushed him up against a wall. "You ungrateful little—"

Nova covered her ears at the string of unpleasant words their father hurled at Nate. She scanned the living room for her little brother, Nolan, and sighed with relief when she remembered he was out with Ma at the store. Nova gulped. That meant she was alone at home with two angry men and no idea how to make them both happy again. She wished that, by some miracle, the fighting would end by the time Ma and Nolan returned.

The loud, muffled sound of her father's and brother's back-and-forth yelling unsettled Nova, but no more than how her father's grip tightened on her brother's collar. How Nate was still able to smirk in defiance — his brown eyes wild as he continued to challenge their father — made Nova want to leave the scene of the battle, but her bunny, Gable, was across the living room from where she sat, and the fight was happening right in between. She couldn't just leave Gable there, but retrieving him would mean putting herself in the crossfire of her family's war of words. Or fists.

Nova stayed frozen on the couch, staring at her stuffed bunny as she tried to tune out the fury of father and son. What was she to do? She took a deep breath and gathered courage before hopping off of the couch and making her way across the room beside the old broken TV to rescue one of her oldest friends. Just as she was about to reach for Gable, however, her older brother stumbled backwards, losing his balance and crashing down the floor, his arm and shoulder swiping her enough to make her go tumbling down with him. Her arm grazed the edge of the side table, making her yelp at the sting of a shallow cut on her skin. Her back hit the wooden floor, followed by the round of her head, her feet swinging up in the air before falling flat with a thump. Nate groaned beside her, his back turned to her. He rolled over to face the ceiling, pinning her arm beneath him.

"Ow," Nova mouthed as she tried to steady her breathing, which had been disrupted by the shock of what had happened. She never should have allowed herself to get caught in the middle of this battle.

Upon realizing she had fallen down with him, Nate sat up and turned to check on her, but before he could say anything, their father took several steps forward to hover over them.

"You and your mother had no one!" He pointed his finger at his eighteen-year-old son. "If I hadn't brought you to this country, both of you would have starved!"

As if not hearing and seeing their father's rage, Nate gave Nova a once-over. "I'm sorry, Nova. Are you okay? Are you hurt?"

Nova shook her head. "I'm not hurt at all," she lied. She wouldn't be surprised to find bruises tomorrow, but Nate didn't need to hear that. She wasn't sure if she was imagining it, but the shade of Nate's brown irises darkened to a near black. His chiseled face tensed, his shoulders heaved, his lean form bulked up, yet he still seemed small in comparison to their father. She held his arm. "Nate."

"Go to the bedroom, Nova," he instructed. In one swift motion, he was up on his feet, standing between her and their father, legs spread wide, feet planted on the floor, hands fisted. "What is wrong with you? What kind of father are you?"

"I've had enough of this disrespect." Dad shoved Nate by the chest. "If I had just left you and Clara in the Philippines, I would be a rock legend by now!"

Nate's glare darkened, and his voice took on a dangerous tone. "If you had what it takes, nothing would've stopped you from your grandiose delusions, but we both know you don't. Stop blaming Ma or us for all your failures."

"How dare you— You would be nothing without me, boy. Nothing!"

Nova's heartbeats paused when Dad lifted his fist in the air. "Dad, don't!" she yelled out.

When Nate realized she was still there, he shifted his anger from their father to her. "Get out of here, Nova! Get out!"

Tears rushed down her face as she leaped to her feet and grabbed Gable. She was about to run toward her exit, but threw her arms around her father's waist instead. "Dad, please don't hurt Nate. He's sorry. He didn't mean all the things he said."

Her father's arm dropped to his side. "I'm sorry you have to see us like this, Nova."

Encouraged by the softness of his tone, Nova continued. "I want you to be happy. I want us to be happy. We're glad you're back home."

Nate scoffed. "How can anyone be happy to have you as a father?"

Her father's body stiffened against her embrace. He pried her arms away from him. "Go to the kitchen, Nova. I refuse to stand here and take your brother's disrespect." He shoved her aside and unbuckled his leather belt.

The sight of it made her tremble, so much so that she feared her legs wouldn't be able to support her. "Dad, no."

"Go to the kitchen." Her father said the words through gritted teeth.

Nate squared his shoulders. The glare he shot at his father made Nova wish she could disappear.

Nova swallowed hard. "Nate?"

He glanced at her and nodded her off. "Go."

Helpless, she backed away from the stand-off happening in the middle of their living room. She was about to get to the archway that led from the living room to the dining room when her back hit the familiar, slender form of her mother. A brown bag of groceries dropped to the floor.

"What's going on here?" Clara asked. "Damien? Nate?"

"*Kuya*[1]!" Nolan yelled in reference to Nate. "Look what I got!"

Nova grabbed Nolan's arm and squinted her eyes. "Let's go to the kitchen, Nolan! We can have a picnic!"

"But I want to show them my drum!"

Nova forced a huge smile. "You can play it for me in the kitchen." She pressed her palms together in a pleading gesture. "I'll even tell you a story."

Nolan's eyes lit up. "Okay, but a new one. I want a new story."

"Deal."

Nova tried to ignore the tension surrounding them and led her little brother past the dining area to the kitchen, shut the door behind them, and climbed onto a stool to reach the pot of chicken adobo Ma had prepared earlier. She lifted the cover from the pot and inhaled the fragrance of the soy-and-vinegar-based stew before using a wooden ladle to scoop a generous helping into a bowl.

"What are you doing?" Nolan asked as his one hand lazily drummed a drumstick on the red plastic instrument hanging on a string around his neck. "I thought you said you'll tell me a story."

---

1 ku·ya /koo-yah/ noun; Filipino word for older brother.

Nova transferred rice into another dish. "I told you. We're having a picnic."

She slid out of the stool and retrieved an old table cloth from one of the cabinets and laid it on the floor next to the counter. With everything set, she sat Nolan and Gable next to each other on the colorful spread with food at the center. Nova sat cross-legged, opposite them.

Something crashed in the living room, startling Nolan.

"I'm not hungry," he said, staring at the food. "I want to eat with Daddy and Ma and Kuya."

"But that can take forever!" Nova threw her arms in the air. "Do you want to wait forever?"

Nolan wrinkled his nose.

Another crash resounded from the living room, followed by more yelling.

Nova winced. "Hey, Nolan. Play me a beat on your new drum. It'll help me tell my story."

Nolan grinned. "Okay." Like a natural, Nolan came up with a steady rhythmic beat, loud enough to drown the muffled sound of the fight happening two rooms away.

Nova shut her eyes and coaxed her mind to drift into a land of stories only she could explore. It was her joy and privilege to share the wonders she discovered from a world existing in her imagination with anyone who would listen. As wisps and talking animals and magical creatures drifted into the forefront of her mind, the all-out battle happening inside her home faded into the background.

Nova smiled and opened her eyes.

Nolan squirmed where he sat. "Do you have a story yet?"

Nova nodded. "I definitely do. Tonight—" she clasped her hands together, widened her eyes, and exaggerated her facial expressions, knowing that animated storytelling would be the only way she could hold her little brother's attention "—I'm about to tell you the story of a girl with trees in her eyes and fire in her hair, and just like our night tonight, her story starts with a BANG!"

Nolan jolted in surprise before he returned his focus on his drumbeat and his sister. He giggled.

Nova grinned. She had her captive audience — a stuffed bunny and a four-year-old — and they were enough to pull herself and them into the safety of a good story.

No matter what horrible things were happening all around her, she could always lose herself in a story. To Nova, this moment was proof of that.

They entertained themselves until they exhausted themselves with nothing but a plastic drum, a stuffed bunny, a good meal, a wild imagination, and a generous dose of laughter. They fell asleep on the table cloth, with Nova hoping that the war in their household would soon come to an end and that her father, mother, and brother could be as happy as she, Nolan, and Gable were.

The next morning, Nova woke up in her bed next to Ma, who gently stroked her palm up Nova's forehead to her dark hair.

"Good morning, Nova," Ma said.

Nova smiled. If she was beside Ma, that meant her father wasn't present. Just as she had hoped, the war had ended, because her father had stormed off late in the evening, retreating from them like he always did. His disappearance restored the peace — at least for the time being — in the Stone household's two-bedroom apartment. Unfortunately, he had left both Ma and Nate with bruises on their faces. Nova asked if they were black, blue, and purple elsewhere, but Ma said not to worry about it, and Nate said not to be so meddlesome.

Nova decided then that no matter how nice he always had been to her, she didn't like her father anymore — not after he had hurt Ma and Nate. Besides, she liked it better when he was away. Something deep within Nova told her she should be missing her father, but she couldn't lie to herself. She didn't miss him at all. She had Ma, Nate, and Nolan, and they were enough of a happy family for her. They had no need for Damien Stone.

Still, as much as she believed that to be true, her dad's absence left a hole in her heart she feared nothing could fill, so once in a while, Nova would imagine for herself a family where Damien Stone wasn't the villain, but the hero they had always needed him to be.

- CALEB, 11 -

All Caleb wanted to do was read, but doing that in the middle of one of Isaac Grant's action scenes was next to impossible. With all six Grant siblings in one room, it was a feat for anyone to concentrate on anything, but Caleb was up for the challenge.

"Okay, okay! Pay attention!" Isaac, thirteen, clapped his hands loudly.

Caleb tuned the chaos out and made himself comfortable in the giant bean bag in one corner of the family room at the second floor of the Grant family home. Propped up by his hands on his chest was the Christian classic his father had recommended to him. Aslan was about to save the day, and Caleb couldn't wait to finish this book and devour the next one.

"Who wants to be the hero?" Isaac yelled over the sudden burst of giggles between their sisters — Hannah, ten, and Deb, six. "Josh or Caleb?"

"I want to be the villain," Josh, Caleb's twin, said.

"Great! Caleb will be the hero then."

Caleb's ears stung at the proclamation. He rolled his eyes. "Can I please not have a main role? I want to be an extra for this one."

Isaac ignored him. "Since you're the villain, Josh, can you tie Hannah up?"

"What?!" Hannah objected. "Why do I have to be the one tied up? Why not Deb?"

Sam, Deb's twin, poked Caleb before sliding into the bean bag with him.

"Sam, come on." Caleb nudged his brother with his shoulder.

"Is that a lion, Caleb?" Sam pushed his head against Caleb's neck to get a better look at the book. "Can you tell Deb and me the story when we go to sleep later?"

"Fine. Now, leave me alone. I'm almost finished."

Sam didn't budge. Caleb groaned when Deb, the other little one, climbed onto his lap.

"Is it a good story, Caleb?" Deb asked as she rolled over and made herself comfortable on the other side of Caleb, leaning her head against his shoulder.

"Where is everyone? Caleb, come on!" Isaac clapped his hands together again. "You're distracting the little ones. Pfft. I guess it's appropriate since Sam is your sidekick."

Sam giggled and kicked Caleb's leg.

Caleb turned his head to the side to narrow his eyes at his little brother. "What did you do that for?" He shut his book, accepting the only way he could finish would be after this whole production ends.

"I'm a sidekick." Sam grinned.

"That's not what sidekicks do, and for that, you shall be punished!" He started tickling the child.

"No!" Sam tried to get away, but Caleb held on to him to keep him in place.

Upon realizing the onslaught her twin was facing from their older brother, Deb jumped onto Caleb's back. "Save Sam!" she yelled.

"Hannah's all tied up!" Josh announced.

"Josh, it's too tight."

"Don't worry about it, Hannah. Caleb will come to save you soon."

"My hands will be blue by then." Hanna's whiny voice grated at Caleb's ears.

"Okay." Isaac pulled Deb away from Caleb. "To your position, superstar. We need our hero."

Caleb finally let go of Sam. He cast a longing glance at his book and sighed. Later. He leaned back on the bean bag and stared up at his older brother. "Why do I have to be the hero again?"

"Because you were lost in Narnia when we did casting calls five minutes ago. Why is it that you and Josh never want to play the hero?"

"It's always the hero who gets beat up in your scenes." Caleb frowned.

Isaac shrugged. "The audience loves an underdog."

"What audience?" Caleb forced a grin. "It'll just be Dad and Mom watching."

"Not quite. We're having people over this weekend, so this has to be perfect. Will you just get up so we can start already?" Isaac extended his hand toward Caleb.

"Fine." Caleb took his brother's hand and pulled himself up to stand.

"Finally!" Hannah exclaimed. "I can't feel my feet anymore."

Isaac barked out instructions and explained what they were supposed to do in his action-packed version of the Prodigal Son.

Every week, the siblings took turns directing a quick skit for their Saturday family nights based on a story or Bible passage they had studied during the week. The youngest of the six siblings, Sam and Deb, usually came up with silly skits involving stuffed toys or a bunch of random props. The four older siblings, however — Isaac, the twins, and Hannah — placed more effort in one-upping one another whenever their turn came.

This particular Saturday, they were having some relatives and friends over, so Isaac was going a bit more over-the-top compared to their usual production quality.

"Why do I die in this story?" Caleb lifted his shoulders and hands — palms up — in a matter-of-fact shrug. "I'm the prodigal son, right? The prodigal son shouldn't die."

"No one's dying, Caleb. You're just almost dead." Isaac proceeded to explain the turn of events that brought the prodigal son's character from riches to rags. "So, you save Hannah from Josh, but Josh gets back at you and ruins your life."

Caleb shrugged. "It sounds like he's better off dying."

"What part do you play?" Josh asked.

"I'm the father." Isaac shrugged. "Sam certainly can't play that part. Josh is already playing the villain and the other brother."

"Wait. What?" Josh stepped forward as he flipped through a pile of stapled sheets. "That wasn't in the script."

"There's a script?" Caleb asked. "How come I didn't get a copy?"

Little Deb scratched her head. "I'm confused."

"Can you please hurry?" Hannah whined, her voice breaking as she wriggled her wrists and ankles within its constraints. "These are too tight. Can we finish this now please?"

"Fine, fine." Caleb relented. "Let's do this!"

They executed the scene as Isaac had envisioned. It ended with Caleb lying on the floor watching Hannah go free while he suffered the wrath of Josh, the villain. By wrath, Isaac directed Josh to give Caleb a sound beating by pretending to hit, kick, and stomp on Caleb, who crouched himself into a fetal position, pretending to writhe in pain. So much for being the hero of the story. Nothing about his role resembled heroism.

"Cut!" Isaac yelled.

Caleb sighed with relief, stretched his legs, and rolled to his stomach. From the corner of his eye, he caught a glimpse of his book on the floor. He reached for it, rolled to his back, and started reading where he had left off.

"I'm not letting any of you tie me up again!" Hannah announced. "I don't want to be part of this stupid skit anymore! My wrists and ankles hurt, and no one even cares!" Her footsteps running down the stairs echoed from the hall up to the family room.

Was she crying? Caleb shook his head and returned his attention to the book where the drama was far more riveting than Hannah's.

"Are you kidding me?" Isaac chuckled. "Caleb, what's with you and these books? You haven't even gotten up from the end of the scene. How do you read through all this noise?"

Caleb grinned as he slipped his hand between his head and the floor. "Skills. It takes skills. If I only read when it's quiet in this house, I will never finish a book."

"Are we done?" Deb asked. "Can I go?"

Caleb oomfed when she plopped herself on his stomach and giggled.

"Boys, what happened to Hannah?" Their father showed up beneath the archways leading to the second-floor family room. "Your sister is in tears."

Caleb groaned as he shut the book again. With their father present and most likely about to huddle them into a family meeting, the odds of him finishing this story dipped down to negative digits. "Deb, get up." He nudged his sister off him.

Deb was more than eager to stand up and make her way to their father. "Josh tied her up too tight!" she announced.

"You snitch!" Josh narrowed his eyes at their little sister.

"Deb is not a snitch!" Sam came to his twin's defense, marching toward Deb.

"Why were you tying your sister up?" Dad asked.

"It's for Isaac's skit, Dad," Josh explained. "For Saturday."

Caleb sat next to his brother on the couch.

"Sam, Deb, go follow Hannah down to the kitchen. Your mom is down there with her. Grab yourselves a snack." Their father shooed the little twins away before setting his focus back on the three oldest boys. He gestured for Isaac to sit on the couch with his brothers before pulling up a chair, so he could sit opposite them. "I've been seeing a pattern here. You boys are getting rougher and rougher, and you always seem to take it out on Hannah."

"Dad, Hannah is just overreacting," Caleb explained, hoping to come to Josh's defense. "I was the one who untied the rope, and it wasn't that tight — not enough to cut her circulation like she was implying. She didn't even bruise."

"That's right," Isaac agreed. "We ignore her, because she has been way too sensitive and dramatic lately. It's hard to take her seriously."

"Josh?" Dad asked. "Do you have anything to say for yourself?"

"I needed it to be tight, so she wouldn't be able to get away, Dad. I didn't think it was too tight."

"Did she tell you it was too tight?"

"Yes, but Dad—" Josh shrugged "—it's Hannah. Like Isaac said, it's hard to take anything she says seriously."

Dad sighed as he leaned his elbows over his knees and clasped his hands together. "Boys, among the three of you, you're used to roughhousing each other. You push and shove each other around and encourage one another to be faster, stronger, and tougher. You've been like this since you were small; meanwhile, growing up, your sister has always just hung back, observing you, probably wondering why the three of you are acting so wild." Their father grinned, a flicker of amusement lightening his expression before his face once again tensed to reflect the somberness of the situation. "I have to admit you're right. Hannah has been more sensitive than usual lately. I'll give you boys that."

Josh exhaled. Caleb shrugged a shoulder. Isaac nodded.

"Your mother and I are trying to get her to open up more, but right now, I need all three of you to be extra careful with her. Be much gentler to her. Especially you, Isaac. As the oldest, you have to set the tone. Try to listen to her and respect her when she says it's too much. It may not be too much for you boys, but it is for her."

"Why do girls have to be so weak?" Josh asked.

"They're not, Josh. In fact, they're stronger than us in ways I pray you will someday fully appreciate." A small smile appeared on their father's face. "Your mother is one of the strongest people I know, and whatever strength I have — whether it is physically or in my character — I want to use that to protect her and the ones I love. Be the kind of brothers who make your sisters feel safe and protected around you."

Caleb and Josh exchanged glances. What was their father talking about?

"Our strengths as men draw out their strengths as women, and vice versa. It's a beautiful give-and-take as the Lord designed it to be. Godly masculinity bringing out Godly femininity. I pray that you boys will grow up into men with wisdom on how to preserve God's design for both man and woman. It all starts with the way you treat your mother and the way you treat your sisters. Treat them well. Love them and protect them. Hannah isn't one of the boys, nor does she want to be. Don't treat her like one."

It would be much later in life before Caleb fully comprehended what his father was trying to say, but in that moment, to the three oldest of the Grant siblings, the mission became clear. They had to protect their sister — from what or whom, they weren't sure. Perhaps it was from themselves, but in a later conversation, the three brothers concluded that the person they needed to protect Hannah the most from was herself.

After all, if she was less of a crybaby, she would be much less annoying and would need far less protecting.

seven

THE ONE WHO RAN AWAY

- ONE YEAR LATER; CALEB, 12 -

His head buried in the pages of a classic, Caleb's mind wandered off to an epic last battle of a fantastical kingdom away from the world he knew. Aslan came to the rescue once again. Something about it both comforted and disconcerted Caleb as he turned the brass knob to the bedroom he shared with Josh. He pushed the door open with his shoulder just as a burst of high-pitched giggles echoed past the hallway.

"Nooooo!" Sam burst out of the bedroom he shared with Deb and ran past Caleb to head for the stairs.

Behind him, Deb held out a doll in front of her as she giggled and ran after her twin. "Angie just wants to play with you, Sam!"

"Get it away from me!" Sam yelled.

Caleb smirked and shook his head in amusement as he pulled his thoughts back to the book he was reading. By the time he shut the door and entered the bedroom, he had already been transported to a world not his own. Only after he sat on the edge of his bed did he realize Josh was sitting on the bay window between their two single beds.

He creased his brows at Josh. What was he doing here, all alone? Caleb shrugged it off, laid back on his bed, and continued to read his book.

The loud crunch of Josh biting into an apple filled the room, followed by Josh's munching.

Caleb tuned it out and lost himself in a realm of adventure, caught in the middle of an age-old battle between good and evil.

Just as he was about to reach a climax, indecipherable yelling ensued in the corridor outside their room. Caleb rolled his eyes. Most likely Hannah and the twins. Again.

"How do you do it?" Josh asked.

"Do what?" Caleb paused his reading mid-sentence to glance at his twin.

"Concentrate with all this noise going on."

Caleb laid the open book over his chest and wrinkled his nose. "It's not a problem for me. Besides, you know a book is great if it can suck you in no matter what's happening around you." Made curious by his brother's line of questioning, Caleb closed the book and placed it on the bed. He turned to his side to face Josh, who was still finishing his apple while seated in the bay window. "In a way, it makes reading more fun when there's a matching energy happening where I am. Especially if there's a lot happening in the book, it helps that there's a lot happening around me as well."

Josh shook his head. "It's tiring sometimes."

Caleb sat up. "What's tiring? You barely read."

"I mean being around people."

"What are you talking about? You love people. You're the friendly one. Everyone always says you're easier to talk to than I am."

"That's because you're so quiet. If you talk more, they'll find out you're much friendlier than I am."

"I doubt that."

Josh blew a breath through gritted teeth. "I don't know. Hannah gets on my nerves sometimes, and Isaac can be so bossy. The twins can be cute, but they're also a handful when they're in one of their moods. Sometimes, I just want to get my energy back."

Caleb made his way to the bay window and sat cross-legged opposite his brother. Josh offered him the half-eaten apple. Caleb took a bite and handed it back to Josh.

Caleb confessed: "It's only Hannah who drains my energy. She's always upset over something or someone. I know Dad and Mom want us to be more patient with her, but it's not always easy."

"Speaking of Hannah—" Josh furrowed his brows and sat up straight, bending one leg, so he could kneel and get a better view outside "—where is she going?"

Caleb followed Josh's gaze and saw Hannah walking out their house's gate and to the street. She had a huge backpack so full of stuff, it looked like if a leaf fell on it or a breeze blew on her the wrong way, the bag might knock her off balance.

"What does she think she's doing?" Caleb frowned.

"Where are those—" Isaac burst inside their room. "Here you two are. I've been looking all over."

Neither of the twins bothered to even glance at their older brother. Instead, Josh waved an arm behind himself to invite Isaac to check out what was going on with their sister. "I think she's running away."

"Who?" Isaac strode forward to peer over their shoulders. "Where does she think she's going?"

"Let's go follow her," Caleb suggested.

"What for?" Josh scowled. "It's just Hannah acting up again."

"Dad asked us to look out for her and protect her, right? Who knows what trouble she might get herself into?"

"Caleb's right." Isaac tapped them both on the back. "Besides, it might do us some good to get out. It's a weekend, and for some reason, we're all cooped up inside."

Josh hesitated, but eventually rolled his eyes and said, "Fine."

Without another word, the three rushed outside, making sure they wouldn't get caught by their mother as she prepared dinner in the kitchen.

It didn't take long for them to catch up to Hannah, who had considerably slowed down, given how heavy her backpack was.

The three boys kept a safe distance behind her — enough for them to duck and hide in case she looked back, enough for them to be able to snicker and whisper to each other without her hearing.

At one point, Hannah paused to readjust her bag, its straps probably already chafing her shoulders. The three boys ducked behind a bush by the sidewalk to avoid getting detected.

"What did she pack for her escape, anyway?" Isaac asked.

"Beats me." Josh shrugged. "Probably dismantled her bed and put all the pieces in the bag."

Caleb tried to hold back his laughter — mainly caused by the idea that it did seem like something Hannah would do. Their sister had a knack for taking things apart and putting them back together. If only she could do the same thing to herself — put herself back together whenever she fell apart.

Hannah started walking again. Several times, she readjusted her backpack on her shoulders.

"Looks like a heavy bag." Caleb frowned. "Maybe we should help her carry it."

"Nah..." Isaac shook his head. "If we approach her, she'll have to go home with us. I want to find out what her master plan is."

"We should take her home," Caleb said. "It's not like we can actually let her leave."

Hannah was already close to the gate leading out of their suburban cul-de-sac. What was her master plan, indeed?

"I'm surprised she would go this far," Josh said when Hannah walked out of the gate. They rushed forward when she disappeared from their sight. They couldn't afford to lose track of her.

When they reached the gate, the first sight that greeted them was the bus stop nearby. Hannah sat alone on the bench under a waiting shed, her legs swaying back and forth, her backpack sitting next to her.

As the boys approached, it became evident that tears were rushing down her cheeks, her shoulders shaking as she sobbed.

Isaac sighed — whether from compassion or exasperation, Caleb wasn't sure. A cautious silence followed as they neared her.

When Hannah raised her eyes and saw them approaching, the way her face fell made Caleb's heart go out to her. Somehow, his immunity to her tears disappeared. Genuine concern for his sister took its place. What was going on with Hannah?

Not knowing what to say to make her feel better, Caleb sat next to her and began stroking her back as she continued to sob, lost in her own despair.

The muscles on Isaac's arm strained when he removed the backpack next to her and laid it on the ground in front of him so he could sit on the spot on her other side.

Josh leaned back on one of the bus stop's posts.

All three of the boys kept silent as Hannah sobbed.

It took at least a good ten minutes before Hannah stopped crying.

It was Isaac who first spoke up. "What are you doing, Hannah? Why are you here?"

"I'm running away," she said.

"Yeah?" Isaac leaned back on the metal bench. "Off to where, though?"

"I don't know," Hannah said in her typical whiny voice.

"What's your plan?" Josh asked. "Just ride a random bus to see where it takes you?"

Hannah nodded.

"Do you have a bus pass?" Caleb asked.

"I took Mom's." Hannah sniffled. She took a tissue from her pocket and blew her nose into it.

"Do you have enough food to last you until you can find a job?" Isaac reached for her backpack and opened it. Upon rummaging through what was inside, he snickered. "Hannah!"

"Don't make fun of me!" Hannah pouted.

"I can't help it!" Isaac was outright trying to hold back his laughter. "Hannah, you brought an entire watermelon with you."

"Wait. What?" Josh stepped forward to peer at the contents of the backpack.

Caleb couldn't help but look as well. Sure enough, beneath her clothes, several snacks, an apple, and a banana, there was a whole watermelon. "Hannah, how did you even get this without Mom noticing?"

"I told her it's for my school project."

"She believed you?" Josh scratched his head. "What school project requires a giant watermelon?"

"I don't know. I don't care." Hannah harrumphed. "I'm sick of all of you making fun of me."

"No one makes fun of you, Hannah." Josh rolled his eyes.

"Yes, you do! You all do. Isaac always teams up with you and Caleb, and Deb and Sam are always together. You all have someone, and I'm just me. Hannah. All alone. I have no one."

"So, your plan to fix that is to run away and be more alone than ever?" Isaac asked, before biting his lip to hold back a snicker.

Caleb sighed before brushing his fingers against his sister's hair. "Hannah, you have us. All of us. We care about you. We just don't understand you sometimes, but if you try to tell us what you think and feel without crying or being too dramatic, we might understand you more."

"I try to tell you, but you never listen!"

"We're listening now, Hannah," Isaac said.

Hannah opened her mouth for a couple of seconds before closing it again. "Well, I don't know what to say anymore."

All three boys chuckled. Isaac threw his arms around their sister. "You're so annoying sometimes, but you're our Hannah, and no matter what it may look like to you, you belong with us."

Just as he finished talking, a bus rolled by and stopped in front of them.

"What's the deal, Hannah?" Josh asked. "Are you going? We can carry your bag — watermelon and all — up for you."

For a moment, her stubbornness made Caleb fear she might actually push through with her running-away idea, but to his relief, the bus left without Hannah budging from the bench.

"So, I guess you're not running away, after all?" Caleb tugged at Hannah's hair.

Hannah pushed his arm away, scowled at him, then nodded.

"Can we go home now then?" Josh rubbed his stomach. "I'm hungry, and I think Mom is making spaghetti and meatballs."

"Who's carrying the bag?" Isaac asked.

"My shoulders hurt," Hannah said.

"Fine. I'll carry it." Isaac lifted the backpack and placed it on his shoulders. He then ruffled her hair. "This thing's heavy. You're strong, Hannah. I can't believe you made it all the way here with this thing."

Her smile made Caleb smile. He placed his arm over her shoulder. "Don't try to run away again, okay?"

Hannah didn't say anything in response, but somehow Caleb understood her answer was a definite yes. They slipped back home and helped Hannah put all the random stuff she packed back to where it all belonged.

When they gathered for dinner, Caleb thanked God for having the family they had. Sure, they all annoyed one another sometimes, but they were exactly where they belonged. They were a family, and Caleb had faith that no matter what life threw their way, they would always be a complete family.

- NOVA, 10 -

Their family was falling apart.

This became clear to Nova one afternoon after school when Nate drove by in their car, Neutron, to pick her and Nolan up. There was something in Nate's eyes that clued Nova in on something amiss — more than the usual, that is. After all, with their father around for a visit, they were almost always in a state of disarray.

"Where's Ma?" Nolan asked as Nate secured him in his car seat.

"She asked me to come pick you up," Nate replied.

Nova shut the car door as she made herself comfortable in the back seat beside Nolan. "Is Ma okay?"

"She's fine." Nate took the driver's seat. "We're going out for a bit."

Nova wrinkled her nose at Nolan, who was, as usual, oblivious to the tension Nate was exuding. Not Nova. She knew her older brother all too well.

"Is Dad staying?" she asked.

Nate's silence didn't give her much of an answer. He could be upset that their father was still around or upset that their father left again — perhaps after having a fight with Ma. Nova could only guess what was going through her brother's mind.

"Where are we going?" Nolan asked, as Nate proceeded to drive.

"I'm not sure. Where do you want to go?" Nate asked. "We can go to the park first and grab some dinner after. Does that sound good to you?"

"Yes!" Nolan threw a fist in the air as a sign of triumph. "Let's go!"

Nova remained silent for the rest of the ride. So did Nate. Apart from the occasional backfiring of clunky old Neutron, only Nolan's humming filled the quiet of the car.

When they reached the park, Nate clapped his hands together after parking. "You guys ready? Do you want anything to eat?"

"I want a balloon!" Nolan yelled.

Nate laughed. "You can't eat a balloon, but sure."

His laughter didn't sound natural to Nova, who unbuckled her seatbelt and got out of the car. Minutes later, they were at the playground, with Nolan running off to the slides while Nova sat on a swing, digging the sole of her shoes into the ground beneath her.

"Swings aren't chairs, Nova." Nate approached her. "Want me to push you?"

Nova shook her head. "I can swing on my own if I want to."

"You'll get higher faster if I push you. You used to love going as high as possible." Nate sat on the swing next to hers.

"I don't want to this time," Nova said, as she leaned her head on the chain carrying the rubber swing. She wished he would just tell her what was going on, but she didn't want to ask either. It seemed she didn't need to.

Nate steadied his feet on the sand and leaned his elbows on his knees. "Dad is home with Ma."

"Thought so," Nova said.

"Can't hide much from you, can I?" He smirked.

Nova smiled.

"Sometimes I worry that you've forgotten you're still a kid, Nova."

She laid her palm over her chest. "I'm ten years old, thank you very much. I won't be a kid much longer."

"That's true, and that's why you should enjoy being a kid while you're still one. You talk like you're sixty sometimes."

She scowled. "No, I don't."

He chuckled before his amusement subsided, and he returned to his usual solemnity.

Nova searched out Nolan, who was now jumping up and down on a trampoline. If it were up to her, Nolan would always be this carefree. A large part of her wished she could be as carefree as he was.

"You can't tell Ma, Nova—" Nate hung his head "—but I'm leaving tonight."

"What?" Nova snapped out of her focus on Nolan and shifted her full attention toward her older brother. "Where are you going?"

"I want to go to Nashville."

"Where Dad lives?"

"Dad doesn't stay there anymore. He's going on tour with his band. That's why he's here to spend time with Ma. His band has been doing very well this year, so he was able to buy a new house for the family to move to in the suburbs. It's a much nicer place, Nova. You and Nolan will love it there."

"But why do you have to go to Nashville, Nate? Why can't you move with us?"

"I need to make it on my own, Nova. I want to make music and prove to Dad that I can succeed just as much as, if not more than, he did. Ma can't always be caught up in all the trouble between me and Dad."

"So it'll be Dad instead of you living with us?"

Nate's jaw tightened as he shook his head. "He came over today just to give her the keys to the new house, Nova. He's leaving again tomorrow to go back on tour. Ma wasn't very happy to hear that he'll be away again. They were fighting when I left the house."

That wasn't news to Nova. Dad and Ma never got along. She wasn't sure why they even married each other to begin with.

"I'll earn money and then come back for Ma, Nolan, and you. I promise, Nova. You believe me, right?"

Almost as a way to hopefully ease the coil of emotions around her chest, Nova began swinging herself forward and back. "I don't like it," she said. "I don't want you to leave."

"Nova..."

Not wanting to talk to him anymore, Nova pushed her legs back into the air to broaden her swing. Back and forth, she moved her feet and strained her arms against the chains to push herself higher. Away from Nate. Away from him and their father, always abandoning them.

If she had anything to do with it, Nolan would never turn out like them.

For the rest of the afternoon, as hard as Nate tried to get her to talk to him, Nova remained quiet. By the time they went out to a diner for dinner, Nolan took over most of the conversation with Nate — a relief to Nova. She didn't want to talk to Nate ever again.

Once they got home, it felt to Nova like the secret Nate had placed upon her was weighing down her entire body. All she wanted to do was crash on her bed and go to sleep, but she still had homework to finish.

"Hey," Ma greeted her when she walked into the apartment. "How was dinner?"

The bags beneath her eyes and the streaks of tears through the powder on her cheek made it clear Ma had been crying. "Fine. I'm going upstairs." Nova headed for the room she shared with her mother. She shut the door and locked it before pulling her homework out of her backpack. It didn't take long before there was soft knocking on the door.

"Nova?" Nate's voice came through from outside. "Can I come in please?"

Nova tried to ignore him, but she knew him well enough to know he wouldn't stop knocking. She huffed before climbing off her chair to open the door. The moment she did, she threw her arms around Nate's waist. "I don't want you to go," she whispered.

Nate's hand brushed against her curls. "I need to, Nova. Please don't be mad at me. I wouldn't be able to stand it if you never forgive me for leaving."

"Please don't go, Nate."

"I can't take Dad's place in this family, Nova. Things are getting better for him. Hopefully, the more his band succeeds, he'll learn to be a better father. As for me, I need to find my place in this world."

She didn't quite understand what he was going on about. Damien Stone could never be a better father, and no one expected Nate to be the father in his place. All Nova expected of Nate was to be there. His place in this world was with his family, but she could tell he was set on leaving, so all she could do was sob into his shirt and pray to whichever God was listening that he would someday return to them.

"I love you, Nova," Nate said.

"I love you, Kuya." Nova's tears soaked into his clothes. "I will write to you every day, I promise."

"You better." Nate pulled away from her to kneel down, so they could look at each other eye-to-eye. "I want to hear everything. Tell me all your stories.

You're a brilliant writer, Nova, and you tell the most fascinating stories. Someday, our dreams — yours and mine — will come true."

She believed him. As her older brother kissed her forehead and assured her that everything would be all right, Nova believed him.

But only because she didn't realize how hollow she would feel in his absence, how painful it would be to find Ma crying as she read his letter the next morning.

Nova had been so used to being abandoned by her dad, she didn't think it would hurt this much when it was Nate's turn to leave, but it did. It hurt a whole lot, and so, that's what Nova wrote to her brother that night.

Dear Nate, her letter read. *It hurts that you're not here. I wish you were, but tomorrow, we're moving to the new house. I hope you can find us there.*

Nova left their old run-down apartment and walked into an unknown future, holding on to a hope that their family would be complete again, that Nate would come to his senses and return to them. Unfortunately, with every day that Nate was absent, a fear grew within Nova — a fear telling her that no matter how much she loved someone, it didn't matter, because she wasn't strong enough, good enough, worthy enough to get the people she loved to stay. Maybe that's why her father and brother kept running away.

eight

THE ONE
WHO HAD
SOMEONE

- THIRTEEN YEARS AGO; NOVA, 10 -

Nova glided her fingers along the edges of her new bed. It was the first time she had ever had a room of her own. She had always shared either with her mother or her siblings. The house they moved into was beautiful — so much better than the apartment they had left behind. In its largeness, it felt hollow. Nova wished Nate was here to see it. She should ask Ma to take pictures to send to Nate.

Nova sat on the bed and let her focus drift outside the bedroom window. She fidgeted with her fingers as images formed in her mind of her older brother in a new city, making music and a name for himself. He had promised it wouldn't take long before he would come over to visit them. She wanted to believe him.

A soft knock on the door yanked her out of her dreams for her kuya. "Nova?" The door creaked open and in came Ma. "Are you okay? You've been in such a sour mood our entire drive here."

Nova's lips quivered as she grabbed the pillow from the bed, hugged it against her chest, and leaned her chin on it.

"You like the house, don't you?"

Nova nodded as she tried to hold back the tears. "Where's Nolan?"

"He decided he wants to meet the family next-door."

Nova forced a smile. "It is so like him to make friends his first day here."

"You'll make some friends too, iha." Ma combed her fingers through Nova's hair. "We get a chance at a new life here. It will be good for us."

"I know." Nova frowned.

"Then why so sad?"

Nova's lips shook harder as she said, "I miss Nate." The moment she said her brother's name out loud, the tears followed.

"Oh, iha. Come here." Ma gathered Nova in her arms. "I miss him too. More than you can imagine."

Nova gave in and sobbed into her mother's shoulder. "I'm sorry I didn't tell you." She wrapped her arms around her mother's neck. "He made me promise not to."

"I understand." Ma rested her chin on top of Nova's head. "Your kuya is all grown up now, and he needs to find his own way. I just wish I could've done more to help make his path easier. Life with me and your father was never easy for Nate."

For a moment, mother and daughter sat inside Nova's new room, silent in their sadness over the one missing member of their family. It wasn't until later that Nova recognized something amiss with how much she missed Nate. The recognition came only after the next-door neighbors dropped off Nolan, who had blue paint smeared all over his face.

"What happened to you?" Ma exclaimed, though her face lit up at the sight of him.

"He and my daughter have been painting," the man who brought Nolan home explained. Beside him was a beautiful woman carrying a platter between her hands. On his other side stood an equally beautiful little girl, right about Nolan's age. She also had paint on her face. "They ran out of canvas, so they improvised," the father explained.

"I can see that!" Ma laughed before laying her hand on Nova's shoulder. "This is Nova, my daughter. Nova, this is Pastor Sam, his wife, Aida, and their daughter, Serene. They're our next-door neighbors." Ma ruffled Nolan's hair. "I hope Nolan didn't cause you any trouble."

Aida smiled. "Not at all. He is such a wonderful boy. I think he and Serene will make great friends. And you—" Her smile widened as she shifted her focus on Nova. "You are so pretty!"

Nova blushed.

Ma nudged her. "What do you say, Nova?"

"Thank you." Nova wanted to hide.

"We're excited to get to know you all," the pastor said.

"Where are my manners?" Ma pressed her palm against her forehead and opened the door wide. "Please come in. It's still messy, but the house came with the furniture, so there isn't much unpacking we need to do."

The neighbors entered while Ma set aside unopened boxes still in the entryway. Nova rushed to help push back a box and then another against the wall to clear up a way for their guests to enter the living room.

"Your home is lovely." The mother held up a platter of food covered by aluminum foil. "We wanted to drop Nolan off and welcome your family to the neighborhood. We thought you might not have everything unpacked yet, so we brought you dinner. I made baked macaroni."

Nova licked her lips as she watched Ma take the platter. Her stomach grumbled. Nolan giggled beside her and patted her tummy.

"We haven't eaten since we arrived," Ma confessed. "Would you like to have dinner with us?"

"We wouldn't want to impose." The pastor smiled.

"Please. We insist," Ma said. "We would love the company."

Within the next hour, the mothers prepared a spread on the wooden table in their new home's backyard. The pastor started a barbecue. Nova helped Nolan and Serene wash the paint off their faces.

When she finished wiping Serene's face, Nova couldn't help but smile. Their family didn't have many friends back at their old apartment. It was refreshing to have some here. If Nate was here, it would be perfect.

Serene tilted her head to the side. "You are so pretty, Nova," she said, before giving Nova a big smile. She pointed at the gap in her teeth, where a tooth should have been. "I'd be prettier if I get my tooth back."

"I think you look pretty, anyway." Nolan leaned his weight on Nova's shoulder.

Nova side-eyed her brother. Did he already have a crush on Serene? Wasn't he too young for that? Nova shrugged it off. "I agree with Nolan." She tucked a strand of Serene's red hair behind her ear. "You're pretty no matter what."

"Kids, dinner!" Ma called out.

They finished washing and headed to the table. Nova rolled her eyes at Nolan and Serene skipping to dinner with their hands clasped together. She would need to have a talk with her little brother about this later.

Nova sat on the chair between her mother and Nolan. Across from her sat the mother, who was sitting between the pastor and Serene.

"Shall we say grace?" she said before Nova could dig into the baked mac.

Nova bit her lip. What did that mean?

"Please." Ma clasped her hands together over her lap.

Nova mimicked her mother.

"Serene, would you like to say a prayer?"

The way Serene's green eyes widened with delight as she nodded was what brought a sense of something lacking toward Nova. At ten years old, she couldn't quite place what it was that made her feel bad. Was it the obvious fact that Serene adored her father, and Nova couldn't care less where her dad was? After all, to her, Nate was a missing member of the family, but she had long forgotten the last time she thought of her father that way. Was the envy within her because of the relationship Serene had with the pastor?

Or was it something more? Something deeper? Something that could explain Serene's delight?

Nova glanced at Ma as Serene prayed. To her surprise, Ma had her eyes closed, her lips moving in quiet prayer.

Nova frowned. When did Ma learn to pray?

By the time everyone said their amens, Nova was no longer just hungry for baked macaroni. She was hungry for something — or Someone — greater.

That evening, when she finally found time alone in her room, Nova wrote a letter to Nate, telling him all about the Sinclairs and how much she longed to have the delight they had.

And for the first time in her life, Nova said a prayer to a God she had never known, but somehow still felt familiar to her — like a magnificent ancient Force Who had known her since the day He had formed her in her mother's womb.

- CALEB, 12 -

"Hey, Caleb." Sam had his face pasted on one of the windows of their family room. "Does Pastor Sam have a son?"

Caleb shook his head. "Not that I know of. Why?"

"He has a kid with him. A boy."

"Yeah?" Caleb approached the window. The first thing he saw was their family van driving away with Mom and the girls to go to ladies' night at church. In their front yard, Pastor Sam was shaking hands with Dad. Not far from them, Isaac and Josh were talking to a dark-haired boy. Definitely not Pastor Sam's kid.

"Do you think I can be friends with him?" Sam asked.

"Let's go find out." Caleb tugged at his brother's sleeve. "Come on."

They rushed down the stairs and on to the front yard, almost bumping into Josh before they could slow down. They arrived just in time to hear the new kid say, "Serene is my best friend."

"Pastor Sam's daughter?" Sam wrinkled his nose. "She's like... five."

"So am I," the boy said. "How old are you?"

"Seven. My sister, Deb, is seven too. She's my twin. Maybe Serene is your twin too."

"I don't know." The boy frowned. "I'll ask her tomorrow."

"What's your name, kid?" Caleb asked.

"Nolan."

"I'm Caleb." He laid his hand on top of Sam's head. "This is Sam."

"Your name is Sam too?" Nolan grinned. "Does that mean you'll be a pastor someday?"

"God, help us if that happens." Josh snickered as he exchanged glances with Caleb.

"Boys!" Dad clapped his hands together. "Come help set up the barbecue. Isaac, go get the food from the kitchen. Your mom said everything should be on the counter top."

"Sure, Dad." Isaac rushed off.

Within the next half hour, everyone helped set up for dinner. After setting the table, Caleb stood by his father, who was talking to Pastor Sam about the Bible as he flipped a steak on the grill.

"We're not after signs and wonders," Pastor Sam said, "but when God's presence abides in us, I believe signs and wonders follow. It just breaks my heart that we don't see more of God's power in today's church."

Dad nodded. "I hear you, Pastor. Naomi and I have been praying for our children—" he laid a hand on Caleb's back and nodded toward Josh who had just arrived to find out what was going on "—that they will encounter God early in their lives and decide to follow Jesus no matter where He leads."

"I'd like to do that," Josh said.

"Do what?" Dad asked.

Josh shrugged. "Follow Jesus."

"Me too." Caleb nodded. "I just don't know how."

Dad exchanged glances with Pastor Sam.

"What do you say, Marcus?" Pastor Sam asked. "Should we introduce Jesus to the boys tonight?"

"We already kind of know Jesus, Pastor," Josh said.

"Yeah," Caleb agreed. "Dad talks about Him a lot."

"But we don't know *know* Him." Josh frowned.

"Well, let's make sure you know *know* Him," their father said.

They finished barbecuing the rest of the meat before they gathered all the boys at the table. Pastor Sam told them what their father and mother had already told them many times before. They had heard it at Sunday School multiple times, as well, but something about that night was different.

Caleb listened and understood. People were sinners. Like so many of the characters in the books he read, everyone had their flaws, their fears, their shortcomings. As Pastor Sam explained further, Caleb asked himself a sincere question: *Am I a sinner? What have I done wrong?*

Glimpses of all the times he complained about his chores or fought with Josh or got angry at Isaac or made fun of Hannah came through his mind. A deep conviction came over him. Yes. He was a sinner, and he needed Jesus.

"Forgive me, Jesus," Caleb whispered even as Pastor Sam and their father led them in prayer. "I want to follow You."

Nothing happened right at that moment. Caleb didn't feel a change within him at all, but he believed Jesus cleansed his sins that night. Dad said so, and Caleb could trust his father's word. If God was anything like Marcus Grant, Caleb could trust Him too.

This unwavering belief in his own father's integrity bloomed into a faith in the Father of Lights, the Giver of every perfect gift, the One in Whom there was no shadow of turning.

From that day forward, Caleb became more intentional in following not just his father, but the Christ Whom his father followed. Little by little, Caleb noticed the changes in himself. One of these was how Caleb's conscience niggled at him a lot more than it used to — like a still, small Voice accompanied by rock solid conviction telling him which way he had to go.

Nova had never been to church before that night, so she didn't quite know what to expect, but Ma was going and Nolan was with Pastor Sam, so she might as well find out what all the fuss was about. The truth was that Nova was beyond excited to go. Her first week at school hadn't been easy. She hadn't been able to make friends as fast as Nolan had, so she hoped she could find friends at this church instead of at school.

Their car, Neutron, backfired again as Ma pulled over at the church parking lot.

Nova blushed. "This car is so embarrassing."

Ma sighed. "Neutron is still running, so he'll have to make do for now until hopefully, your dad gets us a new car."

"Or Nate will." Nova shrugged. "Have you sent him my letters?"

"I have," Ma assured her. "Now, come on. We don't want to be late."

Clara Stone had an air of excitement about her as she got out of the car. Nova held hands with her mother before they traversed the space between the parking lot and the church building, its facade lined with glass panels extending from the ground to the top of the building.

"It's huge," Nova whispered.

"My church in the Philippines was a lot smaller than this," Ma said. "Nate and I used to go, but when your father sent for us here, we stopped going. I miss church."

"You never talked about going to church before."

The corners of Ma's eyes tilted downward as she lowered her eyes. A bitter smile formed on her lips. "I used to love Jesus as a kid, but I walked away from Him after I got pregnant with Nate. Your father was already back here in America. I had no idea how to get in touch with him to tell him that I was pregnant. It was a difficult time. I felt as if God had abandoned me. By the time your father came to visit years later, I had already forgotten my faith. I've neglected it for far too long. It didn't help that Damien didn't like going to church either."

Nova winced. Her father didn't like a lot of things, so that didn't really color her opinion about church. After all, Pastor Sam was a good father, and he went to that church. Maybe Damien Stone just didn't belong where good fathers were. Nova stopped walking just as they were about to reach the church entrance. "Do you think God will let us in His church after not believing in Him for so long?"

Ma chuckled. "I'm sure He will, iha."

Nova shrugged. She hoped God would, because she really wanted to know God more.

"Clara!" Serene's mother pushed the double glass doors open for them. "I'm so glad you and Nova made it!"

"Nova!" Serene leaped past her mother and right at Nova, wrapping her arms around Nova's waist. "You're here! Mama Aida and I made brownies. You'll try them, right?"

"You made brownies?" Nova dropped her jaw to exaggerate her excitement. "That's great. Of course I'll try them."

"Good! Because they're amazing!" Serene pulled her inside and toward the refreshment table.

"You're here again?" A lovely lady with her brown hair in a pretty braid stood behind the table. She frowned at Serene.

"I'm not here to get food for myself, Miss Rhoda," Serene explained, a soft blush tinting her freckled cheeks. "This is my friend, Nova. I want her to try our brownies."

Miss Rhoda gave Nova a reserved smile. "You must be new. Are you with someone?"

Nova pointed at her mother. "I'm with my ma."

"And your father?"

Nova shrugged. "I don't know where he is. He's never around."

Miss Rhoda raised a brow. "Oh."

Serene squeezed Nova's hand. "Here's a brownie, Nova."

Nova took it and let Serene drag her to another area of the church lobby, where other girls sat on a cushioned bench, waiting for whatever was supposed to happen that night.

"Never mind Miss Rhoda. She's grumpy today," Serene said.

"Hi, Serene!" A pretty blonde girl waved at them. "Who's your friend?"

"This is Nova. They live next door to us," Serene said. "This is Hannah and her sister, Deb."

Nova shook hands with Hannah.

"How old are you?" Hannah asked.

"Ten," Nova replied.

"I'm eleven. Deb is seven."

"I'm the youngest!" Serene threw her arms in the air.

"And the cutest." Hannah pinched her cheeks softly.

Deb tugged at Hannah's dress. "Will Miss Rhoda take care of the kids again tonight?"

Hannah shrugged. "I hope not. Mama Aida tells the more interesting stories. Miss Rhoda is boring."

Nova glanced back at the lady by the table. "I think she's beautiful."

"Oh, she is," Hannah agreed, "but she's rarely in a good mood. I think she loves to teach us kids, because she wants kids of her own."

"But she's not married yet, so she can't have any," Deb added.

"Let's be nice to her though." Hannah gave them a resolute nod. "She's a lot kinder and more interesting when we cooperate with her."

Serene held Nova's hand. "Don't worry, Nova. We'll make sure she won't be mean to you."

A wave of dread came over Nova. What was this woman like? When Miss Rhoda gathered the young girls together so the ladies could have time on their own, however, it turned out Nova's apprehension was unwarranted.

Miss Rhoda told them a story from the Bible about a young boy named Samuel, who heard the voice of God.

It was the first time Nova ever heard of such a story. Was it possible for her to hear the voice of God? What did He sound like?

Serene yawned as she leaned her head on Nova's shoulder. "I know this story already. Daddy's name is Samuel too."

"My twin too!" Deb, who was sitting in the other seat next to Nova, giggled. "Why are so many church people named Sam?"

All the kids around her knew the story already, so a lot of them weren't even paying attention, but Nova wanted to learn more about this God and the boy who could hear Him, so she ignored the other kids and hung on to every word Miss Rhoda said.

Later that evening, she wrote a letter to Nate telling him all about the boy, Samuel, and how he could hear the voice of God. After finishing her letter, Nova remained silent and waited until she fell asleep, but she drifted off into a land of dreams without hearing a single word from Above.

In her dreams, however, her family was complete — Damien, Ma, Nate, Nolan, and her — and they were happy. When Nova woke up, the first thing she did was pray to God, asking Him to talk to her like He talked to Samuel. Maybe if she could hear His voice, Nova could one day ask Him how to make all her dreams come true.

nine

THE ONE WHO LOOKED UP TO HIM

- ONE YEAR LATER; NOVA, 11 -

Winsome musings of forest lake adventures and nights of singing together around a campfire were running through Nova's head when she jumped out of the bus that led them from Connect Church to the camping grounds, where they were to hold their church camp — the first one Nova ever went to.

As she stood next to her brother, waiting for their mother to come down from the bus, Nova giggled at Nolan, whose shoes had just been desecrated by the vomit Serene had been holding in throughout the entire ride. The disgust on his face, accompanied by his concern for his best friend, made it hard for Nova to empathize with him. She found the situation too adorable to feel bad about it. Even Nolan and Serene's cuteness, however, wasn't enough to keep Serene's mother from showering their family with apologies.

Not quite interested in their cleanup and the mothers hovering over her brother and his best friend, Nova wandered away from them to check out where this camp was going to happen.

The first thing she saw was what she labeled a rich man's log cabin. The full-length glass windows in front teased the warm lighting and cozy feel of the lobby. Pastor Sam, his assistant, and Hannah's father made their way inside. A lush green garden with well-manicured landscaping surrounded her. Nova's shoulders slumped. So much for the camping-in-the-wild-outdoors image she had painted in her head.

"Hi, Nova." Hannah Grant stepped next to her. "Is it your first time coming here?"

Though a small breath of relief came through her lips at the sight of a familiar face, Nova tried to play it cool. "Yes."

"Are you excited?" Hannah nudged her shoulder.

"I guess. I'm not sure what to expect."

"It'll be fun." Hannah placed an arm over her shoulder to give her a side hug. "We're here every year. It's such a nice place, and there are loads of things we can do between sessions."

"Sessions?"

"Ow!" Hannah yelped when a boy bumped into her. He had dirty blond hair and glasses, and his eyes were fixed on a book. It was the large duffel bag hanging over his shoulder that had hit Hannah. "Watch where you're going, Caleb!"

"Sorry." He glanced at her, making it look like it was torture to pry his eyes away from the book he was reading. "Are you okay?"

Hannah nodded. "What are you reading?"

"*The Count of Monte Cristo*. Alexandre Dumas."

"Is it good?"

"It's interesting," he said before returning his attention to the book. "I'll see you later. Let me know if you need anything, okay?" He stepped aside, heaved his duffel bag to a more secure spot on his shoulder, and walked on, his eyes still glued to his book.

"My brother, Caleb." Hannah rolled her eyes.

"Nova!" Ma's voice rang from somewhere. "Come get your things!"

"I have to go," Nova said, casting one last glance at Caleb, who was already walking toward the cabin. The book must be quite a read if he was so engrossed. What was it again? *The Count of Monte Cristo*?

"Can you believe he brought a book to camp? Why would you read a book in a place like this?" Hannah shook her head. "Anyway, see you later, Nova."

Nova didn't think that to be strange at all. If her imagination could suck her into a different time, a different place, why wouldn't a good book be able to do the same for him? Nova shifted her weight from one foot to the other as she watched Hannah go catch up with her brother. Did he actually mean it? Would he really drop the book to help Hannah if she asked for it? When Hannah reached him, he looked up from his book, smiled at Hannah, and gave her a side hug, pulling her close to him. The sight of brother and sister made Nova's heart ache. How was Nate doing?

While everyone was preparing for dinner around campfires, Nova spent her time writing a letter to her brother and a story she wished someone would someday find as engrossing as Caleb found his book.

When it came time for everyone to gather around campfires, Nova still had an image of Caleb reading his book in her head, so much so that when she noticed him among his family that evening, he put a smile on her face. After helping his father and brothers make a fire and set up their tents, he settled down along with everyone and cracked open his book. Something about that warmed Nova's heart and made her stomach flutter. It made her feel like she knew him, like they had a familiarity between them, even if he didn't even know she existed.

"Nova!" Serene threw her arms around Nova's neck. "Can you braid my hair? I told Mama Aida I want you to do it."

"I would love to." Nova hugged the cute little redhead. "Come sit on my lap."

Serene climbed onto her lap. She then pulled out a long piece of lace and a small comb from her jacket's pocket. "Mama Aida says we can use these for my hair."

"Great." Nova took the comb and started straightening out the kid's tangled red hair. "Hold on to the lace for me."

"Okay." Serene seemed perfectly happy with her position.

"Serene," Nova said.

"Yep?"

"Why does everyone at church call your mom Mama Aida?"

Serene giggled. "Because that's her name, silly."

"Your grandma and grandpa named her Mama Aida?"

"Well, no, but everyone calls her Mama." Serene suddenly tilted her head to the side. "I don't know why."

"Stay still." Nova positioned her head properly and continued to braid. From the corner of her eye, she caught a glimpse of her little brother marching off to Pastor Sam. Not too far away, Ma was having a deep conversation with Mama Aida at a picnic table.

The men surrounding Nolan started chuckling. Nova narrowed her eyes at her brother, who seemed to still be having the most serious conversation with Pastor Sam. Then there was Caleb Grant, face still buried in a book.

Nova couldn't wait to get her own copy of what he was reading. She had never heard of that book before. Nova focused on Serene's braids while her mind drifted off to a story of her own, because the story he was reading was still unknown. Maybe one day, Caleb would read a story she wrote. Would he also forget everyone around him if he ever got to read her stories? Nova would like to someday make up a story like that. The smile on her face spread with the notion.

It was, however, a completely different book — one Caleb also found engrossing — that transformed Nova's life. It was after one of their evening worship sessions at the main hall when Nova was on her way back to their cabin. Nova walked alone, a few steps ahead of Nolan and Serene, who were giggling over Nolan's new guitar. Ma and Mama Aida were further away from them, still chatting.

As they passed by a small flower garden with a gazebo in the middle, Nova heard muffled mumbling coming from the gazebo.

Curious, she pressed her forefinger against her lips to gesture for Nolan and Serene to be quiet. She then tiptoed toward the gazebo to investigate. There was no mistaking it. The mumbling was coming from Caleb Grant — Nova recognized his dirty blond hair and his clothes from earlier. Seated in one of the gazebo's arched benches, he was doubled over, his face pressed against his Bible as he prayed. His shoulders were shaking as he spoke.

Nova couldn't quite make out what he was saying until he said, "I surrender my life to you, Jesus."

Suddenly, shame filled Nova for watching Caleb during such a private moment. He deserved to be alone with Jesus. She turned back to their path, pulling Nolan and Serene with her.

"What was that?" Nolan asked.

"Nothing," Nova said, but it wasn't nothing, because before she laid her head to sleep that night, she wrote a letter to Nate, telling him she had surrendered her life to Jesus, too. After all, Caleb Grant came across to Nova as a smart boy, always reading a book and all. If he thought it was a good idea to give his life to God, maybe he was on to something.

Nova sealed the envelope and hoped she would remember to give it to Ma the next day. Maybe after reading this, Nate would finally respond, because she sorely missed her older brother, but for now, at least she had Caleb Grant to look up to instead.

- CALEB, 13 -

Wonder filled Caleb as he listened to his father speaking on stage about his spirit getting a glimpse of heaven. He hadn't known such a thing was possible.

Even after the evening session, while his brothers fooled around — Isaac daring Josh to tackle him to the ground — Caleb drifted off into contemplation.

What was it like to experience God the way his father did? Something deep within Caleb wanted to find out, so he scanned his surroundings and found his father walking along the same cobblestone path they were on, but still far behind them.

"I want to go talk to Dad," Caleb told his brothers, who didn't seem to even hear him, because they were busy wrestling each other. Caleb rushed over to his father and paused in his tracks when he was near enough to see his mouth moving and his face aglow as he walked.

Dad had his hands in his pocket and for a moment, his eyes crinkled as he shut them tight. Was he about to cry?

"Dad?" Caleb didn't budge from his spot.

His father opened his eyes. "Son." He gave Caleb a curt nod and smiled. "I'm surprised you're not lost in some new fictional kingdom."

"It's too dark to read."

"When has that ever stopped you? I've seen you walk out of your room and to the bathroom at night, holding up a flashlight, so you could keep reading."

Caleb's sheepish smile was far from a reflection of the pride puffing inside him. There was no shame in loving his books so much. After all, Dad himself had given him most of his favorites; still, he hadn't realized he'd been into books so much, it was weird to people whenever they saw him not reading. He shrugged away his father's anecdotal observation of him. "I didn't feel like reading tonight."

"Something on your mind?"

"Did you really go to heaven, Dad?"

Dad's broad shoulders heaved before he extended his arm toward his son, placing his hand on Caleb's shoulder, so they could walk together. "I believe I did. Why do you ask?"

"I want to know God like you do. Not just because I want to have experiences like that — that's great and all, but it's more than that. I can't quite explain."

Dad chuckled. "Few can comprehend, much less explain, the Holy Spirit's work in our lives, so that's okay. Your mom and I always pray for the six of you to have a personal and powerful walk with God, so I'm glad you told me about wanting to know God more."

"What do I do? I've accepted Christ as my Savior, but it's like nothing has changed. I'm still me."

"Sometimes, transformation happens in an instant. Other times, it happens through a process. How about you tell the Lord what you are telling me right now? Surrender your life to Him and talk to Him about the things you want Him to change about you."

Desire stirred within Caleb even as they got closer to their cabin. "Can I do that now?"

"Sure. Find a spot where you can be alone with your Bible and start praying. Also, read John 17."

Caleb did just that. Ten minutes later, he was in a secluded gazebo. At first, it felt awkward as he started to pray. What was he supposed to say? Eventually, the words just gushed out of his mouth in natural and honest confession.

"Lord Jesus, I want to know You better, but to be honest, I don't know how," he said. "I don't talk much to people, so it's kind of hard to talk to You, because You know—" Caleb shrugged "—You're invisible and all, but I know You're there, because You said so. If You said it, it must be true." Caleb paused. What was he saying? He scratched his head.

Now what?

He stared at his Bible, shrugged, and opened it to the book of John, chapter seventeen. He had read those words so many times before, but that night, it was as if the words were jumping off the page and right to his heart. This was Jesus's prayer for mankind — that they would know Him and the Father and make Him known by others. Tears rushed down Caleb's face. Warmth covered his body, and somehow, Caleb recognized it. The Lord was right there with him. The Holy Spirit was within him. When his shoulders shook and he started sobbing, Caleb pressed his face against the Bible and started praying, indecipherable words coming out of his lips.

Caleb had no idea how long he had been there, but he could have stayed forever in the presence of the Almighty. When his tears subsided, he whispered, "I surrender my life to you, Jesus."

He took a breath when he sensed a presence nearby. Was it one of his siblings? Who cared? Caleb lingered in the moment, knowing he had somehow caught hold of something greater than he was — something of eternal worth, and it was so precious, he could give his entire life to pursuing more of it, more of God.

The night felt timeless to Caleb as he leaned back on the bench and observed the moon. Almost as if he was talking to his brother or a close friend, he started telling God about the concerns of his heart.

"I'll be in high school after this summer," he said. "It's kind of scary. Isaac seems to be doing fine, but I'm not like him or even Josh. I'm anxious about it, but I trust You'll be with me, so I guess it will be okay." Caleb then blushed as he spoke about a desire he had never spoken out loud to anyone before, one he had held in his heart since their mom had once told them how she met their father. "Lord, I hope You don't mind me asking, but Dad met Mom when they were in high school, so I was thinking maybe it can be the same for me. Can I meet the girl I will marry when I go to high school?" Caleb shrugged one shoulder. "Just a suggestion. You don't need to make it happen, if You don't want to."

The next morning, a family arrived at church camp. The Meyers had been on the mission field in Southeast Asia for years, and they had just returned in time to join the church's camp. Mr. and Mrs. Meyer had one daughter — Olivia, who was the same age as Caleb.

When their parents introduced them, Caleb shook her hand, his skin looking pale against her sun-kissed tan. "I'm Caleb."

Olivia had one of the most welcoming smiles Caleb had ever seen. She tucked a strand of her wavy dark brown hair behind her ear. "Olivia."

"It's great to meet you." He swayed his head sideways to gesture for them to step away from their parents, who were catching up with one another. "We can go to the lobby. I'm sure your parents will end up there, so they can check in."

Olivia nodded.

He offered to help with her bags. She obliged. Within the short span of time it took for them to get to the reception area, Caleb discovered they were going to the same high school come fall. For the rest of the camp, he and Olivia became inseparable, and through it all, Caleb kept wondering if God had just answered his prayers for a wife by bringing into his life a lovely young woman named Olivia.

ten

THE ONE WHO HAD A CRUSH

- ONE YEAR LATER; NOVA, 12 -

Apart from the icy statement her father had uttered to her mother after the church service, Nova could only guess what was going on in Damien Stone's mind as they drove back home from church.

"None of you will go to church again," Dad had said.

Ma responded with silence.

Nova glanced at her little brother sitting in the backseat next to her. With his focus on the scenery they were passing by, Nolan was seemingly oblivious to the tension brewing inside the car. Had he heard their father's heated statement? Could Dad actually stop them — especially Nolan — from going to church?

Her heart ached at the thought. She wasn't yet sure what it meant to follow God, but she wanted to learn. Besides, both Ma and Nolan smiled a lot more since they all started going.

What was Dad so mad about anyway? Nolan had played beautifully on stage this morning. Everyone kept saying how blessed they were with his and Serene's performance. The painting Serene had come up with while Nolan played was something she would love to have up on her wall. Both children were exceptionally gifted, and any normal parent — like Ma — would be proud of Nolan, but Dad? No. He had left the church fuming, and based on the tense silence filling their car, it seemed he was just about ready to detonate and explode the moment they got home.

Nova gripped her little brother's wrist. Nate was no longer there, and it had been a long while since they had seen their father and mother fight.

"Nova, you're shaking." Nolan stared at her hand on his wrist.

"I'm cold." She faked a shiver and ran her palms up and down her arms.

Nolan wrinkled his nose. "Why?" His gaze wafted past her shoulder and out the window to the sunny day outside.

"I don't know." Nova mouthed.

"You did so well on stage this morning, Nolan!" Their mother's high-pitched voice came across as a poor attempt to sound cheerful. It did little to diffuse the building negativity oozing from their father's broodiness.

Even Nolan, who was never one to complain about being showered with praises, barely reacted.

Nova gritted her teeth. Dad was rarely ever home. Why couldn't he just be kind when he was? Why did he have to ruin everything good they managed to build whenever he was away?

To her relief, the familiar homes of their neighborhood came to view. The house next to theirs, where Pastor Sam's family lived, was still empty. Nova sighed even as longing came over her. It had always been a thing of curiosity for her what families like the Sinclairs and the Grants did after church. It seemed to her like their family was the only one that went straight home.

She didn't have much time to dwell on her curious musings, however, because Dad suddenly hit the brakes to the car.

Their father pointed a finger at their mother. "We need to talk, Clara. I will not have you dragging my children to some religious—" The cussing that came out of his mouth made Nolan gasp. Nova was far more used to it.

"Damien, let's at least have a nice lunch together first. You've been away for so long."

"No. We're dealing with this now. We should have gone to Disney World with the kids like I wanted instead of attending that stupid church. What a waste of my time!" Damien got out of the car and slammed the door shut.

Ma jolted at the sound. From the front seat, she turned toward Nova. She forced a smile, and, in a voice she could barely control from shaking, said, "How about you go to the playground with Nolan? I'll try to get you some food as soon as I can."

Nova nodded.

Nolan groaned. "Noooo... I'm hungry!" He laid his hand on his stomach. "Don't you hear my tummy grumbling?"

Ma handed Nova a dollar bill. "Go get your brother something from an ice cream truck."

Nova took the bill and swallowed back a question about where she was supposed to find an ice cream truck. She would just have to distract Nolan like she always did in situations like this.

"Clara!" Dad burst out of the front door, his countenance dark and his body expanding as he breathed in and out, braced for a fight. "Come in and talk to me!"

Ma's eyes shifted from side-to-side as if to check if any of the neighbors could hear them. She then got out of the car, approaching her husband, saying quiet words to try and appease him. "Let's go in, Damien. Let's not make a scene. We can talk about this."

"You'll just leave these kids in the car?" Damien pointed at Nova and Nolan, who were still seated inside, unmoving.

"They're going to the playground. I don't understand why you're so angry."

At that statement, their father's face took on a fearsome expression, so dark, that Nova wondered if he was part-demon. She hated her father, and she would never forgive him for the rest of her life. Especially now that he had just grabbed Ma's arm was dragging her inside the house.

Nova's immediate instinct when she saw the way Damien was treating Ma was to pull Nolan's face against her chest in a tight hug to hide what was happening from him.

"Nova!" Nolan tried to get away from her embrace. "I can't breathe!"

"Neither can I," Nova muttered beneath her breath, holding her flailing brother in a tight hug until Dad and Ma closed the front door. The moment they were out of sight, she let go of Nolan and breathed a sigh of relief.

"Why did you do that?!" Out of pure instinct, Nolan punched her on the shoulder.

"Nolan!" Nova's eyes widened. Fire filled her as she grabbed her brother's arms and shook him. "Never do that again! You never hit me or any other girl! You hear me?!"

It took a second before she recognized the terror in her brother's eyes. His lips trembled. "You're hurting me."

What had she just done? Nova let go of Nolan. "I'm sorry, but I don't ever want you to be the kind of man who hits women."

"You mean like Dad hits Ma?"

Nova froze. "Why would you say that?"

Nolan frowned. "I think he hit her this morning before we went to church. She had blood on her lips." He crossed his arms over his chest. "I don't like Dad very much. I wish he would just leave, so we can have lunch after church in peace."

"That makes two of us." Nova's face tightened as she shook her head. "I also wish he would just leave and never come back."

"Like Nate?"

It broke Nova's heart to hear Nolan say that. It made her feel like such a failure. She had tried everything she could to shield Nolan from their family's troubles, but at seven years old, he was too observant, too precocious, too smart for his own good. It had become harder and harder to hide things from him, to protect him from how bad their family life actually was. He was too young for this. Nate had tried his best to protect her; now, it was up to her to do her best to protect Nolan. She couldn't quite fight back like Nate used to, so she did the only thing she knew to do to at least distract her little brother from all the negatives of this world.

She laughed.

Nolan scowled at her. "What's so funny? First, you crush my face with your body; now, you're laughing at me."

"I'm not laughing at you, silly." Nova playfully messed with her brother's hair.

"No! Nova! Don't do that. Serene likes my hair this way."

"Well, Serene isn't here, is she?" Nova continued to tug at strands of his hair. "Maybe we should go find her."

"We don't need to find her. I know where she is."

"Where's that?"

"She and her parents are out to have lunch at some fancy restaurant with the Grant people and the new people who came. The Mare people." Nolan sounded whiny, which Nova interpreted as him being upset that he didn't get invited.

"You mean the Meyers?" Nova winced. She had noticed Caleb staring at the Meyer girl at church this morning.

"Yeah. Those people." Nolan huffed.

Nova couldn't help but chuckle.

"You're laughing at me again!" Nolan balled his small hands into fists.

Nova raised a brow at him. "Are you going to hit me again?"

His eyes cleared, and he put his hands down. He glanced at their house and settled himself back on his car seat as he shook his head. "I don't want to be like Dad. When I marry Serene, I'm never going to hit her."

"You're marrying Serene, huh? Does Pastor Sam know about this?"

Nolan stared at her like she had just asked the most ridiculous question in the planet. "I told him at camp last year."

"And he agreed?"

Nova found her little brother's frown precious as he shook his head. "He said I should ask him again when I'm twenty-one years old. I did my maths and figured that's still a long time from now. I'll be so old by then."

This time, Nova actually laughed at him. "You're funny, Nolan. Come on. Let's get out of this car and go to the park."

They got out of the car. After making sure it was locked, Nova held Nolan's hand. Before they could walk down the block to the neighborhood playground, however, Nova stopped by the mailbox to check if there was a letter from Nate. It had become a tradition for her to check whenever she passed it by. Experience had taught her to expect to find nothing but a bunch of white and brown envelopes all addressed to Ma.

To her surprise, this time, there was only one letter inside the mailbox. It was in a pretty black envelope with metallic gold lining. The letter was addressed to her, and the return address was Nate's.

Nova couldn't hold back a squeal as she held the envelope against her chest.

"What is that?" Nolan asked.

"It's a letter from Nate." Nova beamed.

"Open it!"

"We'll open it at the playground." She squeezed his hand and tugged him forward. "Come on."

That was enough to excite Nolan — enough for him to forget that they were supposed to find an ice cream truck to quiet his grumbling stomach.

By the time they reached the playground, however, the moment he saw the slides, monkey bars, and swings, he let go of Nova's hand and ran ahead, leaping into a monkey bar and falling to the ground at the third bar. Nova sank into the bench next to the sandbox, Nate's letter clutched in her hand.

Her chest roiled with how much she missed her older brother even as she opened the letter. She read its contents, took a breath to process what Nate was saying, and then read it again.

Shock overcame her, because she couldn't think of any other time that Nate and Damien agreed on something. In the letter, Nate had written a lot of things — mostly to let her know how he was and what he was doing — but what grabbed her attention the most was the part where he addressed her previous letter about them going to church and her wanting to surrender her life to God.

I don't believe in God, Nova, Nate had written. *Neither should you nor Ma nor Nolan. Don't encourage our little brother to pursue this. Back home, when Ma got pregnant with me, the church didn't take care of us. Not long after I was born, our grandparents died, leaving Ma all alone to care for me. What kind of God would let that happen? In her parents' place, God gave Damien Stone to Ma. Our poor excuse for a father. A good God won't allow the things that have happened to our family, Nova. These church people are just using Nolan's talent. Don't let them. Stay as far away from church and God as possible.*

Nova read those words again and again, and by the end of it, she disagreed with Nate, because if God was so evil, how was it that families like the Sinclairs and the Grants existed? Why did people like Mama Aida and Caleb love Him so much? What if God was good, and the reason they had suffered so much was because Dad and Nate kept disobeying Him?

Nova watched her little brother — innocent in so many ways, but already tainted by the brokenness of their father. Nova clutched her beloved older brother's letter against her chest and once again, prayed to a God she longed to know. "God, if we keep going to church, will You give us a complete and happy family? I would like that very much."

Though Nova felt like she had struck a good bargain with God that afternoon, she would never really find out if He would come through for her, because Ma had decided to stop going to church after Damien left. Not long after, only Nolan remained in church, spending his Sundays with the Sinclairs. After having been pressed by Nate through another letter, Nova stopped going too, and in doing so, she kept wondering if it was her fault her family remained incomplete.

- TWO YEARS LATER; NOVA, 14 -

Upon catching a glimpse of Caleb Grant at the end of the hallway, Nova's gut reaction was to back away until her back hit her locker to clear a path for him and the girl whose books he was carrying. Olivia Meyer. He had eyes only for her, and Nova pushed back her jealousy as the couple passed her by without as much as a glance toward her. Neither knew of her existence, and Nova decided it was better that way. It was enough for her to admire Caleb from afar, appreciate the way he was always so careful to treat Olivia in a way only a gentleman would. That's what he was. A gentleman. Nova sighed. God must really like Olivia if He gave her Caleb.

A mixture of pain and longing gripped her heart when Caleb laughed at something Olivia had said. Nova sighed and shut her locker door.

"Hi." A guy with messy dark hair and a tall lanky build was leaning against the locker next to her. "I'm Knox."

She tried not to wrinkle her nose. Based on his oily skin and hair, she wouldn't have been surprised if he hadn't showered that morning. "I'm Nova."

"I know your name." He winced. "I've had a crush on you for a while now."

"Oh. Okay." Nova shifted her weight from one foot to the other. "Thank you?"

He chuckled. "Not the answer I was hoping for, but I'll take it. Don't worry. I just want to be friends, if that's okay with you."

Nova shrugged. "Sure."

She glanced from Knox to Caleb, then back. They were nothing alike. They might as well have been night and day in comparison, but Knox was here. He could have a crush on her if he wanted.

Meanwhile, Nova could keep dreaming about her crush on Caleb Grant, knowing well he may never even know she existed, but it didn't matter, because that's what made him perfect. As long as they didn't know each other, there was no way Caleb could ever disappoint her.

THE ONE WHO LOST A BROTHER

- CALEB, 16 -

The grand opening of the new mall in town attracted quite a crowd, and the Grant siblings made sure they would be in the mix — even if it meant the teens had to drag their younger siblings with them there on a busy weekend.

As they squeezed their way past all these strangers to get to the arcade, Caleb held on to Olivia's hand to make sure he wouldn't lose her. Foremost in his mind was the desire to ditch his siblings to get his girlfriend all to himself.

His girlfriend.

He grinned upon casting a glance at her heart-shaped face. Her tan from living in a tropical country was already gone, but Olivia was still unquestionably beautiful, and after a lot of parental counseling for each of them and discussions among their parents, the Grants and the Meyers finally allowed Caleb and Olivia to date.

What else would they do? Caleb and Olivia had been spending every spare moment they found with each other.

So, here they were, on their first time going out as an official couple, and they had all of Caleb's siblings in tow.

Olivia inched closer to Caleb when someone started climbing the escalator, squeezing his way past everyone ahead of him. "There are so many people in here."

Upon reaching the top of the escalator, a panicked Hannah yelled out his name. "Caleb!"

"Hannah?" Caleb's brows met as they huddled together in a spot out of the way of mall traffic. "Where's everyone else?"

"Isaac and Kelly returned to the food court." Cheeks flushed, Hannah talked like she had no breath left in her. "Josh is with Deb. They went back to the toy shop." Hannah blew out a breath and paced on the small space she occupied amid the crowded mall.

His sister looked like she was about to have an anxiety attack, so Caleb grabbed her by the wrist. "Hannah, calm down." He gripped her arms, formed a small O with his lips, and drew in one long breath. He exhaled slowly as he nodded at her and brushed his fingers against her soft hair.

Hannah started following him, inhaling and exhaling. When she began to calm down, Caleb smiled at her. "Okay, Hannah. What happened?"

"We lost Sam," Hannah said. "No one knows where he is. When was the last time you saw him?"

Caleb exchanged glances with Olivia. He racked his brain for an image of the last time he had seen his youngest brother. He couldn't come up with a memory, apart from seeing him at home for breakfast that morning. He had been too preoccupied thinking about the possibility of kissing Olivia.

"I honestly thought he was with you." Olivia pointed at Hannah.

Caleb cringed at the guilt on his sister's face.

"The last time I saw him was at the food court, and he was with you guys!" Hannah threw her hands up. "Then I spotted Josh, and he said Sam was with Isaac and Kelly, but when we saw them, Isaac said he expected Sam was with me, because I was going to the arcade, and Sam wanted to go." Her lips trembled. "Did I lose Sam?"

"You didn't lose Sam. We all did. It's not your fault, Hannah," Caleb tried to assure her. "We all should have been paying attention to him. Look. Go to the arcade, okay? Odds are Sam will look for us there, since we all talked about going there. Have you checked if he's there?"

"Josh and Deb checked. He's not there. We'll be in huge trouble with Mom and Dad."

"Relax, Hannah. We will find him. Don't get ahead of yourself. Go to the arcade. Pray. Wait to see if Sam will show up there. The rest of us will search."

To his relief, this seemed to appease Hannah. She nodded. "I'll pray." She twisted her heel and headed for the arcade.

Caleb smiled as he watched her go. Despite all of Hannah's drama, one thing Caleb was certain about her was she loved the Lord. Nothing calmed her like time spent with God.

"Now what?" Olivia asked.

Caleb shrugged. "Any idea where to look?" His heart began thumping against his chest as the immensity of the situation dawned on him. Hannah had every reason to panic, considering how big this crowd was.

Olivia shook her head.

Caleb searched his mind for the last time he had seen his little brother at the mall. Hannah was right. Sam had been dragging himself behind him and Olivia at the food court before they all went to the toy shop. He narrowed his eyes as a possibility struck him. "I may be wrong, but I have a hunch where he might be. Come on." He tugged for Olivia to follow him. Two escalators down, they were back at the food court. There, they stumbled across Isaac, and his girlfriend, Kelly.

"Not at the food court," Isaac said. "We want to check the game shop."

"Great idea!" Caleb said. "We're going to the book store."

"The book store?" Olivia asked. "Sam doesn't strike me as a kid who likes to read."

"Trust me." Caleb winked at her.

Isaac shrugged. "I'm with Olivia on this one, but hey. Josh says he's not in the toy store either, so we're all out of ideas where he might be."

"We'll check there." Caleb nodded.

"Let's all meet up at the arcade in ten minutes, whether we've found him or not," Isaac instructed. "We'll regroup there."

"Copy that." Caleb pulled Olivia forward after Isaac and Kelly left. They proceeded to the bookstore, which was on the way from the food court to the toy store. The moment they entered, despite the urgency of the situation, the smell of books and the warmth of the shop's atmosphere enveloped him. He would love to go back here some other time, but he still had a missing brother to account for. With Olivia in tow, he entered the store and walked past multiple shelves to get to a secluded spot at the back of the store. "Remember when I told you I read an article about this particular bookstore on the newspaper?"

Olivia nodded. "Yeah. You said the store provides reading nooks where people can read books. Something about being able to borrow any book as long as they read it only here."

Caleb stopped and grinned when he saw what he was looking for. At one of the reading nooks, in a giant orange bean bag, was Samuel Grant, fast asleep.

"Unbelievable!" Olivia laughed. "How did you know?"

"I went to the bathroom in the middle of the night last night and saw him in the hallway playing his Nintendo. I doubt he got much sleep. He was all drowsy during lunch, and Hannah was right. He was following us when we left the food court. He might have heard me mention there's a sitting area for readers at the bookstore, so he decided to doze off. It's a long shot, but Sam always finds unique ways to meet his own needs."

Olivia cupped her hands to the sides of her face as she approached Sam whose mouth was wide open, drool dripping from the sides of his lips. "Your brother is so cute!"

"Do you think we should wake him up?" Caleb asked even if the last thing he wanted was to wake up another sibling when he had finally gotten his girlfriend alone.

Olivia leaned against the solid side of a high bookshelf. "I don't know. He might need to rest, but we have to tell everyone else we found him."

"Sam hasn't had that much sleep yet. He might not want to be woken up. Also, they can search for another five minutes. Once they find out Sam's here, it'll be awhile before we can be alone again."

Olivia smiled. "Five minutes then." She brushed her fingers against his cheek.

His lips pressed into hers.

Whether it was five minutes or more, Caleb didn't know, but he drank in every second he got to spend alone with Olivia. It felt good until it didn't.

Something within Caleb objected to what they were doing, so before they could get physical any further, he pulled away from his girlfriend.

Her cheeks pink and her lips red, she cast him a questioning glance as they both tried to catch their breaths.

Caleb told himself it was just because he felt guilty about keeping the others in an anxious panic when they had already found Sam, but it was more than that. He couldn't quite pinpoint why, but as much as he wanted to kiss his girlfriend, something told him it wasn't time for any of that at all.

Weeks later, Caleb understood why.

On a Saturday evening, the Grants gathered together inside the family room.

Caleb fidgeted on his seat beside Josh. "Why is Kelly here?" he asked. "What's going on?"

Josh shrugged.

Kelly sat beside Mom, and Isaac beside Dad on the sofa. Both Isaac and Kelly's faces had drained of all color. Isaac seemed just about ready to throw up.

Without as much as an introduction from the parents as to what was going on, Isaac confessed he had gotten Kelly pregnant, and they were praying about their next step and whether it would be wise for them to get married. They were both only eighteen, after all, just about to graduate from high school.

Their mother started crying. Kelly followed, then Hannah. Deb and Sam had this sad expression of confusion on their faces, their slouched forms on one bean bag conveying they wanted to be anywhere else other than there.

Caleb's older brother, someone he looked up to, someone who had always been so confident and self-assured, could barely lift his head up.

Caleb nudged his twin. The tears in Josh's eyes surprised him. Caleb couldn't quite tear up over the matter. He had this deep sense of grief stuck in his chest, and it wasn't converting into tears. Still, the revelation of Isaac's sin affected him more than someone who didn't know him might have interpreted.

"Son—" their father placed a hand on Isaac's knee "—this shouldn't define you. You made a mistake and have confessed your sin. You and Kelly shouldn't have been sleeping together. Your mother and I wish with all our hearts you both could have waited for marriage, because that would have been God's best for you, but we are here now, and I want you to know this doesn't change how much we all love you."

The moment their father said that, Isaac broke down.

At the image of Isaac's grief, even their father shed some tears. The younger twins followed soon after.

Only Caleb had a dry eye as he kept his stunned stare on Isaac.

He had never seen their older brother cry before. The entire scene ingrained itself in Caleb's memory as he perused the room. He had it all memorized — the remorse in Isaac's and Kelly's faces, the sadness in their parents', the disappointment in Hannah's.

He never ever wanted to experience something like this with Olivia. Caleb wanted to do right by her, to one day stand at the altar with her, knowing they had done it the right way. He didn't want anything like this to be a part of his future, so Caleb resolved to be very careful with Olivia. He needed to be extra cautious when with her, not wanting to go into more temptation than he could handle.

As the sobs filled their family room, Caleb promised himself: the only tears he and his family would shed over his relationship with Olivia would be that tears of joy that they would shed watching her walk down the aisle as Caleb's long-awaited and much-loved bride.

The last place Nova would've wanted to spend her weekend was in a crowded mall, but Knox had insisted, so she relented. What on earth he would want to do there was beyond her, but she enjoyed his company enough to get out of the house, brave the crowds, and hang out with him.

After all, he was the only friend she had in school. Might as well be a good friend to him, especially since she, too, was his only friend.

As they took a leisurely stroll from the bus stop to the mall, Knox dug his hands into his pockets and bumped his shoulder against hers to knock her off-balance.

She giggled as she quickly recovered and bumped him right back. They then walked forward in a comfortable silence. Neither of them had spoken a word since they had seen each other. They didn't need to. After all, what formed a bond between them was a sense of melancholy over the series of heartaches and tragedies their home lives comprised.

The mall was already within sight when Knox broke the silence. "Home?" he asked.

"Same as before. You?"

"Worse than ever," he said.

"Sorry."

Quiet followed. "I should start smoking."

Nova snickered. "Why?"

"I need a vice."

"What for?"

"To distract me."

"Get a hobby or something," Nova said. "Learn parkour or whatever."

"What's that?"

Nova shrugged. "I read about it at the school library. It's a training discipline that allows you to travel through any terrain using balance, agility, precision, and strength. The idea is to find the quickest way to get from one point to the other, despite any obstacle in the way."

"Sounds hard." Knox frowned before his lips slowly formed a smirk. "Could be useful for committing crimes in the future, though."

Nova rolled her eyes. "What is with you and always joking about committing crimes? Is that your goal in life? To become a criminal?"

"It might get my mother's attention. Besides, she's running through her money so fast, we can barely afford anything anymore." Knox shook his head. "I'm thinking of finding a part-time job."

"Is that why we're going to the mall?" Nova scratched the tip of her nose. "It's not my idea of a fun Saturday afternoon to get crushed by a crowd of strangers inside a stuffy mall."

"Better than staying at home."

Nova would have honestly preferred to be back home with Ma and Nolan, but she didn't need to rub that in Knox's face. He never seemed to want to be in his own house — wherever that was. She never could get him to tell, and that was one of the reasons Knox sometimes unsettled her. Sometimes, he gave off the impression that he was this wealthy kid able to buy anything he wants; sometimes, he acted like he was the poorest of the poor. Which of the two things was true, Nova had no way of knowing.

Nova sighed as they walked through the mall entrance. The crowd wasn't a very welcoming sight. She suppressed a groan. She was here now. Might as well find a way to enjoy it. "I can't imagine you working at a mall."

"Why not?"

"You strike me as the kind of person who has never worked a day in his life."

Knox chuckled. "You know me too well, Nova."

They spent the next half hour looking around for job openings. They got a few lists of application requirements for after-school jobs.

"See?" Knox folded up another piece of paper with application requirements and slipped it inside his pocket. "Not a total waste of time."

Nova couldn't object to that, so she just shrugged. "Now what?"

"Let's go to the arcade."

"I only have enough for a snack and a ride home, Knox."

"We don't need money to have fun, Nova. Let's people-watch."

"Huh?"

"Come with me." He grabbed hold of her hand and pulled her toward the escalator. "Let's find a snack we can afford and a spot to sit on. The crowd will be our entertainment."

Nova had never done anything like people-watching before and couldn't figure out how it would be any fun, but she relented for Knox's sake.

After getting one pretzel each, they reached the arcade. They didn't even bother to go inside.

"This is the perfect spot," Knox said. "Lots of traffic here." He sat on the floor, right outside the arcade, and leaned his back on the wall. He then patted the space beside him for Nova to sit on. "Come on." He bit into his pretzel.

Nova sat next to him, her brain commenting on how lame she thought this was. Then again, she figured it deserved a try. "What now?" She sniffed her pretzel before taking a bite.

Knox smirked. "Why do you always smell your food before eating?"

"To make sure it isn't stale." She chewed slowly. Her friend's stare lingered on her. "By people-watching, was it me you intended to watch?"

He muttered something under his breath. Nova could've sworn he said, "can't help it," but she couldn't tell for sure, and if that was what he said, she wasn't sure she wanted to know. While Knox made a great friend to pass time with, he wasn't the type of person she could see in a romantic light, so she let it go, and trusted that if Knox still had this silly crush on her, he would know enough not to act on it. For now, they both leaned their heads back on the wall and finished their pretzels as they watched people passing by.

Whenever they spotted someone who looked interesting, they would point the person out to the other. A woman with a spiky green mohawk and a pink dress, a couple bickering with each other, a gentleman in a suit with the most adorable Pomeranian puppy Nova had ever seen. Both she and Knox stayed silent, but it felt like with every person or scene they pointed out to each other, they developed an understanding about the person by the facial expressions they shared.

Drawn in by the degree of comfort she felt around him, Nova leaned her head on Knox's shoulder, thankful she had found a friend to vibe with in this way. No pressure. No strings attached. Just someone to lean on.

Seated on the floor of a crowded mall, Nova's appreciation for people grew. She got the hang of this people-watching thing. It formed stories in her mind about who these strangers were, where they were going, what their lives were like, what they were feeling at this particular junction of life where somehow, though they were unaware of it, in the smallest way, their existence touched Nova's. She could've sat there forever and enjoyed it, because her imagination introduced her to these strangers, making them more interesting than they probably actually were.

Then, she froze. Alarms went off in her head when she saw the familiar strawberry blonde hair of a person from the church Nova was no longer attending. Hannah Grant.

Was Caleb at the mall too? Olivia? Nova's heart skipped a beat.

Suddenly, Nova couldn't wait to get out of there. For reasons that were beyond her, it still hurt to see Caleb with Olivia. She sat up straight and turned toward Knox. "Are we done? Can we go home?"

His eyes widened. "So sudden?"

"Yeah. My butt hurts sitting here, and Nolan is probably home by now."

"I thought you said he was staying at your neighbor's until dinner."

"He is, but I just want to make sure I'm—"

"Nova!"

Nova winced as she looked past Knox to find Hannah approaching. "Hi, Hannah."

"We've missed you! Will you and your mom ever come back to church?"

Nova's heart warmed at the sincerity Hannah exuded. "I'm not sure. It would have to be up to Ma." That was a lie. Ma wouldn't prevent her from going should she choose to.

"Who's your friend?" Hannah waved at Knox.

He lifted himself from the floor before helping Nova up. After they patted down their jeans, Nova made introductions. "Hannah is from church. She also goes to our school. One year ahead of us." Nova held Knox's arm. "Hannah, this is Knox. He's my best friend."

At that, Knox cast a quizzical look at her. Whether he was pleased by this statement or not, Nova didn't know.

Thankfully, Hannah didn't pay any more attention to Knox. Instead, she drew in a deep breath. "I don't want to be rude, but we can't find my brother, Sam. If you see him around, can you bring him to the arcade? We're all looking."

"We're heading for home," said Nova, "but we'll keep an eye out."

Hannah pressed her palms together. "Please do. Thank you, Nova."

"No problem." Nova turned to Knox. "Let's go?"

"Let's." He nodded.

They waved Hannah goodbye and started walking toward the escalator.

"Church? Didn't think you were the kind who believes in God."

Something about that bothered Nova. "Why do you say that?"

"I don't know." He shrugged. "You never talk about things like faith or religion."

"Fair." She shrugged.

"So? Do you believe in God?"

Nova wished Knox could've just let it go, because she didn't know how to answer him. The image of Caleb's face buried in his Bible as he prayed came to mind. "I think I do," she said. "Do you believe in God, Knox?"

"If He's real, He has not done me any favors."

Nova lowered her eyes at the statement. It resonated with her and etched itself in her mind, so much so that she didn't notice the familiar figure approaching until she bumped half her body into him.

"Oh, sorry." The male voice made her freeze.

She could feel the color drain from her face when she found Caleb staring at her. Her mouth opened, but nothing came out. Her gaze drifted toward the young woman with him. She smiled.

Neither recognized Nova. Why would they? They were lost in a world of their own.

"You all right?" Caleb asked.

Lost for words, she nodded like a dumb person.

Satisfied she was okay, Caleb placed his hand on the small of Olivia's back and moved on, walking past her with his girlfriend keeping in step with him.

Following them was his brother, Sam, who was rubbing his eyes with the back of his hand. Upon seeing Nova, recognition flickered in his eyes. "Oh, hi, Nova." He waved at her.

"Hi, Sam," Nova answered.

Sam mumbled something and sped up his steps, so he could catch up with Caleb and Olivia.

"You know those people?" Knox asked.

Nova tried to play it cool by shrugging a shoulder. "The boy is Sam, Hannah's brother. The one they're looking for."

"And you didn't think to take him to the arcade?"

"I'm sure Caleb and Olivia would know to take him there."

Knox's brow rose. "Who are Caleb and Olivia? Was it the lovey-dovey couple you bumped into? I'm pretty sure they go to our school too."

Nova winced. "Let's just go."

Knox narrowed his eyes at her. "Let me take you home."

"You don't have to do that." Nova shook her head. "I can manage."

"You sure?"

"Family drama back home."

His jaw twitched, but to her relief, he shrugged and let it go. "I got you."

"Thanks, Knox."

"I'm here for you, Nova." He sighed. "Even if you keep on trying to run away."

The statement rubbed her the wrong way. "What do you mean by that?"

He shrugged. "Never mind."

"No. What do you mean? I'm not running away from anything. In fact, I'm the one people always leave behind. My dad, my brother. They were the ones who ran away."

"Don't read into it too much. I was just thinking about how interested you were in parkour, and to me, it just sounded like a fancy word for running away. You don't have to run away from me, Nova," Knox said. "I'm not going anywhere. I'll always be here for you."

Nova couldn't explain to herself why his words both comforted her and unsettled her. Knox's statements brought about a sense of unease, almost a sense of foreboding.

When Nova reached home, her trepidation grew the moment she stepped into the entryway, though she didn't exactly know why she felt that way. She closed the door behind her. No one seemed to be home. "Ma?! Nolan?!"

The phone rang.

Nova peeked into the kitchen. No one was there. She headed to the living room to pick up the phone.

"Hello?"

"Hi," a male voice spoke up. "I need to speak to Nathan Stone's mother."

"She's not home. I'm his sister, Nova. Who's calling?"

"I'm his bandmate." There was a pause on the other side of the line. "Something terrible has happened." His voice broke. "I think I should talk to your mother instead. When can I call back?"

"No. Please," Nova said breathlessly, her pulse racing and her body growing numb. "Tell me instead. What happened? Is Nate okay?"

A long pause accompanied slow breathing on the other end of the call. "I'm sorry, Nova. I hate to be the one to tell you this, but Nate is gone. Your brother is dead."

The moment she heard the word, 'dead', Nova collapsed on the floor, her knees giving way beneath her. Tears stung her cheek as she let out a silent scream before sobs racked her body. The man didn't go on any further. If he had tried to explain to Nova what had happened, she wouldn't have understood anyway, because devastation had already taken over.

It was half an hour later when Ma and Nolan arrived from the supermarket, and Nolan found Nova in a heap of tears at their staircase.

Knox had been right. If God was real, He certainly hadn't done any of them any favors. That night, fueled by grief and anger over Nate's death, Nova swore she would get her revenge — against whom, she had yet to figure out. Was it possible to exact revenge on God?

That night, anger brimming from within her, Dr. Edge came to being as Nova poured out her rage and her pain into a fictional world where those who have suffered injustice can rise to bring suffering to those who have brought them pain.

After having written an entire scene, Nova crumpled on the ground and cried out in anger to a God she had abandoned for far too long. As she drifted off to sleep, the one notion percolating in Nova's head was the idea that God was crying right along with her, because for the first time in Nova's life, her one prayer was for God to somehow end her life.

twelve

THE ONE
WHO GRIEVED
A LOSS

Neither the light of the sun nor the darkness of night had the ability to fill the hollowness that had formed within Nova upon losing Nate. Even the brightness of a rare blue winter sky failed to comfort her as she watched her brother's coffin being lowered to the ground.

Nolan was sniffling beside her, while just like her, Ma stood there, expressionless, no tears left to shed, because they hadn't been able to stop crying since finding out about the deepest loss they had ever experienced.

Pastor Sam spoke about times and seasons, about grief, something meant to comfort and appease the dreadful questions roiling in their minds.

The lower the coffin sank, the more people cried, the more Nova's hopelessness transformed into anger. At the final thud of the casket on the ground, Ma sobbed beside her. Nova clenched her fists. She fought back the urge to cry. It would do nothing. Nate was gone, and he was never coming back.

What she had to do now was to find who was responsible for this growing void in the depths of her soul — a space her older brother used to fill.

The rest of the day happened as if every sensation experienced was happening outside of her, like she was simply an observer. When Nolan buried his face in her stomach, his arms clutched around her waist, her arms hung limply on her sides. She couldn't feel his tears soaking through her clothes or his tight embrace straining her breath. Surely it was happening to someone else. Not Nova, not her family, not Nate.

She pried her brother's arms away from her, relieved when Ma noticed and coaxed him away from Nova, who wanted to get out of the house Nate had never been to, the house that held not a single memory of him. Panic filled her. Would she forget? Would the very memory of him, his very essence, die in this house?

Suddenly, Nova's breaths grew ragged, like the oxygen was being pulled out of her body, and she had to fight to draw it back in. She stumbled as she tried to walk away from the house, holding on to the doorpost for balance. The front door invited her outside for a gasp of fresh air. She hobbled toward it and bumped into Mama Aida, whose kind eyes and gentle demeanor had made her crumble multiple times over the past week. This time, their sweet neighbor's gaze went right past Nova, because she was no longer there. She had checked out. She wanted nothing to do with these people, these people who had never even known her brother and could never have the chance to know him now that he was gone.

Nova rushed out of the house, slamming the front door shut, before rushing into the front yard, gasping for breath.

"Nova!" Ma's voice called out to her before a familiar feminine figure wrapped a coat over Nova's shoulders. Soft hands held hers. "It will be okay, iha. It hurts right now, I know, but we'll be okay."

The words incensed Nova, and she stiffened against her mother's attempt to embrace her. Okay? How could they ever be okay again after this? She pushed her mother away and pulled the coat over her body before running as fast as she could. The faint sound of both her mother and little brother calling out her name faded away as she attempted to escape the sorrow their presence now only highlighted.

She reached the empty playground, where she allowed herself some release — not of tears, but of screams coming from the depths of her pain. Her knees dropped to the sandbox, the fine grains of sand cushioning her legs as she pulled the coat around herself like an embrace and let out another yell. And then another.

The sound of her harried breathing followed, grating her ears, before footsteps grew louder to indicate an unwanted presence.

Next to her, someone knelt on the sand. Not one word was spoken. No attempts to touch her or comfort her.

Knox just stayed there next to her and yelled to echo her pain — and perhaps his as well. After he finished letting out a guttural yell, it was Nova's turn again.

For the next few minutes, that's what they did. One person screaming their guts out, releasing all the pain and frustration, before it was the other's turn again. They did it until their throats were sore, and they couldn't yell at the brutal world anymore.

When silence came, Knox leaned over and kissed her.

Nova's mind cried out against the invasion, so she pressed her palm against his chest to push him away.

Knox backed off, but when their eyes met, his gaze reflected her pain, and somehow, she knew he understood. Despite all her attempts to ward anyone away from her, she didn't want to be alone, so when he leaned forward to kiss her again, Nova gave in.

She needed someone, anyone. Knox was there for her. He understood her, so why not let him in to fill some of the space in her life Nate had once occupied? Not all of it, just some of it — just enough to make her a little less hollow inside.

Her first day going back to school after Nate's funeral, Nova made quite an entrance after she had chopped off all her curls almost to her scalp. She hated how everyone looked at her like she was wounded, so she put on a defiant front, but upon reaching Knox — her one true friend — all he did was grin at her and pat her head.

"You shouldn't have taken your anger out on your head, though. That's quite a haircut, Nova." He sighed. "It will be okay."

For some reason, it sounded horrible when Ma had said it, but believable when it came out of Knox's lips. After he said the words, Nova caught a glimpse of Caleb and Olivia with hands clasped together, passing by them at the hall.

For the first time, it didn't bother her to see them together, mainly because she was too numb to care. Was that it? Or was it because now that she had Knox Cartier, she no longer needed the illusion that was Caleb Grant?

Discomfort roiled in Nova's gut, unsettling her, because she felt nothing for Knox. Truth was, after she had given herself over to sorrow upon Nate's death, she didn't feel much of anything at all.

Caleb couldn't believe his ears. Did Olivia just say that? He leaned his shoulder against his locker and stared at his girlfriend's face for a few minutes before shaking his head and chuckling. "Very funny, Olivia." He faced his locker and dialed in the combination to open it.

"You're not hearing me." Olivia tugged on his sleeve. "I'm serious."

The words numbed him. He turned to face her, his eyes burning into hers. "Please explain."

Upon eye contact, she lowered her eyes, unable to meet his confused gaze. "We should break up."

Caleb's mind spun. He had heard right the first time. "I don't understand. What did I do wrong? Why are you breaking up with me?"

Olivia kept her head bowed as she spoke. "Caleb, our family is moving back to the Philippines. Dad and Mom decided to continue the ministry they started there, but in a different area. It's best if we break up, because we'll be so far apart, and it'll be hard to keep the relationship going." She winced. "I like you a lot, Caleb. Please don't get me wrong, but I think it would be in both our best interests if we cool off a bit."

"Olivia, just because you're moving to another country, doesn't mean we have to end our relationship. We can still keep in touch, call each other, email. There are so many ways we can keep our relationship strong. I'm passionate about what we have, Olivia," Caleb said. "We can survive this."

"We're sixteen, Caleb, and we have our whole lives ahead of us. I think we don't need to make such great commitments right now. Not to each other, not to anyone. I hope you understand where I'm coming from. We might have rushed into this. That seems to be the case now that everything's changing, and we're moving halfway across the world. I love what we have, Caleb, but how do we make this work?"

He clasped her hands in his. "We'll find a way, okay? We can make this work."

"Are you sure?" Olivia lowered her gaze. "I want to believe it's possible, but we're young. What if you find someone else you like? Maybe it's better if we're free to explore other options, so neither of us gets hurt in the end."

Caleb tried to hold back all the violent objections within him, screaming for this not to happen. How could Olivia not see they were perfect for each other? He forced himself to keep his head on straight, to process this rationally despite the devastation he felt over what she was saying.

He gently cupped her face between his palms. "I love you, Olivia. There is no one else to find, because

I've already found you. I understand your concerns, but know that I want to be with you, and I'll be waiting for you. When you return, I will be here, because I have no doubt in my mind you are the girl for me, Olivia Meyer."

This time, Olivia raised her eyes to meet his. "Explain that to me, Caleb. Why are you so convinced we belong together? We're so different. Why do you think we're compatible?"

That took Caleb aback. How were they so different? They had the same values, the same faith, the same ways of thinking. How could she think they weren't compatible? Before he could further the conversation with her, the school bell rang, indicating the start of class.

"Let's give each other space for the next few days," Olivia said. "We can pray over what we ought to do."

Not knowing what to say, Caleb just nodded his agreement. Despite his attempts to locate her and talk to her for the rest of the day, he wasn't able to grab a moment with her again.

When he mentioned what Olivia had said to Josh and Hannah as they drove home at the end of the day, his siblings exchanged glances.

Hannah angled herself sideways in the front seat to get a better look at Caleb, who was seated in the back. "She kind of has a point, though."

"What?" Caleb scowled.

"You two are incompatible, and you're so intense about this relationship. Especially with both parents involved and hovering over you both to make sure what happened to Isaac and Kelly won't happen to you, I can understand if it's becoming a little suffocating for Olivia."

"Has she spoken to you about this?"

Hannah shook her head. "Of course not. I have eyes, Caleb. I can see."

"Why are we not compatible?"

"For one thing, you want to get a career, find a wife, settle down, and raise a family behind a white picket fence," Hannah said. "Olivia wants to travel, maybe become famous someday, live a life of adventure. Those two aspirations don't mesh."

"I can raise a family while getting involved in missions." Caleb shrugged. "I don't see what the problem is."

"Is that what you want or is that something you're only agreeing to, because you're into Olivia?" Josh asked from the driver's seat.

"I don't know, but isn't that what relationships are about? Compromise? Adjusting to each other and making space in our lives for the other to influence us and change us? Besides, let's say we are incompatible. There are plenty of incompatible couples who find a way to make it work." Caleb was brewing inside. Why was everyone going against this? He had already prayed about this, and even their parents — both Olivia's and his — agreed to them being together. What further confirmation was necessary?

"You asked what we thought about the whole thing," Josh said. "That's what we think."

"I can't believe you're saying that, man. You're supposed to be on my side."

"I am!"

"We are!" Hannah exclaimed. "We're just trying to help you see this from Olivia's point of view." Hannah sighed. "I'm sorry she's leaving, Caleb. That can't be easy, but what if she has a point? What if it's better to break up until she comes back?"

Caleb shook his head and shifted his focus past the car window. "I don't want to talk about this anymore."

Silence followed, but it lasted only a few minutes, because Hannah wasn't very good at shutting up.

"It's so sad what happened to the Stones." She sighed. "Have you heard?"

Josh tsk-tsked. "Did you see Nova at school today? What she did to her hair?"

It didn't register to Caleb who they were talking about and why he should care. Something about a tragedy with people at church or in school or wherever. Tragedy was happening everywhere. It was happening to him at that very moment. Olivia had just shattered his plans for the future!

It wasn't until later that night in the comfort of their bedroom that Josh knocked some sense into him.

"Sorry, bro," Josh said. "It sounds to me like you're more upset about your plans being disrupted than you are about possibly losing Olivia."

Caleb was about to object, but he realized it was true. He was in love with the idea of Olivia, not with Olivia herself. Caleb tossed and turned in his bed as he talked to God about his relationship with her. Wasn't she the one for him? Was Josh right? If she wasn't the person for him, why couldn't he imagine a future without her?

"God," Caleb whispered, "I will miss her so much. I hope she wouldn't break up with me. It isn't necessary, but whatever happens, Your will be done."

The next day, as soon as he arrived in school, Olivia approached him, kissed him on the cheek and said, "I prayed about it, and if you're convinced we can make it work even through the distance, then you're right. We don't have to break up."

Caleb smiled at her, but though he wouldn't admit it to anyone — perhaps even himself — his confidence had wavered. Could they survive the time and distance apart? They would have to, because he had promised to wait.

Weeks later, on the drive back from the airport after waving his girlfriend goodbye, the sense of loss he had inside rattled Caleb into silence. It shook him to realize how much of a space he had given Olivia in his life, so much so that when she left, it felt like a loss he needed to grieve.

Perhaps it was all for the best, because he needed to get to a place where God, not Olivia, could fill the needs of his heart. "God, help me," Caleb prayed before loosening his grip on the future he once wanted to have with the girl he had been convinced would someday become his wife.

thirteen

THE ONE WHO WAS WILLING TO WAIT

With a single, long-stemmed white rose in hand, a smile on his face, and a hopeful heart, Caleb sought the object of his affection among the crowd. Around them, families were gathering to snap pictures and exchange hugs. The atmosphere of celebration encouraged him as he approached the pretty brunette who had captivated his heart and mind for the past four years.

Upon seeing him, Olivia's face lit up with a smile. She waved at her friends and skipped to him, the hem of her yellow dress sweeping over her knees. When she reached him, she tipped his graduation cap to the side.

"Congratulations, Caleb!" She threw her arms around his neck. "I'm so proud of you!" She kissed him on the cheek.

"I'm so glad you're here for this." He wrapped his arms around her waist and spun her around before setting her on the ground to take a good look at her. "You look amazing."

"So do you!" Her eyes sparkled. "Is that for me?"

"Nah." He shook his head. "It's for Josh."

She laughed. "Where is your twin anyway?"

"He had to rush off to Pastor Sam's house for orientation on the mission trip they're going to this summer."

"He's still set on going to Bible school?"

Caleb nodded, then grinned as he handed her the rose. "This is yours, by the way."

She snickered and took it from him, breathing in a whiff of the petals before smiling at him.

Caleb's heart leaped. He had been waiting for so long to be with her. It had been so difficult over the past two years weathering their long-distance relationship, but here they were. Still going strong. "That's not the only graduation gift I have for you, but you'll have to wait until our summer trip to get it."

Her smile faded, and her eyes took on a pensive expression as she regarded him.

"It's still on, right?" Caleb couldn't keep the tone of worry from his voice.

"Of course!" she said. "Road trip with my boyfriend and one of my best friends in the whole world? I wouldn't miss it for anything."

"Everything all right then?"

"Yeah. I just—" She shifted her weight from one foot to the other. Her eyes downcast, she opened her mouth to say something, but shook her head instead.

"Olivia?"

She beamed at him. "It's nothing. It's your day, Caleb. We can talk about everything some other time. I'm just thankful to be here with you on such a special day."

Caleb tried not to flinch. What was there to talk about? Everything had been fine, as far as he was concerned. In fact, everything had lined up perfectly with her coming home just in time for his graduation. He cupped her face with his hands. "Stop worrying so much, Olivia. It will be a great summer. We will have a blast, and we can both look forward to a glorious future together."

In response, she took hold of his hand, stood on her tiptoes, and planted a kiss on his cheek. "You're amazing, Caleb Grant. I don't think I'll ever deserve you."

His happiness over her presence and the celebratory atmosphere surrounding him overshadowed the strangeness of her last statement.

She smiled and subtly pointed at some of the girls in their graduation class. "I don't understand why you have eyes only for me, when any of these girls would love to be in a relationship with you."

Caleb lowered his eyes to look at his feet before raising his gaze to peer at her through his lashes. "I know what I want, Olivia, and I tried to not want you, but I still do. If I didn't believe with all my heart that God meant for us to be together, I wouldn't still be here so deeply in love with you."

"That's just it, Caleb. How are you so sure?" she asked. "I'm unsure about so many things. What I long to be, where I want to go, what I intend to do for the rest of my life. How is it that you are not worried about these things like the rest of us?"

He shrugged. "I just know." He squeezed her hand and leaned over to plant a kiss on her cheek. "Take your time, Olivia. You can go ahead and figure out who you are and what you long to be, and through it all, I'll be here, waiting until you're ready to take the next step with me."

He was close enough to her to feel her tremble at his words. To his surprise, Olivia reached forward, cupping his cheek with her hand, and strained upwards to press her lips on his. The kiss deepened, and it was Caleb who pulled away. Olivia gasped when he did, her eyes darkening with what Caleb interpreted as passion. It was nice to know he still had that effect on her.

"I love you, Caleb," she said.

With those four words, she solidified his resolve to fight for their relationship, to believe that it would stand the test of time, because Caleb placed all his faith in God and Olivia and trusted she would be worth the wait.

That summer was one of the best he had ever experienced. He spent every minute he could spare from those precious few months with Olivia. Their road trip with Hannah ended with a tour of Caleb's university, where he intended to earn a degree in literature. His goal was to be just like his father, getting a job as a literary agent at Frontier Press.

Meanwhile, he still had no idea what Olivia had planned for her future. Caleb didn't care, as long as he remained a part of it. If she chose to stay with him, then even better. Should that be the case, Caleb decided he would propose to her as soon as his first semester in college was over.

However, that wasn't what Olivia had in mind.

On the last day of their road trip, he, Hannah, and Olivia hung out in the girls' hotel room, preparing to watch a movie. Caleb and Olivia sat on the couch waiting for Hannah to finish her shower when Olivia finally brought it up.

"I've been thinking about what I want to do." Olivia shifted on the couch beside him as she took a bite from a strawberry. She tried to hand him the bowl she had gotten it from. "Want some?"

"No thanks." He stretched his arm over her shoulder and pulled her closer to him. "Have you figured it out? Have you decided to live in the dorm with me?"

"You're going to live in an all-boys dorm."

"I can find a way to hide you."

Olivia snorted. "Very funny. No. I want to take a gap year. There's this internship I can get in South Korea. My dad has connections there. I can teach English for a while." She shrugged. "What do you think?"

Caleb struggled to process what she had just said. So she wasn't staying? She actually wanted to return halfway across the world? Could he bear a few more years of a long-distance relationship? He swallowed hard. "I don't know, Olivia. I was hoping you would decide to stick around. There are so many opportunities available for you here. You can pursue a degree in photography, you can even start work as a photographer."

Olivia placed the bowl of strawberries on the wooden coffee table in front of them before angling herself to face him. "We made it through two years apart, Caleb." She frowned. "I'm not ready to settle down yet. Can you give me another two years?"

Caleb sighed. "It's not what I was hoping to hear, but I'll wait for you for as long as I have to, Olivia." He gave her a quick peck on the jaw before lifting his forefinger in the air as a gesture for her to wait. He rose from the couch to reach for his backpack on the floor. From it, he retrieved a box wrapped in glossy paper with a ribbon around it. He handed it to Olivia.

"What's this?" she asked.

"Open it." He smiled.

Olivia tore away the wrapping and found a professional digital camera inside. She gasped. "Caleb, this is too much."

"I saved up for it for quite some time," he said. "It's disappointing to hear that you'll leave again, Olivia, but no matter where life takes you, I'm sure you'll take amazing pictures. You'll be behind the camera and in front of it, and either way, this camera will capture beauty — that of yours and others — wherever you go. And once you've had your fill of the world and all its beauty, you can come back home to me."

She stared at him — a stare that lingered long enough for him to become uncomfortable. A tear ran down her cheek. She smiled and leaned forward to kiss him.

Caleb didn't pull away. He enjoyed the strawberry taste of her lips over his. Olivia pushed further, drawing closer to him. It took several minutes before Caleb summoned the presence of mind to stop, before the temptation to go further would be irresistible. He looked up to see a strange expression on Olivia's face. She looked almost hurt, tears rushing down her cheeks.

"Hey. What happened? You okay?" Caleb asked as he wiped the back of his hand against her cheek.

Olivia nodded, allowing the tears to fall, some of it pooling on her delicate chin. "I have something for you too," she said, "but you have to open it later when you're alone in your hotel room." She scribbled something on a piece of paper, slipped it inside a glossy black gift bag, and handed it to him. "Thank you for all the memories, Caleb."

He chuckled as he took the bag from her. "Why do you sound like you're saying goodbye?"

She laughed dryly as she wiped away her tears. "Because I am, silly. I'm going to Korea, remember?"

"No goodbyes." Caleb stroked her hair. "I'll be waiting for you."

"I know," she said.

The way her hair cascaded down her shoulders and framed her heart-shaped face etched itself in his memory. Once again, Caleb told himself she deserved the time and space to be her own person. If he was convinced they belonged together, then he would have to bear the wait.

Later that night, in his hotel room, Caleb opened the gift bag and retrieved the square album inside. He flipped through the pages and found picture after picture of him, Olivia, their families. Each page contained trips they had taken together, afternoons they had spent at each other's houses, screenshots of the messages they had sent each other while apart. All the things that had convinced Caleb they belonged together.

At the very last page was a Polaroid of just the two of them, along with the note Olivia had scribbled earlier: *You're the best friend anyone could ever ask for, Caleb. I adore you and want only the best for you. Keep praying for us, because the last thing I would ever want is to make you wait for nothing, but from the bottom of my heart, thank you for being willing to wait. Love, Olivia*

Caleb didn't know how to interpret the note. A tinge of fear hit his chest and spread over his soul. Was there still a possibility in her mind they wouldn't end up together?

The worry lasted as long as it took for Caleb to remember the taste of strawberry on his lips. After she had kissed him like that? He smirked. No. Olivia would come back to him. There was no way in the world God or Olivia would allow him to be waiting for nothing.

- TWO YEARS LATER; NOVA, 18 -

Nova didn't know what it was about the winter break of their senior year that transformed Knox Cartier, but when she saw him come spring, it was like he was a whole other person. The moment he stepped into the hallway of their high school, he grabbed the attention of more than a few people he passed by with the shades he had on, the brown leather jacket he wore over a crisp white shirt and dark denim jeans. His dark hair slicked back over his head. Short stubble accentuated his firm jaw. It was like he had popped straight out of a magazine.

As he approached, Nova could swear several girls swooned. Their class president had her jaw wide open as she nudged her friend and asked, "Is that Knox?"

Was it Knox, indeed? Nova couldn't believe her eyes.

The smirk on Knox's face was enough of an indication of how aware — and proud — he was of his transformation.

Nova raised a brow. She couldn't deny he looked great, but something about it rubbed her the wrong way, and she couldn't quite pinpoint the reason behind her trepidation. She narrowed her eyes at him. "You're different."

"That's all you can say?" He lifted his hands, palms up, as if to present himself to her.

"What do you want me to say?"

His face fell, his shoulders sagging. "Well, hello to you too, Nova Stone. Seems not much has changed. You're still as sullen as ever. I'm glad you survived the winter with all your curls still intact." He tugged at the end of her curls. "You don't look that much different."

"Sorry." Nova tried to soften her tone. "Dad was home this morning."

"Yikes." He genuinely looked disgusted. "I'd be in a sour mood too."

"You look amazing." Nova wanted to change the subject. "You should have told me you were going to get an extreme makeover. I would have done something to keep up with the changes around here." She pressed her palm against his chest to nudge him backwards. "I did miss you."

"We were on the phone every day."

"Only because you kept calling."

He shrugged. "Not my favorite way to spend the time being with my dad's other family."

"Come on. Your stepmother can't be that bad. Didn't you get along with any of her kids?"

"They're monsters, every single one of them. As for her, well, she threw all that money on me, so I can look like the stud I am, so I can't complain."

"Ah, so that's why you don't resemble Frankenstein anymore."

Knox rolled his eyes. "And you are still the same old you."

"You've already said that. Not all of us have a guilty stepmom desperate for our approval."

"Hey. I said you still look the same." Knox shrugged. "I never said you didn't look amazing."

That brought a smile to her face. "I missed you. I wasn't receiving enough compliments with you gone."

"Glad to be of service."

Nova tugged at his leather jacket and gave him a complete look-over, nodding as she inspected him. "I'll have to make adjustments once you take your pick from all these ladies swooning over you."

"Oh please, Nova Stone." Knox winked. "You know I have eyes only for you."

She rolled her eyes. Just as she was about to respond with some snark, she gasped when he leaned forward and pressed his lips against hers. She stood there, barely able to comprehend what was happening, much less decide what to do — push him away or respond to his advances?

Since they kissed at the playground, they had never done it again. It had been a vulnerable moment for her, and she had made it clear to Knox she wanted to stay as friends. He had never brought up a relationship again, nor had he tried to kiss her again, so this out-of-the-blue kiss brought her nothing but shock.

"What was that?" she whispered after his lips left hers, his forehead still pressed against hers.

"I want to be with you, Nova." His hands found hers. "Not just as your friend. I want more, because I need you. You have no idea how desperately I need you in my life."

The words sounded wrong to her, even if she felt like she needed him, too. After all, they had been through so much together.

"I'll wait if you want me to," Knox said, "but you and I belong together, Nova." He kissed her again. "Don't make me wait too long, okay?"

Nova's mind raced for a response. She didn't want to be in a relationship with him, and as much as she cared about Knox and enjoyed his company, she didn't see him that way. The only person she had ever entertained a romantic notion about was Caleb Grant, and he was long gone. Was it time for her to open herself up to the idea of romance? Was Knox the right person? Why not? He was one of the few people she trusted and loved.

Once again, she studied his outfit, trying to figure out what it was about it she found so off-putting. It wasn't until he walked away from her to grab something from his locker that it hit her.

It wasn't just his outfit. It was the way he carried himself, the way he made her feel safe, the way he made her laugh.

Knox reminded her too much of her father, or at least the way Ma talked about him whenever Nova asked about how they had fallen in love. Nova adored the fact she could run to Knox whenever she was afraid or vulnerable, whenever the situation at home got too tough, but there was a darkness in him as well — a darkness Nova had recognized in

Nate and her father. He had the same dangerous edge to him as they did, always just on the surface, waiting to break out. Could she handle being in a relationship with someone like them?

Nova shook her head to get rid of the questions flooding her mind. This was Knox she was talking about! The person she had always been able to lean on. He had never done anything to hurt her before, so why did she think he was anything like her father and brother?

When Knox extended his hand for her to hold, she held his wrist and lowered it to his side. She pulled off his sunglasses. The stern expression on his face surprised her.

She smiled at him to ease the tension as he put the shades inside his jacket's pocket. "There's no sun here," she said. "Let me think about everything you said, okay?" She stood by his side and nudged him by the shoulder. She drew a breath when he gripped her wrist.

In a low, dark tone that sent shivers through her body, he brought his lips closer to the shell of her ear. "Don't make me wait for nothing, Nova. I won't know what I'll do if you ever break my heart. It will be the end of me."

He let go of her and as if nothing happened, he nudged her right back on the shoulder and laughed.

Had he just threatened her?

Nova never said it out loud to anybody — especially not to Knox — but it felt like she lost her best friend that day. In his place was a walking threat — someone who needed her and was waiting for her to give him what he wanted. What if she decided she didn't want to be with him? What then?

"It will be the end of me."

Seven words were all it took for Knox to shatter the faith Nova had in him. Just like that, Nova was alone again, her soul more hollow than ever, and in the weeks to come, all Nova could think about was how much she missed the security of knowing God was on her side. She had turned all her anger toward God when Nate had passed away. She had asked God to let her die.

Did God feel as manipulated as Knox was making her feel every time he told her it would be the end of him if he couldn't get what he wanted?

Not knowing who else to turn to, Nova started writing letters again, but this time, not to Nate, but to God. She told Him everything, and though she didn't hear Him answer, it was at that junction of Nova's life that she once again revisited the story of Dr. Edge and began weaving opportunities for redemption to rescue a heart that had once been bent on revenge.

fourteen

THE ONE WHO SAVED HERSELF

For the rest of their senior year in high school, the pressure mounted with every significant event they went through. Nova dreaded prom night because Knox was her date. She even tried to convince him not to go. He insisted on going, and like Nova had expected, it didn't go well. The anger in Knox's eyes when she resisted his attempt to kiss her made her shudder. She scolded herself for agreeing to go to a private spot with him. What did she think he would try to do once they were away from everyone else?

"Knox," she said. "I want to wait. Let's at least graduate high school first. I don't want to rush into things, and—"

"I've been waiting, Nova," he hissed, his lips so close to her ear, she could feel his warm breath. "It's driving me crazy how much you're making me wait this long. Why can't you see we're not meant to be just friends? We should be together. Besides, it's just a kiss! It's not like I'm even pressuring you to—"

"I know, I know." Nova kept her voice low to appease him, her fingers brushing against his arm. She missed her friend — the Knox she had been able to depend on. This person wasn't the same person she had met in her freshman year of high school. "I appreciate how patient you've been, Knox. It's just that—" The words got stuck in her throat. Did she have it in her to tell him she couldn't see a future with him on their prom night? That she didn't see him that way? Was this the right moment?

He swore under his breath. His clenched fists made his torso bulk up.

She backed away from him. "I'm so sorry, Knox."

He stepped forward, looming over her. For a fraction of a second, she feared he would hit her, so she clenched her fists as well. There was no way any man — or anyone — would be able to treat her the way her father treated her mother. She would fight back with every bit of strength left in her. They stared each other down until something shifted in the way Knox was looking at her. His eyes softened, his lips twitched.

Suddenly, there was hurt in his eyes, and Nova's determination turned into guilt.

"I can't believe you, Nova," he said. "After everything we've been through, no matter how many times I've told you how much I love you, how much I need you in my life, you're still putting me through this. You're not even some sort of religious nut who has all these ideas about staying pure before marriage, so I can't understand why you're doing this."

"Knox, I care about you. I love you, but not the way you want me to. It's not like that between us. We've always been friends, and I can promise to be your friend for the rest of our lives, but I'm not on the same page as you right now. I'm not ready for a relationship. Please understand." Nova tried to hold his arm, but he pushed it away.

"Nah. I'm sick of this." Knox shook his head. "I'm taking you home."

"We don't have to go, Knox. We can still enjoy the rest of the night. It's prom! A night like this won't happen again for the rest of our lives." She held his hand. "Knox, please."

He lowered his eyes, as if to consider it. He then slowly raised his gaze, so it swept over her from her foot to her face. "I can't," he said as he shook her hand away from his. "You look stunning, Nova, and you won't even let me touch you."

"Don't be like this."

Knox walked past her, turning his back on her. "I'm taking you home. Hurry up!"

Nova would've done anything to get back the Knox she had once known, but he had changed so drastically, and it felt like there was no way to retrieve the old him.

Upon reaching her bedroom, Nova sank into her bed, tears rushing down her face. A knock on her door made panic shoot through her as she quickly tried to wipe the tears away.

"Nova?" Nolan's voice came through from the hallway. "Are you all right? Why are you back so early?"

Nova gasped. The last thing she wanted was for Nolan to find out what she had been going through with Knox. He had enough on his plate, given all the drama he was dealing with at church. The very thought of it left a bitter taste in Nova's mouth. Nolan had served that church since he was a little boy. What was with all these rumors about him and Serene when everyone knew they were just best friends?

"Nova? You there?" Another series of knocks followed.

Nova got out of the bed and checked her appearance in the mirror. Why Knox was so obsessed with her, she couldn't figure out. There were a lot of girls in school who would love to be in a relationship with him. Why was it her that he needed? Nova pushed the thought away, took one deep breath, opened the door for her brother, and flashed a huge smile.

She should win an award for acting, because the worry on her brother's face disappeared after seeing her.

They spent the rest of the night watching a movie, with Nolan assuring her things were getting better at church. Miss Rhoda had already stopped expressing concern over his friendship with Serene after Pastor Sam assured her they were only friends.

"Is that true though?" Nova asked her brother. "Are you and Serene only friends?"

"Of course."

The smirk on Nolan's face told her otherwise.

For a moment, as much as she loved her brother, she wondered if he was just like Knox. That's when she realized what an awful image she already had of the guy she had once considered her dearest friend. That's when Nova decided she had to end whatever hopes Knox had of them being a couple. She couldn't keep him waiting. It was time to be honest, and whatever the consequences of that honesty, she would find a way to face it.

- CALEB, 20 -

Caleb had never experienced such devastation. Part of him wished Olivia would have found it in herself to lie, to string him along, to let him hold on to the hope they would be together, but that wasn't what Olivia had told him over the phone. No. She had instead given him the truth. She had found someone else, someone who made her feel the way he had never been able to, someone she was certain was the one in a way she had never been a hundred percent sure with him.

She cried during the two-hour-long phone call, every minute of which had shattered his heart. Her. She had been the one who was crying. Was it out of pity for him?

Caleb dragged his feet along campus grounds. Couldn't Olivia have waited a few more weeks? At least until the final exams of his sophomore year were over? That way, he could at least spend an entire summer drowning himself in all this misery.

How had this happened? Where had he gone wrong? He had done everything right. His relationship with Olivia was something he had prayed over, sought counsel for. It was something their families approved of. He had been so certain she would one day become his wife.

Was she making a mistake? Should he fight for this?

"Caleb?"

He turned to find his sister walking toward him. It was strange how annoying they used to find Hannah when she had been such a blessing to him since she had started her freshman year in the same university.

Hannah stopped walking a meter away from him. She heaved a sigh. "I'm sorry."

"How did you know?"

"Olivia called. She wanted to make sure I check on you, in case."

"In case what? I won't do anything stupid, Hannah."

"Of course not." The patronizing way Hannah said that made Caleb want to pull his hair out.

"I'm fine. I'm in shock. That's all. I'm trying to process everything." He started walking forward, past her, his eyes set ahead, his heart wishing it would be just as easy to move on from Olivia.

Hannah spun on her heels and walked in step with him. "Don't be too hard on yourself, okay? Olivia shouldn't have strung you along all this time."

"What do you mean?" Caleb asked. "How long has she known that she doesn't want to be with me?"

"Caleb, she has always adored you, but she was never as fully invested in your relationship as you were. This is just me speculating, but I wouldn't be surprised if she has known since you graduated high school. I guess she was hoping you would find someone else once you go to college, but you kept waiting."

"She should've told me."

"She didn't want to break your heart."

"And what do you call what she did now?"

"Caleb..."

"What if I'm right about us belonging together, Hannah? What if she's making this huge mistake being with this other guy?"

"Come on." Hannah linked arms with him. "There are so many other women out there. The right one is somewhere. I don't think it's Olivia."

"You don't think I should fight for her, for what I believe I heard from God?"

Hannah sighed. "We both know that if it's from the Lord, both people should hear the same thing. Olivia listens to God, too. Why is it that you're the only one God is speaking to about something as life-altering as marrying her?"

The blow to his ego was shattering him, but Caleb refused to shed a tear. This was humiliating enough. "So I've made a mistake hearing from Him then."

"You're passionate and sincere in your convictions. You're also human, so you should cut yourself some slack and accept that things don't always go according to plan." Hannah leaned her head on his shoulder. "You're amazing, and any woman would be lucky to have the same dedication and respect you have given Olivia."

"All of this is so embarrassing. I was so sure."

"At least you're not in a heartbroken heap of sobs," Hannah said. "How about I take you out to dinner?"

"Yeah, I guess. If I can't have Olivia's company, you'll have to do. Will you carry me home if I get drunk?"

Hannah slapped him on the shoulder. "Since when do you drink?"

"I figured I would try tonight. Drown out the sorrow and all that."

"You don't look very sorrowful. You deal with heartbreak the way some people deal with a bad grade. It's like you're used to it."

The statement shook Caleb. His mood grimmed, and he stopped walking. "There's no way I could ever get used to this."

That was all he had to say for Hannah to get the meaning behind his words. He may not be able to show it to her, but he was crumbling inside. There was, however, nothing he could do other than to keep going.

So, Caleb squared his shoulders and prayed God would broaden them, so he could handle the heartbreak and disappointment life had thrown at him. He would get through this. No matter how long it took, or how many tears he needed to shed in the shower, he would get over Olivia Meyer. That was a promise he made to himself, because Hannah was right. There was another woman out there waiting for him.

"You're making a huge mistake, Nova."

Knox's face darkened, the contours of his face taking on a sharper edge as he rose from their favorite spot at the mall — the floor by the arcade entrance.

Nova leaned her head on the wall. She had chosen the mall for a reason. It was less crowded than usual, but even with only a handful of people around, there was a lesser chance Knox would make a scene, which was the last thing she wanted. Still, despite all the strangers straggling past them, Knox stood in front of her slouched form on the ground. His eyes dark, his fists balled, his stance domineering.

Compared to him, Nova felt small, but she needed to stand her ground, so she lifted herself up from the floor and stood perpendicular to him, facing his shoulder. She sighed and pressed her forehead on his shoulder blade, the tension oozing out of him coming at her in waves. "We were great as friends, Knox."

"We can be even greater as more than friends, Nova, but you never even gave it a chance. After all those times I've been there for you, this is how you repay me."

Nova shut her eyes. This rhetoric of him having been there for her during her darkest moments had been something he held over her like it was something she owed him for, not something he had done only because he cared, because he was her friend. "You know I care about you," was her lame attempt at trying to comfort him.

"Then why are you hurting me this way?" His voice broke.

His brokenness touched a tender part of her heart. The last thing she wished to do was to hurt him, but it was better this way. "I'm sorry, Knox."

"Are you?"

Suddenly, he moved his arm, his elbow slamming against her gut, knocking the breath out of her. Had he meant to do that? She couldn't tell for sure. Whether or not it was intentional, he certainly didn't care about hurting her, because he was already walking away, his imposing form moving farther and farther away from her.

Not knowing what to do, Nova stayed rooted to her spot, her hand clutching her stomach. Knox was just hurt. It was probably a knee-jerk reaction. He didn't actually mean to hurt her. He might not have even noticed.

Nova debated with herself whether to follow him or not and eventually decided to go home instead. He needed space to let what she had said sink in. She hoped he would see it from her perspective, that her honesty about what she felt for him — or the lack of it — was meant to protect him from getting hurt even more if she kept leading him on. Hopefully, by Monday, when they get back to school, they would have a sincere conversation about it and decide how to move forward from there.

Nova still wanted to be his friend, if that was at all possible.

Come Monday morning, the sight of Knox eradicated all her hope of keeping her dearest friend after breaking his heart. Bruises marred his face, a white bandage wrapped around his fist. When she approached to ask him what happened, he brushed right past her.

Throughout the rest of the day, she kept getting questions about what had happened to Knox. After all, people expected her to be the one in the know, especially considering how, throughout high school, Knox barely said a word to anyone in school apart from her. If only they knew how much she wanted to know as well, but Knox had been dodging all her attempts to talk to him, so she knew about as much as everyone else.

Towards the end of the school day, Nova gave up on even seeing Knox, because he had skipped all the afternoon classes they had together. Guilt kept trying to consume her, but she successfully warded it off as she assured herself she did what needed to be done. Whatever trouble Knox had gotten himself into over the weekend was his fault. Not hers.

Knox, unfortunately, had different ideas about the whole situation, and he made this clear to her when he slipped into the passenger seat inside her car in the parking lot.

"I'm black, blue, and purple, Nova," he said, "and it's all your fault."

Nova's grip on the steering wheel tightened. She hadn't yet started the car. She then took a deep breath and looked at Knox. "What happened to you? I've been trying to talk to you all day."

"Can you blame me if I don't want to talk to you? You did this to me."

"No." She had seen her father try to guilt her mother over his bad behavior far too many times to let Knox do that to her. "Whatever happened to you, Knox, I had nothing to do with it."

"You have everything to do with this, Nova. I told you I needed you in my life, or I wouldn't know what would happen. You don't understand, Nova. You make me better. I need you. If I don't have you in my life, this—" he pointed at his broken face "—is what happens. At least just give us a chance."

To her shock, tears started falling from his eyes.

"Nova, come on. How can you not see we're perfect for each other?" He grabbed her arm and pulled her toward him.

"Ow! Knox! You're hurting me!" She tried to push him away, but he was stronger. Before she knew it, her body was twisted at an uncomfortable angle as he forced a kiss on her. This time, she didn't stay frozen in shock over his advances. She tried to get away from him, but both his hands were now gripping her arms, his lips pressing on hers so hard, it hurt. She tried to speak out her protests, but only gave him room to deepen the unwanted kiss.

Helplessness swept over her as she flailed about, doing everything she could to get away from him.

Agitated, he pulled away from her, grabbed both her shoulders, and tried to shake her into submission. His tears kept falling as he tried to explain to her, "I don't want to hurt you, but I need you to understand how much I love you, how much I want to be with you."

The frantic look on his face was enough indication he wasn't in his right mind. Fear took over Nova, bringing with it a rush of adrenaline as she used all the strength she could summon to push him away from her. "Let go of me! Get out of my car! Get out!"

He backhanded her. The force of his brute strength coming at her made her neck snap to the side, her jaw bumping against the steering wheel. Her breath knocked out of her, Nova fought hard to regain her senses.

The sight of blood on her face cleared Knox's dark eyes. "Nova? I'm so sorry. I didn't mean to hurt you. Please forgive me." He reached out to touch her.

She knocked his hand away. "Get out," she said darkly.

"Nova, I lost my mind a bit. It's only because I'm so hurt. I can't imagine life without you. Nova—"

"Get. Out!"

Grim darkness overshadowed the frantic expression on his face. She had seen this shift in countenance far too many times in her father and Nate. For the first time in a long time, with fear coiling around her chest, trying to squeeze the life out of her heart, Nova prayed. *Help!* With that one word circling her consciousness, she prayed silently to a God Whom she hoped still cared for her enough to rescue her from the dangers of a man's viscerally violent tendencies, the same type of danger oozing out of Knox at that moment, a warning for her to get as far away as possible.

Nova grabbed for the door handle, but as she was about to open her car door, Knox's eyes cleared and remorse took over the dark expression on his face.

For a moment, it was like he was there again. The unsure teenager she had met four years ago, the one who was broken up about his father's affair and his mother's drunkenness, the only friend she had who understood her pain, the one who made her feel protected even if he himself proved dangerous to her.

"I'll go," he said, to her relief. "I'll go." He opened the door and stepped out of her car. "I'm sorry, Nova," he said. "I hope someday, you'll find it in your heart to forgive me." He shut the door.

The moment he did, Nova locked the car doors and drove out of there as fast as she could. She needed to get as far away from him as possible. She kept driving until she reached the familiar comfort of their driveway. That's where she allowed herself to fall apart. She cried, her sorrow stemming from a deep root of betrayal from all the men in her life. She knew in her heart of hearts she could never let Knox into her life again, and though she had already prepared herself to lose him when she had decided to tell him the truth, she had never expected for things to get to this point.

A mixture of fear and grief swept over her, and she gave in to every emotion that had been bottled up inside for so long. She broke into sobs, unable to stop herself even when Nolan appeared from the neighbor's house and noticed her inside the car.

He peered through the window and saw her crying. He tried to get in, but the doors were still locked. "Nova? Let me in."

"Leave me alone, Nolan. I'll be fine."

"No. Let me in. Why do you have that bruise on your face? Are you bleeding?"

The question tore her apart and her sobs started to rack her entire body. There was no hiding this from her little brother.

"Nova, please let me in."

She reached forward and unlocked the door to the passenger seat Knox had occupied earlier. The moment Nolan was in, she threw her arms around his neck and sobbed into his shoulder.

"What happened? Tell me." His voice went way too deep for a thirteen-year-old. He almost sounded like Nate.

That notion only made her cry even more. "Nolan, I can trust you, right? You'll protect me if you have to, right? You'll be nothing like Dad. Promise me that. Promise me, Nolan."

Nolan pulled away from her embrace so he could look her in the eye. "I promise, Nova. I'll be nothing like Dad or Nate. You've looked out for me all these years. I will do the same for you."

That brought her the tiniest degree of comfort, because she still felt like she should be the one looking out for her little brother. After all, that was a promise she had once made to Nate.

"Did Knox do this to you?" Nolan asked.

Nova nodded. "Knox. And Dad. And Nate. They all did this to me."

"I'll kill him."

She let out a laugh that sounded sorrowful even to her. "Who? Knox? Or Dad?"

"Whomever did this to you."

"I did this to myself, Nolan." She sniffled. "I shouldn't have trusted Knox. It was foolish of me to think he was someone I can lean on. Not when he's just as broken as we are."

Nolan sighed. "Pastor Sam said we don't always have to be broken, Nova. God can make us whole."

At that, Nova snorted. "Do you believe that, Nolan? Do you really believe in this God?"

"I want to believe it. I want to believe in God. It can't hurt to believe that a benevolent God can make us whole. It's certainly better than hopelessness."

The words had come out of the teenager's lips in a way that made it sound like Nolan wished with all his heart it was all true. God. The promise of wholeness.

Listening to him, Nova found herself wanting to believe as well, but they called God, Father. Based on Nova's experience with her own father, how could she believe God wouldn't just abandon her, too?

As she stared out her car window at their front yard, a flicker of sobriety brought to memory the one-word prayer her mind had uttered back in the car. A plea for help. Knox had relented right after. Had that been God's answer to her prayer?

Nova couldn't tell for sure, so she tucked it in the back of her mind and faced the consequences of rejecting Knox. In the months that followed, Knox harassed her endlessly. He never touched her again, but he did everything he could to get her to talk to him, then a couple weeks before graduation, he disappeared without a word.

As much as she once loved him as a friend, whenever Nova thought of Knox, she thought, "good riddance." He had been a warning to her to keep her head on straight. She couldn't rely on Knox, nor could she rely on God. She had her mother and her brother. That's who she had. She wouldn't be made a fool twice by getting her to trust someone else again. She wouldn't let even God make a fool out of her.

As far as Nova was concerned, one Knox was enough for her to learn her lesson and never repeat her mistake of trusting a man again.

fifteen

THE ONE WHO RAN TO GOD

- THREE YEARS LATER, CALEB, 23 -

The Grant family house was once again brimming with life as guests — family friends mostly from church — crowded the living room, the kitchen, and the dining area. At first, Caleb had wanted to skip the gathering as he had just gotten back from a year-long stay in Ancoria, helping Joshua out in the work he was doing on an island south of the country. Hannah had insisted, saying it would be a great time for him to reconnect with everyone. So, there he was with his five-year-old nephew, Kenneth, trying to build an airplane out of Legos. Next to Kenneth, this new kid whom Caleb wasn't familiar with was peering over Jeremy Sinclair's shoulder as the pastor's kid played with his Gameboy.

His sister-in-law, Kelly, sank into the sofa, her belly looking like it was about to burst open to reveal their new baby girl. She was having what looked like the deepest conversation with Hannah and Deb, who was preparing to go to university with her twin soon. Where Sam was, he could only guess.

"Uncle Caleb, I want to go to the islands when I grow up," Kenneth said. "I'll visit Uncle Josh. That's why we need to build this airplane."

"Right." Caleb nodded. "That sounds like a plan. Do you want to be a pilot?"

Kenneth wrinkled his nose. "What's that?"

"You know. The guy who flies airplanes."

Kenneth shook his head. "Does Uncle Josh fly airplanes?"

"No. He just rides them."

"I want to be like Uncle Josh."

Isaac's laughter caused Caleb to turn and find his older brother sinking on the couch behind him. "Kenneth had a chat with Josh over the phone, and Josh was making it sound like he was having the time of his life, so my son is now determined to become a missionary someday."

Caleb grinned and lifted himself up from the floor so he could sit beside Isaac. "There are worse things he could aspire to be, and to be fair, Josh is for sure having the time of his life."

"Yeah? How was your time there with him?"

"It was amazing. It was good to see the work he's doing there, and on a personal level, I needed the time away to gain perspective before diving headfirst into a career I've always wanted. Once my work at Caine Corp starts, I doubt there'll be many chances for me to leave the country again. I need to work hard to earn a spot as agent at Frontier Press. The timing was perfect, but..." Caleb's words drifted off when it became clear by the way Isaac kept diverting his eyes from Caleb to the women that Isaac was struggling to pay attention.

"I'm sorry, bro. I want to hear all about your experience, but the girls keep looking our way, and I'm genuinely wishing it's you they're talking about. If it's me, then it makes me worry if I somehow got myself in trouble without knowing it." Isaac leaned forward and lowered his voice. "Kelly has been a tad bit high-strung lately, pregnancy and all."

"What are you telling Caleb about me?" Kelly shot her husband a glare. "What did he say?"

Caleb lifted his hands in the air in mock surrender. "I'm staying out of this."

"I was telling him about your pregnancy, honey." Isaac winked at her.

Kelly's eyes narrowed. "What about my pregnancy? Let Caleb answer."

Caleb panicked, so he blurted out the first thing that came to mind. "Are you girls talking about me or about Isaac?"

Hannah smirked. "What makes you think we're talking about either of you?"

"You keep glancing this way," Isaac said.

Hannah looked Caleb straight in the eye. "Olivia is back."

His heart stopped.

"She's with her husband," Deb added.

"Deb!" Kelly and Hannah said in unison.

"What?" Deb shrugged. "Might as well rip it out like a Band-Aid."

Caleb kept his cool, but even he was surprised by how much it still stung to hear that Olivia had a family of her own now, a family Caleb once hoped to have with her.

"You all right?" Hannah asked him.

"Of course. It's been three years. I'm just surprised to find out she's already married. No one told me."

"It didn't seem like something you would want to find out via email," Deb said. "It would've been a weird tack-on to a family email, you know. P.S. Hey, Caleb. Did you know Olivia got married? How are you dealing with that? Do you need us to send you a hug?" Deb nodded in agreement with herself. "See what I mean? It reads weird."

Despite how everyone was treating him like he was wounded all over again, Caleb managed to laugh at his youngest sister's entire bit.

"I only found out now, too." Hannah raised her hands in defense of herself, even if no one was questioning her about it. "Just in case you were wondering."

"Guys, Olivia is free to do whatever she wants. We haven't been together for years." Caleb wished someone would disrupt the conversation and change the subject.

As if hearing his plea, his mother called everyone in to pray, announcing that dinner was ready. It took at least five minutes before everyone could be rounded up in the backyard where a generous spread of food was available on a buffet table.

"Naomi would like to have a short word with everyone before we pray," their father announced.

With her hands clasped together and a brilliant smile on her face, their mother started talking. "I'd like to thank my beautiful daughters for all the preparation they did today. Kelly, Hannah, Deb."

Isaac elbowed Caleb on the rib.

"Ow," Caleb mouthed before giving his brother a glare.

Isaac tossed his head back, his chin angling to their right. Caleb turned and found the Meyers coming through their backyard. Olivia and her husband trailed behind. Upon seeing her, the girls immediately approached to hug them and welcome them.

The only thing Caleb wanted to do at that point was to duck and hide, but he squared his shoulders, approached Olivia's parents first, and gave them a hug. The entire exchange was awkward, but he pulled himself through it until it came time to face Olivia.

Her bittersweet smile made him feel wounded, pathetic, but Caleb managed to smile and nod. "Olivia."

"Caleb. This is my husband—"

The sound of glass breaking resounded from inside the house.

"It's probably the boys," someone said. "They're not here."

Jeremy Sinclair and his friend weren't around.

Caleb was quick to jump at the opportunity to get away from there. "I'll go check on them." He shot a pleading look at his mother. "You guys should go ahead."

Naomi seemed to get his drift, because she clapped her hands to get everyone's attention.

Caleb rushed inside their family home and found pieces of a broken vase scattered on the ground. On the floor beside it was a Frisbee, which Jeremy's friend was crouching down to pick up.

"It's not Max's fault!" Jeremy declared, his face red with shame. "I threw him the Frisbee, and it hit the vase."

Caleb stared them down for a few more seconds to intimidate them a little before taking a deep breath. "It's just a vase. If you want to play, the best place to do it is in the front yard, so you don't get your disc in the food. You two go ahead. I'll follow."

"Thanks, Caleb!" Jeremy said as he rushed to the front yard with Max, who had the disc in hand.

Caleb proceeded to get the broken glass out of the floor while whispering, "No. Thanks to you for providing me an escape."

It seemed he wasn't the only one trying to escape, because just as he was about to throw the pieces of the vase from a dust pan to the trash can, he bumped into Serene Sinclair. When she saw him, her eyes widened, but her finger was still moving on the keypad of her phone. "Oh. Hi, Caleb. Just wanted to go to the bathroom."

Caleb narrowed his eyes at her, but gave it no further thought. After disposing of the vase's remnants, he stared past the backyard door. He was over Olivia, he was sure of it, but why was this still so strange and awkward?

As he walked out the front door to spend some time with the boys, Caleb surrendered his heart and his plans to God. It was a new season of his life as he was now about to start his career, and he didn't want to make a mistake like he had with Olivia next time he opened his heart up to the idea of a relationship with someone, so his prayer was simple that evening.

God, wherever she is — the right woman for me — take care of her, and let Your plan, not mine, be fulfilled in our lives. Amen.

- NOVA, 21 -

Nova pulled an over-sized T-shirt over her leggings. After a long day at work, and after finding out her father wanted to take them to some vacation somewhere, the only thing she wanted to do that evening was read a good book in bed. A shadowy figure lurking past her bedroom window foiled her plans. She parted her curtains.

Nolan froze. A wide, toothy grin appeared on his face.

Nova raised a brow. "Where do you think you're going?"

"To a party."

"What are you sneaking around for? It's not like Ma won't let you go."

"I don't want to explain. It's a long story."

"If you don't tell me what you're up to, I'm telling Ma."

His face fell. "Come on, Nova. Weren't you sixteen once?"

"Yes, and I never snuck around like you're doing now. This is suspicious behavior."

"Right. I remember. You were the most boring teenager to ever live." Nolan groaned. "Fine. I'm crashing a party at the Grants' place."

Nova frowned. "Why?"

"Serene will be there."

Nova narrowed her eyes. "You already broke up with Serene." She threw her head back after noting guilt in Nolan's cringe. "Nolan! No! You're still dating her? Who else knows about this?"

Nolan's face reddened. "Nobody! No one can know. If Ma finds out, she'll tell Pastor Sam and Mama Aida, and it'll be a huge mess. Dad's coming tomorrow to take us on this vacation thing. I want to see Serene before we go."

"Who else will be there?"

"I don't know. It's like a welcome party for Caleb Grant and the Meyer family or something. A bunch of church people will be there, for sure."

Nova's ears perked up at the mention of Caleb Grant. Welcome party? Where had he been? Were he and Olivia still together? She hadn't been to church in years, and from the way Nolan had been talking about how Connect Church had treated him, she figured it was for her own good that she hadn't been going. But Caleb would be there, and something in her leapt at the thought of once again seeing the one guy she still had a massive crush on.

"So?" Nolan asked. "Can I go?"

"I'll go with you."

"What?" Confusion twisted her younger brother's handsome features. "Why? You don't even know most of the people there."

"I don't care." Nova opened her window and climbed out. "Come on." She brushed past Nolan. "Hurry."

"You're going dressed like that? Nova, you're wearing bunny slippers."

"Doesn't matter. No one will see me. I'll be invisible. Like a ninja." She strode toward his car.

"What kind of ninja wears bunny slippers?" He caught up with her and walked in stride with her. "You're not still taking those self-defense lessons, are you?"

"Why is that relevant?"

Nolan shrugged as he opened the car door for her. "Ninja."

Nova smirked. "Let's just go."

He circled the trunk of the car to get to the driver's seat and tried to back out of the driveway as quietly as possible. Fifteen minutes later, he parked the car across the street from the Grants' family home.

Nova swallowed hard at the sight of the huge house. All these years, she had wondered what kind of home the Grants lived in. Here it was. A mansion compared to their home.

The keypad of Nolan's phone made a ping sound with every button he pressed.

"Texting Serene?" Nova asked. "You're not even going inside?"

"She says she's stuck in a conversation with her parents and Caleb." Nolan groaned. "They're talking about Godly relationships or something." He leaned his head back on his seat. "This will mess with her again. If not for church, Serene and I would have fewer problems being in a relationship. This whole Christian thing is making everything so complicated."

Nova didn't respond, because she didn't know what to say. Mr. and Mrs. Grant lived by "this whole Christian thing", and they had the loveliest family she had ever encountered. She could say the same thing about the Sinclair family next door. Maybe it was Nolan and Serene who were making things complicated. Nova sighed.

Right then, the front door swung open, and two boys came running out. Jeremy Sinclair and a boy unfamiliar to her ran to the front lawn. They started tossing a Frisbee around.

"Who's that kid with Jeremy?"

"His new best friend," Nolan said. "Max Owens. Big fuss in church about Max and how Jeremy led him to Christ the first day they met in their school playground. Cool kid."

Right behind them, Caleb followed, his eyes closed, lips moving. Nova drew a breath at the sight of him. Was he praying?

She leaned her temple against the window and bit her lower lip. She hadn't seen him in years. He had stubble on his jaw, and his usually clean-cut hair appeared tousled and unkempt, but he still looked so handsome, so refined. Nova's stomach fluttered. She checked herself and rolled her eyes.

"No way!" Nolan snickered. "Nova!"

"What?" Nova frowned, her eyes still fixed on Caleb.

"You stalker! Seriously? After all these years, you're still into Caleb Grant? That's why you came? Super Nova, I'm disappointed. All the while, I thought you just wanted to hang out with me, but no. You're here for Dr. Edge himself!"

"Don't call him that!" Nova slapped her brother's arm, ignoring the heat rushing to her cheeks. She never should have told Nolan she was writing a novel and that the main character's appearance and noble character was loosely based on a former crush. She hadn't actually realized how aware Nolan was that Caleb was the only crush Nova had ever had. "Shush, Nolan."

"Why don't you go say hi?"

"I'm wearing bunny slippers. Why don't *you* go say hi? If Caleb is out here playing Ultimate with Jeremy and Max, then it means the relationship talk with Serene is over."

Nolan's eyes widened. That was enough to divert his attention back to texting his forbidden sweetheart.

Meanwhile, Nova took one last glance at Caleb and leaned back in her seat. She smiled. She would forever put Caleb Grant on a pedestal. And, because they had never actually met each other — and they most likely never would — he could always be her ideal man, the one who would never have the power to hurt her.

- ONE YEAR LATER; NOVA, 22 -

The irony of it all wasn't lost on Nova — how much her father and brother detested each other, yet it was uncanny how similar they were. Even in the way they died. Where they were different, however, was how Nova didn't cry for Dad the way she had for Nate. The tears she shed upon the death of her father were tears coming out of regret more than sorrow. Nova mourned the sense of loss left behind by all the years Damien Stone had wasted trying to chase after stardom at the expense of his family.

They could have been a beautiful, happy family if only Dad had given loving his family half the try he had given chasing his dreams.

Nolan's sunken eyes made Nova cringe as he sat next to her on the pew of the funeral home, where they were about to conduct a service that evening. He was taking their father's death much harder than Nova. After all, Damien had been making an attempt to reach out to him, develop a relationship with him over the past two years. To be fair, their father had tried with Nova as well, but she was less open to him than Nolan.

He had asked for forgiveness far too many times. Ma had forgiven him far too many times. The only reason Nova ever agreed to spend time with him was to avoid drama, especially since he wasn't hitting Ma or yelling at her anymore. Not since Ma almost sent him to jail for the fight they had after Nate's death.

"He's gone," Nolan said. "How can he do something like this? Especially after the way Nate died."

Like father, like son. Nova didn't say the words out loud, because Nolan was Damien's son too, and her prayer still remained: that Nolan would grow up nothing like Damien. But would God answer the prayers of someone who begged for His help when she needed it, but barely acknowledged His existence the rest of the time?

"Do you still believe in God, Nolan?" Nova asked.

"I don't know," Nolan admitted. "After everything we experienced as kids and everything I learned at church, part of me still believes there's a Higher Power out there Who cares for us, but after how I've been treated at church, it's getting harder and harder to trust in Him."

Nolan could've fooled Nova, because during the service that evening, with tears in his eyes, he worshiped God like he still believed in Him with all his heart. He sang It is Well with My Soul with that beautiful voice of his, and as he did, something shifted within Nova.

It was perhaps Nolan's tears or her mother's pain or the sudden gush of realization that at this point, Nova was the only one left providing for the family with a job as a waitress. Whatever inheritance they receive from Dad would probably go to paying for Nolan's college tuition.

Suddenly, Nova felt like she once had as a child whose primary goal was to distract Gable and her little brother with a sense of wonder Nova no longer had.

Tears came down Nova's face as Nolan sang his song. How could it be well with his soul, all the things they had gone through as a family? When she started to sob, Ma, seated next to her, began sniffling too. Knowing there were no more people to run to for comfort — not her mother, not her brother, not even the friend she once cherished — Nova brought her anger to a God looking down at her from the heavens.

Where was He? Did He care?

Nova searched for a prayer in her soul. If He was real, what did she want to tell God? What could she possibly ask of Him?

Nolan kept singing the song, Nova kept crying, and by the end of it, she offered God her anger in exchange for something she had lost growing up. "If you're there, God," she prayed in a whisper only she and God could decipher. "Bring back my sense of wonder. I want to believe and hope again."

The answer to her prayer wasn't immediate. In fact, she barely noticed it happening until a year later, her professor at the community college she was taking night classes from recommended her for a temp job at Caine Corp. On her first day at work, the first person she saw was Caleb Grant, and somehow, since then, little by little, her childlike wonder returned and so did her belief and hope in a God Who had never once abandoned her.

PRESENT DAY
CIRCA 2000'S

sixteen

THE ONE
WHO TRIED TO
TALK TO HER

- PRESENT DAY: CALEB, 25 -

Surreal was the only word that came to Caleb's mind when Nova and her mother walked into the lobby of Connect Church. Nolan wasn't with them, so Caleb assumed he had already gone to church earlier to prepare for worship. He had been attending Connect since he was a boy. How had he never noticed Nova before? How was it he was aware of both Clara and Nolan but not Nova? Especially with her looking as stunning as she did in the royal blue dress she had on. Did she look like this every Sunday?

Caleb stepped forward to approach her, but before he could get anywhere, an usher started calling everyone in, because the service was about to start. Caleb figured he could catch Nova by the end of the service. He entered the sanctuary and sat in his usual spot.

As if to taunt him, Nova and Clara sat a few rows nearer the stage, somewhere to his right, so that Caleb had a clear view of Nova's face in profile. He gulped. "God, she's so beautiful."

"Bro." Someone poked his shoulder.

Caleb turned his head to find Isaac standing in the aisle with Kelly and their kids. Caleb stepped back to give them room to occupy their usual seats.

Isaac took the seat beside him and nudged him on the shoulder. "Just ask her out already."

Caleb swallowed hard. "Not sure what you're talking about."

"Right." Isaac chuckled. "All our brothers and sisters can get away with playing dumb, Caleb. Not you." He tapped his forefinger against his temple.

Nolan took the stage and started leading worship. Caleb tried his hardest to stay focused, but still found himself catching glimpses of Nova. Had she and her mother always taken those seats?

Nolan belted out a note on stage and snapped Caleb back to attention. Nova was the sister of the best worship leader Connect Church ever had, and he hadn't even known she existed all this time. "Focus, Caleb," he mouthed to himself as he closed his eyes. "Church is about keeping your eyes on God, not Nova. You'll see her at the office tomorrow. Stop gawking at her until then."

Caleb made a conscious effort to take captive his every thought, his soul, and his heart, so he could submit it all to God. He was there to worship his First Love. Not even a beauty like Nova should be able to distract him from God. As he lost himself in worship, Caleb was able to give his entire attention to the God of the universe, but that lasted only until the worship ended. The moment they sat down to listen to Sunday announcements, Caleb was once again endlessly glancing at Nova.

Partway through the preaching, Isaac snickered. "Caleb, come on," he whispered.

"What?" Caleb pried his eyes away from Nova and back on stage. What was Pastor Sam talking about? Something about hiddenness. "I'm listening."

"Please." Isaac snorted. "I know you, bro. You're most likely already praying about her, so why not just go for it?"

The question made Caleb take pause. He scanned the large crowd of people surrounding him — his church family — until he caught sight of Olivia and her husband. She was rocking their newborn baby to sleep. That image was the reason why, Caleb told himself. He had been so sure that Olivia was the right girl for him, and he had been wrong. Did he even think Nova could be the right person for him? If not, then why would he date her?

These concerns continued to circle his head as he made his way to the lobby after the service ended. Right before he could reach the lobby, he found his father and mother shaking hands with Rhoda Petersen. Her husband, Robert, stood next to her, exchanging small talk with Marcus, while their daughter, Rachel, straightened the skirt of her pink floral dress. Caleb couldn't help but grin. What a miracle it was that Miss Rhoda now had a family of her own! Many doubted anybody would be able to handle her high-strung nature. Perhaps God really prepared someone for every person.

Caleb cleared his throat as he approached his parents, just as the Petersen family left. "Dad. Mom." Caleb kissed his mother's cheek.

"Caleb." Naomi squeezed her son's arm.

"Can I have a short word with Dad?"

"Sure," Naomi said. "I'll go have a chat with Aida and Annette."

"Son?" Marcus beamed at Caleb after Naomi left.

"I wanted to ask a question."

"I'm always open to hear what you have in mind."

"Have you met Nova Stone?"

"Clara's daughter?"

Caleb nodded.

"I don't know her personally," Marcus said, "but from what I've seen, she seems to be a lovely young woman who loves the Lord."

"I've only begun to notice her a few days ago. She is a temp at Frontier Press, and she's a brilliant author. I can't wait to share her work with you."

"That sounds great." Marcus grinned. "So, what's the problem?"

"I can't get her off my mind," Caleb admitted.

Marcus chuckled. "I thought that might be the case. So? What are you planning to do? It's been a while since I last heard you show interest in a young woman."

Caleb shrugged. "That's my question, Dad. What should I do? Especially after what happened between me and Olivia, I feel so unsure about jumping back into the dating waters."

"You may be overthinking this, Son." Marcus patted Caleb in the back. "You've always known what you wanted, Caleb. It's an instinct you've had since you were a little kid. Your brothers can be so fickle and indecisive, but you." Marcus grinned. "You, my son, have always had such a security about you and what you want that I've always admired. It's like you never went through a phase of striving to please people. You lost a bit of that when you lost Olivia. It's like you suddenly became unsure of yourself. Especially when it comes to pursuing a woman. This young lady is the first person who seems to have brought back that instinct in you about what feels right and what doesn't. Get to know her, and see where it goes, and don't let some ideal in your head dictate where the relationship should lead." Marcus tapped his earlobe. "Listen. You can recognize God's voice. Let Him guide you."

Caleb gulped when he realized then what he wanted to do. "Thanks, Dad. I have to go."

Marcus laughed. "Go then. I'll see you on Wednesday for family dinner."

"I'll be there!" Caleb jogged to the lobby, hoping to find Nova there. He arrived there in time to see her walking out of the building with her mother.

Caleb sped up his pace, brushing past Hannah, who might have been talking to him about something, but he rushed right past her. "Nova!" he called out when she was already within earshot.

She turned around, and her big brown eyes widened at the sight of him. Her hand — clasped together with Clara's — tightened around her mother's grip. Her throat moved ever so slightly as she faced him. "Caleb?"

Suddenly, he didn't know what he ought to say. His throat felt dry, and all words abandoned him. He had just gotten her attention. Now what?

Nova tried to ignore her heart thumping against her chest and the beads of sweat wetting her palms. Caleb combed his fingers against his hair as he tried to catch his breath. His blue eyes grazed her face before he smiled and nodded at Ma.

"Hello, Caleb," Ma greeted, when neither of them said anything. "How are your parents?"

Caleb's shoulders straightened at Ma's question. He gave Ma a curt nod before responding. "They're fine, Mrs. Stone." He used his thumb to point backwards over his shoulder. "They're still talking to friends. Usual post-Sunday service fellowship."

"Is there anything we can do for you?"

The color drained out of Caleb's face as his eyes met hers. "I'm not sure if this is too sudden or out-of-the-blue, Nova."

It definitely was, but she wasn't about to tell him that.

"I'd like to be intentional about getting to know you better. If it's okay with you and Mrs. Stone—" Caleb shifted his gaze from Nova to her mother and then back "—I would like to ask you out on a date."

Nova couldn't believe her ears. This man! The man whom she had admired from afar for over a decade had been the inspiration to many of her stories' heroes — including Dr. Edge from the novel he had been gushing about. She bit her lip as she lowered her gaze. Completely tongue-tied, she begged for her brain and her heart to somehow make an agreement about what to do, so she could say something — anything — to Caleb.

At the awkward silence, Caleb cleared his throat and shuffled on his feet. "I'm sorry this is so sudden. I understand there may be a conflict of interest — especially if we end up working together — but

I wanted to get that out there. It won't hurt my feelings if you say no."

"No, Caleb." Ma tapped his arm.

Nova's mouth dropped open as she tried to shoot her mother with questions using her eyes. What was she going on about? "Ma."

"Let me finish," Ma said. "I meant to say no, Caleb. You don't need to apologize. I'm sure my Nova would love to go on a date with you. You should join us next weekend. It's Nolan's graduation. And Serene's too, so we're planning a family get-together with the Sinclairs. You can be Nova's plus-one."

Nova shut her eyes and swayed her head from side-to-side. If only the ground would swallow her up whole. She and Caleb hadn't even been on a first date yet, and Ma was already inviting him to meet not only the entire family, but their next-door neighbors too! Sure, Caleb already knew Pastor Sam's family, but still! She cast an apologetic look at Caleb, but he didn't seem to take it as an apology.

"That sounds wonderful to me," he said. "But only if you're okay with that, Nova."

What was she supposed to say? "I guess it's a date." She winced. Finally, she was able to speak, and of all the things to say, she had to come up with a cliché.

"Great!" His handsome face lit up, and Nova's heart melted. "I'll see you tomorrow at work, Nova. Mrs. Stone, I'll see you on Saturday."

"Perfect." Ma tapped the small of Nova's back as Caleb returned to the center of the church lobby to mingle with his family.

Once he was out of earshot, Nova confronted her mother. "Ma, why did you do that?"

A bemused smile highlighted Ma's deepening wrinkles. "Because I know you want it, Nova. Am I wrong?"

Nova's shoulders sagged. She rolled her eyes. "Well, no, Ma. You're not wrong, but—" She sighed. "Never mind." How could she explain to her mother how Caleb made her feel when it didn't make sense even to her? "It's okay. Let's go."

They made their way to the parking lot and to Nova's car. Just before she got inside, Nova turned her head to find Caleb coming out of the church building with his siblings.

She got in the driver's seat, shut the car door, and gripped the steering wheel until her knuckles stretched her skin. *God,* she prayed in her mind as she backed the car up, *help me keep a level head and see Caleb for who he is and how You made him, not what I built him up in my mind to be. He doesn't deserve a relationship built on delusion, and neither do I.*

It took a full drive from their church to their home before Nova recognized the hope blossoming within her — hope that maybe Caleb wouldn't disappoint her and that he would be the kind of man her father, brother, and Knox had never been and never could be.

Hannah's eyes widened in surprise when Caleb told her later that evening that he had asked Nova out on a date. She then narrowed her eyes at him. She shifted on their living room couch, so she could bend one knee and lean her side on the backrest to face him. "What is going on with you?"

"What do you mean?" he asked.

"You're never this impulsive. You've only really known Nova for a few days."

"Yet I should have known her far longer than that. Also, I can't get my mind off her, Hannah."

"Yes, but you work in the same office. You want to be her agent and take her on as a client. Have you considered what it'll be like if things don't work out? Actually, even if it does work, it complicates a lot of stuff for you and her professionally. Are you ready for that?"

Caleb winced. He had definitely acted on impulse, but it felt like the right thing to do at the time.

"It's just strange, Caleb, because you usually think things through before you jump into decisions like this. Even in your relationship with Olivia, you were so careful to make sure that you were both following the rules, that you had both our families' blessing."

Caleb blew out a sigh. "I've already asked her though. In front of her mother. I can't quite take it back, can I?"

"Look." Hannah sighed. "Nova is great. I like her. I've told you that already, but I don't want to see you get hurt again. And Nova... Well, we all know everything her family has gone through, so she may have a lot of baggage we can't even begin to unpack."

"What are you saying, Hannah?"

"Just that I know you, and I know when you fall in love, you fall hard, and Nova seems to have quite an accelerated effect on you. In a lot of ways, it's similar to how Olivia got to you. Don't make the same mistakes again, okay? I do think Nova is a lot more fragile than Olivia was, and you're not as sure of yourself as you were in high school."

Caleb snorted. "Dad said the same thing."

Hannah shrugged a shoulder as she twirled the ends of her blonde hair with her finger. "Nova is a great person, but she's been through a lot, Caleb. Tread carefully with her. Make sure it's what God wants, not just what you want."

Her words struck Caleb in a different way, mostly because they rang true based on the limited interactions he had shared with Nova since she had gotten on his radar. She had come off to him as guarded and protective. Were her walls only for herself or also for the people she loved? Caleb sighed. "I'll keep everything you said in mind, Hannah. Thanks for that. I am praying about this. Trust me."

"I do trust you—" Hannah reached forward to ruffle his hair "—more than our other brothers, to be honest, but don't tell them that. Now, let's watch this movie, shall we?"

Caleb grinned. "You'll love it." He grabbed their DVD player's remote control and pressed play. He found it unbelievable that Hannah still hadn't watched the first movie of *Lord of the Rings*, when the second one had just come out. Caleb took it upon himself to amend that travesty.

As they watched the film, Caleb gave thought to what Hannah had said. An image of Nova walking away from that guy in a leather jacket played through his mind. He smirked at the part where her elbow connected with the guy's jaw. He could only wonder at the story behind that altercation, but he didn't feel like he was in a position to ask Nova when they had been in the pantry.

Caleb blew out a deep breath. He definitely needed to pray more about this date before he ended up leading Nova — and himself — on.

The same way Olivia had once led him on.

seventeen

THE ONE WHO SECOND-GUESSED A PROPOSAL

Caleb tossed and turned on his bed, kicking his blanket off him before a shiver made him pull it back over his body again. Like a highlight reel, scenes involving Nova Stone played in his mind. Her smile and the dimple on her cheek, the boy's head ramming into her stomach, her standing in his office in a superhero costume, the conversation they had from office to parking lot, her elbow connecting with that stranger's jaw, her expression when he had asked her out on a date. Each scene warmed his heart, but disturbed his soul, as it all culminated in Hannah's words echoing in his ear.

"Nova is a great person, but she's been through a lot, Caleb. Tread carefully with her. Make sure it's what God wants, not just what you want."

What was he doing?

He was going out on a date with Nova that weekend, that was all. How had Hannah turned it into something so much more? Like she had dropped this immense sense of responsibility on him — one he wasn't ready to carry. Was it up to him to deal with Nova's baggage? All he wanted to do was get to know her! How could he not when not a waking moment passed by without her somehow squeezing her way to the forefront of his mind? Had it been this way with Olivia before?

Caleb pushed his blanket aside and stood to his feet. He pulled a hoodie over his bare torso before sauntering to the kitchen to pour himself a glass of warm water. The clock on the wall was ticking past midnight. Caleb sighed before leaning forward to grip the edges of the counter, stretching his arms and arching his back. The weight on his chest grew by the minute, so he inhaled one long breath and exhaled through his nostrils.

He shut his eyes. *God, what is going on? Why do I feel this way? Should I not date Nova? Is this not what You want?*

He smiled at the recollection of the dimple on Nova's cheek. The memory created an ache of longing within him. Something about her enticed him. She had a mystique about her that he found irresistible, but if it wasn't what God wanted... Caleb gritted his teeth. He paced the floor, paused to take a gulp from his glass of water, and paced again.

What should he do now? Should he back out on their date? What about the proposal he was to present to her tomorrow? Should he not represent her as her agent as well?

Caleb finished his drink and placed the glass on the sink before returning to his bedroom. He sank on the edge of his bed. "God, please. Tell me what to do," he prayed. "I don't know what You want me to do."

He closed his eyes and waited for something, *anything*, to give him direction, but no answer came. Caleb sighed. Was he spiritualizing this too much? He shrugged and lay back on his bed.

It took another hour before Caleb fell asleep, and when he finally did, he found himself in a land of dreams where he sat on a porch of a house he believed to be his own and a little girl with curly dark hair sat on his lap. The idyllic scene didn't last long, because a frantic young woman in a white dress, torn and tattered, came running to him, pleading for him to save her. The faces of both the little girl and the young woman were none other than Nova's.

Nova opened her eyes to find the bright sun sending warm rays of summer light into her room. She snuggled her cheek against the pillow as a smile as bright as the morning spread on her face. She bit her lip even as an image of Caleb's face drifted into her mind. Had her lifelong crush really asked her out on a date?

Equal parts dread and anticipation made her heart thump an erratic beat against her chest. She pushed away the apprehension and embraced the eagerness. The truth was, she couldn't wait until Saturday. She was about to go on a date with Caleb Grant!

Nova leaped out of the bed and shimmied her shoulders to bask in the sunlight she was convinced was cascading over her like a promise of blessings sure to come. The phone on her bedside table vibrated. She picked up the small sky blue gadget and found a message from Caleb.

> **Caleb:** Good morning, Nova. Sent you an email. Can't wait to spend time with you on Saturday. Have a great day!

Upon reading his message, a satisfying calm left her breath-taken as her thumb flew on her phone's keypad to send him a reply. She typed a response, erased it, then typed another one, and another one before settling for:

> **Nova:** Good morning! Will check the email once I get to work. See you on Saturday. Have a great day as well!

She had half the mind to get to her computer to read his email immediately, but opted against it. After all, she had a scheduled appointment with him to discuss her manuscript and the proposal he mentioned he would present to her.

Nova went about her morning feeling like she was floating.

Vienna's brow quirked up upon seeing her at the office. "You look different," she said. A grin formed on her face. "Does that huge smile have anything to do with your meeting with a handsome literary agent later?"

Nova's smile grew. Her lashes fluttered. "Maybe." She settled herself in her cubicle and booted up her computer.

Vienna left her cubicle and made her way to Nova's. "You have to tell me all about it."

"I think a lot of these meetings at this stage are supposed to be confidential." Nova double-clicked on the icon for her email software.

"Yeah, but Nova, this is me. You can tell me anything."

The desire to tell her friend about her date with Caleb grew within her, ready to burst out of her lips, but she mustered the will to hold the news back and asked instead, "Anything?"

Vienna narrowed her eyes at Nova. "Anything."

Nova sighed as she clicked on Caleb's email. Just as she was about to respond to Vienna, she read the first line of the email. "He canceled our meeting today," she said. Her eyes sped through his short email, explaining that he was working on the proposal, and it was taking longer than expected. They'll talk about the novel by next week. He then repeated how excited he was to see her on Saturday.

"What?" Vienna leaned over Nova's shoulder to read the email herself. "He seemed so sure and excited about it. I wonder what happened."

Nova fidgeted in her chair. Did the sudden delay have anything to do with their date?

"Why are you seeing each other on Saturday?" Vienna asked.

"My mother invited him to attend my brother's graduation party," Nova said. At least she hadn't lied. That much was true. Sitting in her cubicle with her coworker hovering over her, Nova then realized the precarious situation she was in.

"You two are getting close," Vienna said before returning to her cubicle. "Things are happening fast here at Frontier."

Nova winced as she tried to reel back all the concerns running through her mind as the ramifications of dating in the workplace hit her. She swiveled her chair left to right, then back, as an unsettling thought came over her. Was Caleb only interested in her novel, because he wanted to date her? What if their date ended up a mess? How would that impact their professional relationship? Could they still work together as agent and author?

Nova tried to push away the distrust, but as if to remind her of the many reasons she found it hard to date and trust men, another email popped up.

Nova gritted her teeth, deleted it immediately, and blocked the sender. She wanted nothing to do with Knox Cartier.

Once upon a time, Knox had her full trust, and now, he was one of the main reasons she was finding it difficult to trust even a guy she had always admired, because the reality was what did she really know about Caleb? What made her think he wasn't like any other man in her life?

The rest of the week went on, and Nova didn't hear from him nor see him around the office. The disappointment sank in, but she fought the urge to message him. She didn't want to appear desperate or clingy. Especially since they haven't even had their first date yet. She would just have to wait until Saturday.

"What's going on with you?" Nolan asked over dinner, Wednesday night.

"What do you mean?"

Nolan pointed at her plate.

Nova looked at her food and found it almost untouched while Ma and Nolan were already done eating. "Oh. Nothing. I got a lot on my mind, that's all."

Ma tapped her arm. "Your sister is just nervous about her date on Saturday."

Nolan's brow rose. "Date? No one told me about a date. My graduation ceremony is on Saturday. Have you forgotten?"

"Like I would ever forget." Nova rolled her eyes. "I'll be there, Nolan. I wouldn't miss it for the world."

"So, what about this date of yours?"

"I'm bringing a plus one to your graduation." Nova shrugged.

"Who's this guy?"

"You'll see," Nova said.

"It's Caleb from church." Ma smiled.

"Ma!"

"What?!" Nolan started laughing and clapping his hands loudly. "No way! Caleb Grant?! How? When did this happen? Why has no one told me about this until now? Nova, it's like all your dreams are coming true!"

The heat rushed to her cheeks as Nova shut her eyes. She buried her face in her palms.

"Aw, Nova. What are you hiding your face for?" Nolan reached forward to twirl a few strands of her hair in his fingers.

"I'm embarrassed."

"Why?"

"Yes. That's what I'm thinking. Why?" Ma was nodding her head profusely. "Caleb is a wonderful young man, who belongs to a great family." She sounded mighty pleased with herself. "He's better than that boy Nova used to spend so much time with."

Nolan flinched at the mention of Knox.

Even with her palms still plastered to her face, Nova identified the sudden awkward tension at the dinner table, so she lifted her eyes to face her mother and brother before forcing a smile. "Okay, fine. I admit it. I'm nervous about Saturday. So what? Nothing weird about that."

"Of course." Nolan's grin grew. "I'm happy for you. Caleb's a great guy—" he wrinkled his nose "—or at least that's what Serene says. I don't know him that well, to be honest. All I know is he was loyal to Olivia all those years they were together, so I'm assuming he'll be loyal to you. He better be. You deserve only the best, Nova."

"I agree." Ma squeezed her hand. "Now, finish your dinner."

Nova wanted to say she wasn't hungry, but she didn't want to trigger further questions, so she started eating. She might have fooled her mother, but Nolan was harder to trick into believing she was perfectly fine.

In this case, even her attempts to fake enjoying her dinner didn't convince him everything was okay, because he remained even after their mother had excused herself and had gone to bed.

Nolan tapped his hands over the wooden table. "What's wrong, Nova?"

"I know not what you speak of."

"Right." His eyes narrowed. "There's something you're not telling me."

"You and your wild imagination," Nova said.

"I'm not buying it." Nolan leaned back in his chair, crossed his arms over his chest, and smirked. "Besides, between you and me, you are the one with an overly active imagination. Spill it, Nova. What's bothering you?"

What was she supposed to say? Her stalker was back, and she was about to dive into an office romance with a man whom she had admired and tried to avoid for years — the same man who had the potential to make or break her career. And her heart. Also, Caleb hadn't even bothered to talk to her since his last email. The last thing she wanted was to talk about either of them to Nolan, so she had to figure out a way to change the subject.

Nova stared at her little brother. He wasn't so little anymore. He was a man now, about to go to college, thanks to the inheritance Dad had left them, the same inheritance she had reserved for Nolan's future instead of her own. "I can't believe you're leaving soon."

Nolan's brown eyes softened. "You'll always be my Super Nova. You know that, right? I've never thanked you for all the times you've protected me. I don't want you to think I don't recognize how much worse my life would have been if you weren't here. Vienna and Miles might have bet you into wearing a superhero costume, but I've always seen you for the selfless hero you are, and if Caleb Grant is the man who can treat you like you deserve, then I'm all for it. But for now, I'm still the main man in your life, and if he ever hurts you—" Nolan hit his left palm with his right fist.

At that, Nova laughed. "Please. I can hit better and harder than you, plus you won't want to ruin those pretty long fingers of yours. Those are meant for guitars and grand pianos, not fights."

Nolan snorted. "You calling me weak?"

"No." She shook her head. "I just think I'm more of a fighter."

"Are you bragging about all those self-defense lessons you took?"

Nova shrugged. "Ninja."

He laughed before a pensive expression took over his usually fierce and broody countenance. "I hope it works out, Nova. You and Caleb. I like him for you, and let's face it—" he smirked "—you like him for you, too."

Nova lowered her eyes. "We'll see."

Nolan took a deep breath. "I already told Ma, and I've been looking for a chance to tell you, but—" He rubbed the back of his neck with his palm.

"What is it, Nolan?"

"I want to propose to Serene on Saturday."

Nova could swear her brain short-circuited. What was Nolan going on about? "Propose what?"

Nolan deadpanned. "Marriage."

"Nolan, you're eighteen."

"Old enough, and far too in love not to take the leap. Serene's the girl for me, Nova."

"You're crazy. Pastor Sam and Mama Aida would never agree to this!"

"I already told them."

"They said yes?"

"They have their reservations, of course—" Nolan shrugged one shoulder "—but I think they realize how difficult it is to keep Serene and me apart."

Nova huffed. "It's impossible."

Nolan grinned. "See? So, as in love as we are, they're worried about me and Serene going to college together. The temptation might be too much to resist, so why not get married?"

Nova rushed to process the information. Was this the right thing for Nolan and Serene? "Have you prayed about this?"

Surprise flickered in Nolan's eyes. It wasn't a question that Nova had ever asked him before. "Yeah, I guess. I mean, Serene and I have already gotten this far. I assume God approves. Why wouldn't He?"

Nova's heart sank to hear his answer. "Nolan, I don't want you to make a mistake you'll regret someday. This is huge."

"I know, Nova, but I want this."

Nova winced. "Is there even anything I can say to convince you not to do this?"

"Nova, your blessing is important to me."

She couldn't figure out what to say. "I want you to be happy, Nolan. I want Serene to be happy. You both mean a lot to me."

"Does that mean you're okay with this?"

Nova wished she could say she was, but something about it didn't feel right. "Can't you wait a few more years?"

"I guess." Nolan shrugged. "But what for? This is what I want, and I believe it's what Serene wants as well."

Nova tried to smile, but the smile faltered. "This is scary, Nolan. It sounds foolish."

"All I'm asking is that you trust me. I know what I'm doing."

She bit her lip as she reached forward to embrace her brother. It felt as if she was losing another man in her life. "I love you, Nolan."

"I love you too."

When they pulled away from each other, Nova forced a grin at him and changed the topic to avoid having to give him her blessing for something she wasn't sure he should do. "You're doing dishes, right?"

Nolan chuckled. "Only because you didn't object to my wedding."

Deep inside, a million objections were going on inside Nova, but she held herself together until she was in the privacy of her bedroom, where the moment she was alone, she fell on her knees and cried out to the only Father she had.

"God," she prayed, with her knees on the floor, her hands clasped together, her elbows propped up on top of the bed, "Knox is back. I have no idea what he wants, and I honestly just want him out of my life, but a huge part of me also wishes he would find happiness and satisfaction in You. He terrifies me, but I once called him my best friend, and deep inside, he's broken like I am.'

"Unlike Caleb, who is probably a lot more whole and put-together than Knox and I combined. He hasn't spoken to me since he asked me out on a date, nor has he said anything about what's going on with him or with the proposal he says he wants to pitch to me to represent my work. I'm sure he talks and listens to You more than I do, so I hope You can speak to him and lead him. Whether or not You mean for us to be together, teach him how to treat me right, and teach me how to honor him and not place on him the distrust my dad, Nate, and Knox planted in me.'

"And then, there's Nolan. He's about to go to college, and now he's proposing to his girlfriend, which I think is insane, but I'm not sure there's anything I can say to dissuade him from this. He's been in church longer than I have, so I don't know how to explain to him this unsettled feeling I have within me. God, protect my brother. I sometimes wonder if he needs protection from himself, but God, You know him. I pray for only the best for him."

Nova was about to close in prayer when a question captured her thoughts. *What about you?*

She froze even as the verse she read that morning came to her.

Ask and it will be given to you; seek and you will find; knock and the door will be opened to you. Matthew 7:7

Nova wasn't sure what to ask for. Hadn't all those prayers been for her? She searched her mind for something to ask on her behalf, and this was the prayer that came out of her lips:

"Bless and preserve my family, God — Ma, Nolan, and the families we have yet to form. Heal my heart, refine it, make it clean. Most of all, help me delight myself in You, so that no matter what happens in the situations I have with Knox, Caleb, and Nolan, my heart can still rejoice in knowing I am Yours, and You are mine."

With those words said, a smile formed on Nova's lips. Peace beyond her understanding embraced her, and a God, Who was Friend, Lover, Father, assured her the road ahead was not one she needed to walk on her own.

He would be right there with her.

Caleb shifted uncomfortably in his seat as Ethan Caine's stare shot jagged slivers right through him. He had always known his boss as a calm, reasonable, and fair man, but his request was neither reasonable nor fair, and if his pulse rate was any indication, Caleb wasn't calm either.

"Let me get this straight." Ethan sat straight in the executive chair behind the large mahogany desk separating boss and employee. "You're telling me you discovered a manuscript by a young and upcoming author you are willing to stake your career and literary integrity on, but you're not willing to represent the author? Caleb, from what you've told me of this story, it sounds like a book tailor fit to your area of expertise. All the contacts and connections your father handed over to you will greatly benefit this book and this author. Why are you suddenly backing out of this project? Help me understand this decision."

Caleb straightened his shoulders and willed himself to keep his gaze directed on Ethan's. "I've met the author. She was the employee from the marketing department who pitched her novel to all the agents in a superhero costume, an outfit that would make a lot more sense had the other agents read her manuscript up to the end. One of her coworkers from the marketing team read her book and left her manuscript on my desk the first day I became an agent for the company."

"I see." Ethan's brow rose. A slight smile lifted the corners of his lips. "Alex Orwell is a woman."

"Her name is Nova Stone. She apparently goes to my church, as well, and without thinking it all through, I asked her out on a date." Caleb swallowed hard. Was it wise for him to divulge such a personal matter to his boss? It didn't matter now, because it was done. He took a deep breath to ease his nerves. "I've been thinking and praying about what I would rather do — date her or represent her. I would honestly like to do both, but Mr. Caine, I don't know how that will impact our professional work, so—"

"Do both."

"Excuse me?"

"Mr. Grant, I grew up as a part of this company, and even as a boy, I have seen your father's work ethic and integrity. Marcus Grant did good by all the authors he signed. He gave their work the best it deserves and went over and beyond what was called for. I am confident there is no other person who can represent this young woman and her work the way a Grant man can. As long as you do not compromise your existing clients — the ones your father worked hard to support and represent — then I don't get why you shouldn't represent this new author."

"But what about—"

"I'm not a God-fearing man, Mr. Grant. My family doesn't bother much with religion, but I've always respected how your father lived by his faith. He was a man of integrity. The fact we're having this conversation gives me a lot of confidence you won't do anything to stain the legacy of not only your father, but of your God." Ethan grinned, his eyes flickering with a naughtiness Caleb had never seen before. "Quite a predicament you have gotten yourself into, Caleb. Your relationship with Nova Stone might just cause a few more bets to go around this office."

At that, Caleb balked. He shook his head to show his disapproval of such a practice. "I wouldn't want anyone to know we're dating, Mr. Caine."

Ethan brushed his forefinger over his sealed lips. "I won't say a word, but let's not be naïve. It's only a matter of time before word gets around you're dating your newest client, who also happens to be working as a temp at the marketing department." The dark-haired man whose often serious demeanor caused intimidation in most people had a child-like streak of mischief in his eyes that made Caleb wonder if he was even talking to the same person who had hired him. "If worse comes to worst, maybe we should fire her, so she can focus on her book."

"Please don't." Caleb frowned. He didn't even know anything about Nova's financial situation. The last thing he wanted was to get her fired from her job.

Ethan laughed. "I'm joking." He pulled out his drawer and took out a manila envelope. He dropped it on top of his desk and pushed it toward Caleb. His expression shifted from jovial and relaxed to the more typical somberness he brought into the workplace. "I've reviewed the proposal you want to offer to her, and I'll be honest. I'm surprised you're taking a lower agent commission than your dad used to take. Is this only because you're attracted to this woman or do you plan to take a lower cut from all your clients?"

"I didn't think I should take a cut as large as my father's." Caleb took the manila envelope, assuming it contained the proposal he had for Nova. "I may have inherited a lot of his know-how, but I'm not as seasoned as he is."

"But you also have a direct line to all his knowledge and experience, Caleb. My grandfather built Caine Corp from the ground up. You don't see me taking a pay cut because I'm not as experienced as he was. Don't sell yourself short." Ethan nodded him off. "Now, go back to work. And good luck on your date with Nova Stone."

"Thank you, Mr. Caine." Caleb rose to his feet and fought the urge to rush to the marketing department to check on Nova. It had been so difficult trying to avoid her this whole week to clear his mind and seek God about what to do about the situation he had dragged them into, but as he left Ethan Caine's office, a weight rolled off his shoulders, a sense of release. Still, Caleb held a prayer close to his heart. A protectiveness over Nova had been growing in his heart as he continued to not only pray but also dream about her throughout the week. "God," he whispered as he made his way back to his office, "help me do right by her."

He checked the clock on the wall. Nova would be on her way home by now. He rushed to his office window and looked down at the ground below, where he could see the outdoor parking lot. Right on time, Nova walked out of Caine Tower and made her way to her car.

Caleb smiled, took out his phone, and called her. It took several rings before she responded.

"Hello?"

"Hey, Nova. I was wondering if we could have an early breakfast before heading off to your brother's graduation. Would that work for you?"

Apart from her gentle breathing, there was nothing but silence from the other side of the line.

"Nova?"

"Sure. I would like that."

"Does five o'clock work for you?"

"That's super early."

"Six?"

"No. Five will do."

"I'll see you tomorrow then."

"I'll see you."

Caleb hung up and watched as Nova drove her car out of the parking lot. That wasn't a very enthusiastic response from her, but at least she said yes. Long after her car had gone, Caleb stood there, praying, fully aware of how precious she was in God's eyes, how precious she could someday be to him.

Hopefully, his boss's confidence in him wouldn't be for naught. After all, the last thing Caleb wanted to do was stain not only the legacy of his father but also of the God he served. Caleb whistled out a sigh. No pressure at all.

eighteen

THE ONE WHO OPENED UP

The orange, blue, and violet hues of the dawn struck Nova and wrapped her in a warm and inviting glow, causing Caleb's breath to hitch. She pulled a beige knitted cardigan over her powder blue dress while exiting their front door. A timid smile formed on her face when Caleb stepped back on their front porch to give her space.

"Did I wake you?" Caleb asked.

Nova shook her head. "No. Everyone's up already. Ma and Nolan will have breakfast in an hour with the Sinclairs next-door. They're heading over to the graduation ceremony together."

"Should I maybe tell your mother where I'm taking you?"

"I don't think they would want to face a guest in all their morning glory."

Right about then, the front door swung open. Nolan leaned against the doorpost wearing a black shirt and checkered pajamas. He fixed his stare on Caleb.

"Good morning, Nolan." Caleb extended his hand for Nolan to shake. "Congratulations on your graduation."

Nolan took his hand and squeezed it hard. "Take care of my sister and don't underestimate her. She may look a little mousy sometimes, but believe me when I say she's a formidable opponent."

"I don't doubt that." Caleb glanced at Nova. "Though the last word I would think to describe her is mousy." He shifted his weight from one foot to the other. "I'll look out for her. We'll see you at the ceremony."

Nova hugged her brother, who whispered something in her ear before letting go. Nolan snickered, while Nova's cheeks turned bright red. She rolled her eyes and lightly tapped his jaw with her fingers. She then faced Caleb, but kept her eyes lowered.

Against the light of the dawn, with the way her curls framed her face, Caleb found himself breathtaken by her. "You're so stunning."

Nova's eyes widened before shooting up to meet his. Her cheeks reddened further, as her mouth parted to say something before a smile appeared, and she looked away again.

"I'm such an idiot for having never noticed you before." Whatever was on her mind, Caleb could only guess while he tried to recover from the realization he had just spoken those words out loud.

Nolan's brows flicked upwards before he let out a laugh. "I can't disagree. You're kind of an idiot. Always baffled me how this—" he pointed his fingers at them, swinging back and forth between them "—hasn't been a thing before now. Have fun. Don't do anything you'll regret." He pointed two fingers at his eyes, then at Nova as a gesture to inform her he was watching. He then returned to their house and shut the door behind him.

"Let's go?" Caleb swept an arm across the air to point at his car.

Nova pulled her cardigan around herself once again before walking in step with him.

"Cold?" he asked.

"Not so much." She huffed and let go of her cardigan, dropping her arms to her side, her shoulders stiff as she marched beside him.

"You okay?" Caleb narrowed his eyes at her as he opened the car door for her.

"I'm a little nervous." She slipped inside his car.

He smiled at her. "Don't be. It's just me." He shut the door and made his way to the driver's seat.

Once inside, he winked at her as she pulled the seatbelt and clasped it in place. Her profile highlighted the soft angles of her face, her black curls cascading down her shoulders on to her delicate waist. What was going through her mind? The same mind that had come up with Dr. Edge. Her straight shoulders, her hands clasped together over her lap, her gaze directed outside the window. Everything about her posture told him she was uncomfortable, or more likely, guarded.

Caleb wanted nothing more than to put her at ease. But how? He barely knew her. The same way he had barely known Olivia when he had first started seeing her. He drew a breath, which caught her attention.

Nova's eyes grew wide upon realizing how he had been staring and that they hadn't gone anywhere yet. She didn't say anything. She just stared back at him with an unspoken question behind her gaze.

Caleb pulled his seatbelt on and grinned. "Are you hungry?" he asked.

"Not so much," she said.

"Good. It'll be about a half-hour's drive to the city, so get comfortable."

She fumbled with her fingers and swallowed hard.

Caleb had the urge to reach forward, hold her hand, and tell her to relax, but his own protective instinct told him not to, because he wanted her to feel safe around him, and she didn't seem to. That notion unsettled him, because he couldn't help but wonder what had happened in her past that made her so walled up.

He started driving. Though he kept second-guessing if the uncomfortable silence was a good sign for their second date, Caleb forced himself to remain quiet, to not ask questions first, to get her more relaxed around him. For the entire thirty-minute drive, he prayed a prayer that didn't involve words, because he didn't know how to pray about a woman he wanted so badly to get to know better, but for some reason, couldn't seem to get comfortable around him.

When he turned a corner to a place that couldn't have been more familiar to both of them, Nova finally spoke. "Are we going to Caine Tower?"

Caleb grinned. "Just its parking lot."

"What?"

"You'll see." He tapped the steering wheel before hitting the brakes. He then got out of the car and opened the door for her. "We have quite a few hours before your brother's graduation, so I figured I'd take you somewhere special." He reached out his hand for her to take.

Nova stared at it for a couple of seconds before taking his offer and stepping out of the car. He closed the door and headed to the trunk of his car to retrieve a picnic blanket and a picnic basket. "Hannah helped me prepare it."

"You live with your sister?" she asked.

It was good to hear her ask him something about his life. "Yeah. We share an apartment together." He cradled the blanket in the crook of his elbow and held the basket with his other hand before motioning for her to follow him.

"Let me help," she said, before pulling the blanket from him.

"The apartment is a shorter drive to work than living in the suburbs. Also, it was meant to be a shared apartment between Josh, Hannah, and me, but we had only been there a few months when Josh flew off to China. It's just me and Hannah now." He glanced over at her. "You? Must be quite an adjustment for you and Clara now that Nolan is going to university."

Nova hugged the picnic blanket against her chest, her head bowed as she walked beside him. "It's difficult to process, but I've been praying about him, about us. God will take care of us."

"Do you mind telling me what brought you to church? I believe you guys didn't go for a while, but I should have noticed when you did. I'm honestly still amazed I haven't met you earlier."

The corner of her lips tugged ever so slightly upwards. When she spoke, her words sounded calculated, like she was choosing each one carefully.

"Nolan was the one who has been faithful. Ma and I stopped going because of my father and older brother. They didn't believe in God, and they were pretty jaded about church. It was after my dad died that I started going again. At first, it was because of Nolan. He was going, and I figured we needed to go as a family. I wanted to feel closer to Ma and Nolan. I also missed the community I had at Connect Church. It was just that, at first. A longing to be with people, to not feel so alone, especially seeing how much help the Sinclairs were to my mother and brother. At some point though, all that longing for community and belonging brought me closer to God."

"What brought you to that point?"

"A lot of it was seeing the lives the people at church led. The Sinclairs, especially. The kind of marriage Pastor Sam and Mama Aida have, the way they lead their lives, how they raise their children. Your family, as well. I've always admired the relationship your parents have and how they have raised you guys, especially considering there's so many of you."

Caleb laughed. "That's true. There's quite a bunch of us."

Nova's irises took on a brilliant glow. "Your family, as well as the Sinclairs... It's nothing like the family I grew up with. I think it was at one of the church camps when I came to a point where I told God about the kind of family that I want, the kind of family I wish I grew up with, the kind we weren't. There's this spot at the camp site our church always goes to. The gazebo."

Caleb's breath hitched. He remembered that gazebo all too well. After all, it was the site of the night he surrendered his life to the Lord.

"One night, I went to that gazebo and told God I would serve Him. I would give my life to Him, but I wanted to someday be a part of a good family, have a good husband who will be a good father to our children one day." Nova's smile grew, her gaze distant. "I was still trying to bargain with Him, still trying to figure out what I could get out of Him, but from that night on, I became more faithful and intentional in getting to know Jesus. Once I did, I fell in love. At some point, it ceased to matter whether He gives me what I want or not, because I wanted His desires to be mine. I wanted to learn what it was like to delight in Him." She shrugged. "I'm still learning."

"Aren't we all?" Hearing her story, Caleb couldn't help but be drawn to the sincerity of her heart, as well as honored that she would share it with him. Caleb had stopped walking, and so did she, but it didn't seem like she had even noticed they were by the park bench in front of the water fountain where he had first seen her. "You really are super, Nova."

Nova glanced up at him. Her cheekbones flushed pink. She smiled. "So are you though." She then looked around, and upon realizing where they were, much to his delight, for the first time, Caleb heard her laugh.

The laughter bubbling out of her lips was nervous energy brought about by the realization of where they were and the recollection of the scenario that brought Nova's existence to Caleb's attention. At the memory of her appearance that day, Nova buried her face in the blanket. "I can't believe you brought me here. I was so embarrassed!"

"Why? You looked magnificent. I'm serious, Nova. I can't get that scene out of my mind. The way you were running after that kid with the outfit you had on. It was glorious!" He tugged at the blanket. "Come on. Let's have breakfast."

She lifted her face from the blanket. Certain her knees would give way beneath her when he pulled the blanket from her to lay it on the ground, Nova shifted her balance before snapping to attention and taking the picnic basket from the bench where he had laid it, so she could help set up. With the checkered red blanket on the ground and the picnic basket in the middle, she and Caleb took their places on it, leaning their backs on the edge of the bench opposite each other, both facing forward with the basket between them.

Caleb took out triangle sandwiches, a round plastic container with watermelon slices in it, a box of apple juice for each of them, a thermos, and a couple of plastic cups. "Brewed coffee." He winked as he tapped on the thermos.

"I love it."

"Let me pour you a cup then," he said.

Something about the simple breakfast in a place that already had meaning to them made Nova's heart leap. There was a familiarity about it that drew her closer to him, made her more at ease. She didn't even know how it had happened, but somewhere in between the trip from their house to the park, Caleb had managed to ease her tension and make her feel comfortable enough to keep talking about whatever it was she had been blabbering on about.

"It's still piping hot." He placed a sleeve on the cup of hot coffee before handing it to her.

"Just the way I like it." She took the cup and blew on its edge, enjoying the warmth between her palms as she watched him pour himself a cup as well. She stretched her legs and crossed her ankles as she leaned back on the bench, enjoying the early morning privacy of the park and the gush of the water fountain in front of them. "I've never been here this early before," she told him.

"This is my spot." With coffee in one hand and his arm stretched along the edge of the bench, the tips of his fingers brushing against her hair, Caleb's refined and chiseled features relaxed as he surveyed the scene around them. "I enjoy reading right here in this bench. If I could have it named after me, I would."

Nova laughed. "What makes this bench so special?"

"It was my dad's spot, too. He told me that whenever pressure at the office became too much to handle or if he needed space to think, to ask God what to do, he would come here to pray. When I joined Frontier Press, it became my spot, as well. I love reading here."

"Seriously?" Nova took a sip from her coffee. "It gets so busy and crowded in this park. How do you concentrate?"

He flicked his brows at her. "It's my superpower." He tapped on the bench. "I was sitting right here, reading your manuscript, when you showed up looking like Agent Snow." His chest puffed out, as if he was extra proud he had recognized the reference.

Meanwhile, Nova tilted her head to the side. "I honestly didn't even realize the outfit I wore that day was a lot like how I wrote Agent Snow."

"Are you serious? Didn't you design the superhero costume you were wearing?"

"No." Nova threw her head back. "Vienna designed it. Now, it makes sense. She has already read the manuscript! But wait—" She bit her lip. "She hasn't read the ending yet. Only you have."

Caleb grinned. "I'm flattered to be the first person to read the ending, because it's perfect."

"You asked for it, so I delivered." Nova shrugged.

"Tell me. Will she become the love interest of Dr. Edge?"

Nova smiled at him. "Maybe. You didn't take me here to talk about work, did you?"

Caleb brushed a hand against his dirty blond hair. "With you, it's kind of hard not to blur the lines between personal and professional."

"I can understand that." Nova lowered her eyes.

He took a huge gulp from his coffee before setting it down, so he could angle himself to face her. "That day I saw you here, you blew me away. I had no idea if I would see you again, then you showed up at my office. When I found out you were Alex Orwell, you became irresistible. I had to get to know you. Even more so after I found out everyone in my family knew you, except me. How that happened, I still don't understand."

Nova could barely bring herself to look at him. What was she supposed to say? Could she tell him she had admired him for so long? Was it even appropriate to admit something like that on a first date? Wouldn't that only scare him away?

She took a deep breath and let the words roll out of her tongue. "I've been avoiding you, that's why."

At first, Caleb thought he had heard wrong. Did she just say she had been avoiding him?

"What?" Caleb's brow lifted. "Why?"

"I've known you since I was a kid, Caleb. The first time I noticed you was at church camp. You remember the one where Nolan got his first guitar, and he learned how to play it by the end of camp?"

"How could I forget? Yes. That was the camp I gave my life to the Lord."

"I know," Nova said. "At the gazebo."

Caleb threw his head back in surprise.

"You were also reading The Count of Monte Cristo during that camp." Nova smiled. "I read it soon after."

Silence followed as Caleb tried to piece it all together. A vague recollection of a campfire and a girl braiding Serene Sinclair's hair came to him. He had paid little attention to Hannah's friends back then; his sister had been enough to deal with. Caleb smirked, but something was still missing from Nova's story. "That still doesn't explain why you've been avoiding me."

Nova took a sip from the cup of coffee in her hands before responding. "I liked so much of what I saw in you back then, Caleb. You became the archetype of a hero to me. A lot of the good traits I infused in Dr. Edge's character were traits I imagined you to have. A lot of the darker traits were ones inspired by men who have disappointed me. My father. My brother." She held back her tongue before she could mention Knox. "I avoided you, because I didn't want to give you the chance to disappoint me like they did, but then I made that bet with Miles and Vienna, so here we are."

The story was coming together, and Caleb was desperate to find the missing pieces. "What was the bet?"

"When your father retired, I bet you would never come to work at Frontier Press as an agent."

Caleb cocked his head to the side. "Why would you make that bet?"

"I don't know." Nova's gaze drifted downward to her fidgeting fingers. "Ethan Caine had never hired someone as young and inexperienced as you are, but more than that, I guess part of me was hoping you wouldn't take the job. It would've been harder to avoid you if you did. Another part of me wondered how things would pan out if I lost the bet and finally got to meet you." She sighed. "It must all sound so creepy to you."

That last statement jolted him into awareness of how vulnerable it made her to open up about all those things. "Not at all," he said. "If anything, I'm flattered you would think of me in that way. I hope God gives me grace to live up to what you built up in your head, but—" Caleb gulped "—if I'm to be honest, I think I'll disappoint you eventually. It's inevitable, because I'm a sinner too. It would be unfair of me to entertain the idea that I'm more than what I am — a person redeemed and living by God's grace."

Nova took another sip from her coffee, and then another.

Caleb allowed everything that had been said to hang in the air.

"I've been praying." Nova put her coffee cup down. "I don't know how this date will go, Caleb, or if you would even want to date me after everything I opened up to you, but honesty is important to me. You deserve that from me. That's why I said what I did, and you're right. I can't put all that expectation on your shoulders. Trust that it's a burden I'm placing at the Lord's feet."

It meant the world to Caleb to hear the words she said, but it also increased the pressure building up within him — not because he felt he needed to live up to her expectations, but mostly because he wanted to. The same way he wanted to honor the legacy his father left at Caine Corp, he wanted to be the kind of man Nova could draw strength from. He longed to be the guy who would break the cycle of disappointment the men in her life had placed her in. He repeated his prayer to God in a hushed whisper, "Lord, help me do right by her."

Raindrops falling from an overcast sky drove them out of the park before they could finish the watermelon slices and Caleb's story about Hannah once trying to run away with an entire watermelon in her backpack.

Nova was still laughing as they entered his car before they got soaking wet. After tossing the blanket in the back seat and laying the picnic basket on top of it, Caleb gave her a long look.

Nova's laughter subsided. Suddenly, her questions about what happened to Hannah and her watermelon didn't seem to matter anymore.

Caleb reached forward and pulled back her curls to the side of her face to get a clearer view. His smile showed his pleasure at what he saw, and never before had Nova felt as beautiful as she did then.

In turn, she took the opportunity to study his face. She smiled upon realizing she had never been this close to him before. His blond hair mixed with highlights of brown and his blue eyes had streaks of gray in it. Nova gathered her courage and lifted her thumb to trace it against the fine line of his jaw, his short stubble brushing against her skin.

Caleb leaned forward. Nova drew a breath, bracing herself for a kiss. Instead, he reached past her and pulled the seatbelt over her.

When their eyes met, he gave her a teasing smirk before he buckled her seatbelt, leaned back in the driver's seat, and pulled his seatbelt over him. He then met her questioning gaze. "I'm intent on pursuing you, Nova," he said. "I'm praying about you, and I hope you'll begin praying about me too, because I do want to explore the possibility of having a future with you. For now, I would love to get to know you more."

"I would love that, Caleb." Nova choked up a little, even as hope blossomed in her heart over the degree of straightforwardness and intentionality in the words he had just spoken to her. She pushed back her apprehensions about how pursuing a relationship with each other would impact their working relationship and allowed herself to just enjoy the rest of the day.

Somehow, with Caleb around, the day went by easier. Even if Nolan was about to leave, she had someone there with her. Even through Serene saying no to Nolan's wedding proposal — much to Nova's relief, especially since Nolan seemed to be perfectly okay with that — Nova was more at ease that Caleb was present, nurturing her hope that he could be someone for her to lean on. After all, stepping into Caleb's world and with him stepping into hers, there was only one Person Nova trusted to protect her heart through all this: her Savior.

So, she laid her head to sleep that night with a smile and a prayer for God to watch out for her as she opened herself up to the possibility of falling in love with a man who until only recently had only been a dream she never thought would ever come true.

nineteen

THE ONE WHO NEEDED TRUST

Sunday morning, Nova couldn't wait to get out of bed and prepare herself for church. Way before anyone else was awake, she was already in the kitchen making French toast with a side of watermelon slices left over from her date with Caleb the day before.

The clock had just ticked seven o'clock when she heard light footsteps from the staircase. Seconds later, Nolan's head popped up beneath the archway, a long yawn coming out of him. His eyes widened upon seeing his older sister in the kitchen. "Someone's excited to go to church today. I'm guessing your date went well?"

Nova beamed in response. "He's coming over for breakfast before we all go to church together."

The corners of her brother's eyes crinkled as his huge smile mirrored her own. "Check out Super Nova getting what she wants. No need to act all ninja around him anymore. No lurking in the shadows watching him from afar."

"You make me sound like a stalker." She flipped the French toast on the non-stick pan.

"You kind of were for a while." Nolan sauntered toward the kitchen counter.

"No, I wasn't!"

"Sure, you weren't." He propped himself up on the bar stool and drummed his fingers over the counter. "Remember that one time we hung out outside the Grant family's house, because you wanted to catch a glimpse of him?"

"That was one time!" She slid the toast onto a plate and placed it on the counter in front of him. "Plus, I was only there because you were so desperate to see Serene." She placed several slices of watermelon into a bowl and slipped it beside his plate. "From my point of view, you're the one who's more of a stalker."

"Can you believe that was only a few years ago?" Nolan tore a piece from the French toast and popped it inside his mouth. "So much has changed since then."

"Thank God." Nova breathed out as she dipped a piece of bread on the batter and placed it in the pan. The sizzle masked her words a bit. "I'm hopeful for our future. I'm just praying you and Serene won't do anything you regret while at university. How are you taking her saying no to your proposal? Are you sure you're okay?"

Nolan shrugged. "For sure. We're still together, anyway. It's only a matter of time before Serene realizes we're really meant for each other." He folded the French toast and bit off half of it. He chewed on it for a few seconds and swallowed. "And seriously. Don't worry about us. We'll behave, I promise." He popped the rest of it in his mouth before rubbing his fingers together to dust off crumbs as he rose from his seat. "I need to prepare for church. I'm leading worship this morning. You look great, by the way." A teasing smirk formed on his face as he perused the dress Nova was wearing. "Someone is inspired!"

Nova rolled her eyes, but the smile on her face spread anyway as she slipped another piece of French toast onto a plate. The doorbell rang.

"I'll get it." Nolan rushed to the front door while Nova dipped another piece of bread in the egg mixture before transferring it onto the pan.

"Hey, man," Nolan's voice boomed from the entry way. "She's in the kitchen. You should get her tulips next time. She likes those."

"Thanks for the tip," Caleb said. A few seconds later, he appeared in the kitchen with a bouquet of red roses. "I didn't know what kind you liked." Seeing she was preoccupied, he placed the flowers on the counter. "Do you have a vase?"

Nova pointed at one of the cabinets. "Ma keeps one there. Thank you so much, Caleb. The roses are lovely."

Caleb headed to the cabinet and opened it to retrieve a clear glass vase. He glanced at her over his shoulder as he lowered the vase. "Nowhere near as lovely as you."

"Thank you," she said.

"Sleep well?" He walked past her toward the kitchen sink, where he put water in the vase.

"I did." It had taken a while before she had been able to drift off to sleep, but once she had, it had been a good sleep, so it wasn't a lie.

Caleb removed the roses from the wrapping paper and placed them in the vase. "Where do I put this?" He lifted the crumpled paper in the air.

Nova slid the toast onto another plate. "Could you fold it up? I'm sure Ma will find some use for it later. You can place it on the counter after."

"Sure thing."

Nova couldn't keep the smile from her face as Caleb did as instructed and placed all the satin ribbons over it. Within the next fifteen minutes, she finished making breakfast, with Caleb moving around to help her get everything ready.

Ma's face flickered with delight when she walked into the dining area to find breakfast waiting for her, though Nova doubted her happiness was because of the food, more than it was because of Caleb.

Breakfast breezed by pleasantly enough, with Nolan grabbing another piece of toast and gulping down a glass of orange juice before rushing off to church ahead of everyone else.

"Are you helping with the kids today?" Caleb asked Nova.

"Yes. Hannah and Olivia asked me to help out." Nova winced upon mentioning Caleb's ex. She had never asked him about that.

He didn't react to the name, so she didn't think to pry.

"I was wondering if you guys would like to join us for lunch at the family home after church."

"The Sinclairs invited us to have lunch with them, but Nova can go with you," Ma said. "I'm sure Pastor Sam will understand."

Nova blushed even as she thanked God for her mother, because she wanted nothing more than to spend time with Caleb's family, find out what they were really like.

The rest of the morning passed by smoothly as they cleaned up after breakfast and headed off to church. It wasn't until after the worship service that Nova left her mother's side to go help Hannah and Olivia with the children's ministry. She passed by Caleb, who was seated with his family, on her way to where they held Sunday School. They exchanged glances. He winked. She winked back. "See you after church," he whispered. She nodded.

The moment Nova walked through the main hall's exit, like a cold splash of water jolting her back to reality, she found a familiar figure in the hallway, his back leaned against the wall, his arms crossed over his chest.

Nova tensed as she approached him. "Knox, what are you doing here?"

He smiled at the sight of her. The way his stare roamed her body before settling on her face left her uneasy. "You look so beautiful."

"Knox." She shook her head, grateful the hall was empty. "Don't make a scene here."

"I'm not here to make a scene. I'm here to find out why you're so into this place. Is it because of him? Caleb, is it? You've had a thing for him since we were in high school. Does he know that?" He reached forward to tuck her hair behind her ear.

She slapped his hand away. "Knox, why are you doing this? Stop showing up like this. The messages have to stop. This has to stop."

"I want another chance, Nova." He took a step forward, closer to her, his height towering over her smaller frame. "I was in a dark place back then, but I'm better now. Give me a chance to prove myself to you. It was once me and you against the world, Nova. No one will love you like I do."

Nova pushed him away. "Leave me alone, Knox."

"Everything okay here?"

Nova turned toward the direction of the voice. She was mortified to find Hannah looking at them. What could she possibly be thinking about this scene? Nova nodded to acknowledge Hannah before casting a pleading glance at Knox. "We're fine. I was just about to head over to Sunday School."

Knox pointed at the main hall. "I'm off to church. Was just saying hi to my old friend over here."

Hannah narrowed her eyes at him before glancing at Nova. "Didn't he go to school with us? You hung out with him all the time."

Nova winced. "Yes. He was my best friend."

"I've never seen him at church before."

"Neither have I."

"Are you sure you're okay?"

"Yeah." To Nova's relief, Hannah didn't pry any further. They headed past the hallway and the lobby to the extra rooms reserved for the children's ministry.

By the end of the service, Knox was nowhere to be seen, but Nova felt like she had some explaining to do to Hannah, and she wasn't exactly sure what to say, because the last thing she wanted was for Caleb — much less his family — to be caught up in all of Knox's drama.

After the service, Caleb left the main hall to find Nova and Hannah in the lobby waiting for him. He was their ride to the Grant family home.

Hannah was carrying their niece, Jael, while Nova was having what appeared to be a very serious discussion with their nephew, Kenneth — at least that's what it looked like from afar based on the somber expressions on their faces.

"Sure." Nova nodded. "You can do that, but don't you think you need to learn how to fly a plane first before you go buy one?"

"But I already have a hundred dollars saved up. I can't learn how to fly a plane if I don't have one yet."

Nova stroked her chin. "Why do you want to fly a plane again?"

"I want to visit my Uncle Joshua. He's in a jungle somewhere, and I want to go on adventures like he does."

"Sounds like a plan."

"I'll go on that adventure." Caleb smiled at Nova. "Especially if it's with you."

"Okay!" Hannah held her little nephew's shoulder. "I'll take these two to their parents while you guys plan an adventure together. I'll meet you both at the parking lot."

"How was Sunday School?" Caleb asked Nova after getting her all to himself.

"It was okay." Nova averted her eyes from side-to-side, as if in search for someone. "How was the service?"

"Eye-opening. Are you waiting for somebody?"

"No." She shook her head.

"Do you need to say goodbye to your mom and Nolan?"

"No need. They're aware I'm with you. Let's go?"

Caleb pushed aside the concern she was hiding something from him and nodded. "Sure. We can wait for Hannah in my car."

Minutes later, they settled inside his car in the parking lot. Caleb turned the engine on, so they could put on the air conditioning. "Looks like we're in for a hot summer."

Nova didn't respond. She had her eyes out the window, worry traced in her eyes.

Who was she looking for?

Caleb shifted in his seat. What was going through her head? "Nova?"

"Hmm?"

"You seem tense."

Her lips slightly parted as she inhaled before prying her gaze from outside the window onto him. "It's nothing." A smile appeared on her lips, but Caleb had already seen what a genuine smile looked like from her. This wasn't one of those. "I'm just nervous to meet your family."

He accepted that explanation. At least for now. Something still seemed amiss, but he would have to wait until she was more comfortable before prying further. "Don't be. They like you, and they're excited to have you over."

This time, the soft smile on her face was genuine. "I'm glad to hear that."

Out of a desire to distract her from whatever was bothering her, Caleb brought up the only other thing they had in common. "Are you busy with the marketing department tomorrow? Do you think Steve can release you for a short meeting with me in the morning?"

"I'll have to ask, but I'm sure he can spare me for even just half an hour. I can make up for it by extending my hours in the afternoon."

"Just a reminder, if you accept the offer tomorrow and sign me on to represent you, we need to work on the manuscript for a few weeks before I send it out to publishers. We want to make sure it's the best it can be, so I have a few notes for you to consider."

"I'm up for it. It won't make Steve happy if one of his temps is working on a manuscript at the office, so I'll have to work on it in my spare time."

"Of course. If you want, we can work on the manuscript together at your place or in mine. Or if it works better for you, I can just send you notes and—"

"No." Her smile grew. "I'll grab any reason to spend time with you."

At that, Caleb couldn't help but return her smile. Knowing she felt that way was an ego boost he would welcome any time. Before he could say anything in response, however, Hannah showed up and made herself comfortable in the back seat.

"Let's go," she said.

The rest of the day flew by wonderfully. It was amazing for Caleb to see Nova around his family. He didn't want to get ahead of himself like he had done with Olivia, but a part of him hoped and prayed for a future with Nova, even if so much of her still remained a mystery to him.

The mystery only grew later that day when, after he dropped off Nova at their front step, he returned to his car to find Hannah moving to the passenger seat.

Right after he drove away from Nova's house to the thirty-minute drive to their apartment in the city, Hannah huffed.

"What's the matter, Hannah?" Caleb asked.

"Do you remember the guy Nova always hung out with back in high school?"

"Uhhh... no." Caleb kept his eyes on the road but his heart skipped a beat at the mention of a guy Nova always hung out with once upon a time. "I don't even remember Nova being in our high school."

"Oh yeah. Still so weird." Hannah frowned. "Everyone in our family knew her."

"We've been through this. What about the guy?"

"He was at church this morning. I saw him talking to Nova in the hallway after worship, right before she headed off to Sunday School. I've been trying to ask questions about it, but she's kind of dodgy. Don't get me wrong. I don't think they're together or anything like that. She seemed tense about their encounter, but it's been bothering me, so I figured I'd tell you. Better you find out earlier rather than later."

Caleb stopped the car at a red light and drummed his fingers on the steering wheel. "I'll ask her about it." He couldn't sort out what he was feeling. He was aware Nova had a bit of a jaded past, but he didn't understand to what extent. The heaviness on his chest grew as he drove further. Was he jealous? "What's his name?"

"I don't remember, but I can ask around if you want me to."

Caleb took a deep breath. "Never mind. I'd rather hear it from Nova. Thanks for telling me about it."

"Just looking out for my brother," Hannah said, "but handle Nova with care, okay? Don't jump to conclusions. We don't know the full story."

"Right." The weight on his chest grew as it hit him that he was once again getting ahead of himself. He needed to reel himself back in and get to know more about Nova before he went ahead and planned a future with her.

He told himself to wait until seeing her the next day to ask, but upon getting home, it took him less than an hour before his self-control gave way, and he sent a message to Nova.

> **Caleb:** Thanks for hanging out with us earlier. My family loves you.

Her response arrived immediately, which made Caleb grin as he relaxed on the couch and continued exchanging messages with her.

> **Nova:** I had an amazing time! Thanks for inviting me. Your family is lovely. So much better than I imagined.

> **Caleb:** Hey, I have a question.

> **Nova:** Shoot.

> **Caleb:** Hannah mentioned you had a run-in with some guy at church earlier. She said you seemed tense. Who was that? Are you okay?

He blew out a breath after pressing send on that last message. When there wasn't an immediate response, he inhaled deeply. She must have gotten distracted by something, Caleb reasoned to himself.

He placed the phone on the glass coffee table in the middle of their living room and headed to the kitchen to get a drink and grab a snack. Five minutes later, he returned to the living room and checked his phone. Still no reply from Nova.

He conducted an inner debate on whether or not to send another message and eventually ruled against it, as he gave himself one reason after another why she wouldn't respond.

A quarter of an hour later, Caleb was sitting on the edge of their living room couch with his elbows over his knees and his hands clasped together in front of him. He fixed his stare on his phone, still on top of the coffee table, willing for it to vibrate. Once it did, he grabbed it and checked the message. His stomach turned. The message came from Isaac. Something about whether or not Nova was joining them for their Wednesday family dinner. Isaac and Kelly were hosting that week.

Caleb clenched his jaw. How would he know what Nova planned to do when she wasn't responding to him? Caleb returned the phone on top of the coffee table, only to pick it back up again seconds later to re-read his exchange of messages with Nova.

Even re-reading the texts, Caleb saw nothing wrong with what he had messaged her. Why then wasn't she replying? Why wouldn't she tell him about this guy?

Caleb tossed his phone on the empty space on the couch beside him. He leaned backwards, the back of his head resting on top of the couch. He blew out a breath as he brushed both his hands against his hair. What was wrong with him? He was acting like a crazy, jealous ex-boyfriend, and he had only been on one official date with Nova. Why was this getting to him so much? He was acting like a besotted teenager, waiting on a text from her.

"I need to shake this off." Caleb stood up and bounced up and down to ease his nerves.

"Shake what off?" Hannah skipped out of her bedroom to join him in the living room.

Caleb cringed. "Nothing." He plopped himself right back on the couch.

"Mm-hmm..."

"I'm fine."

"I didn't say anything." Hannah slipped into her favorite velvet-lined Jensen chair, with her legs tucked beneath her thighs. "Why are you being so defensive?"

"I'm not being defensive."

"Sure, you're not." Hannah's blonde hair cascaded down the backrest of her seat as she leaned back and smirked at him. "This has nothing to do with what I told you about Nova, does it?"

Caleb flinched. "Of course not."

"Riiiiight."

He hated to admit defeat, but Caleb gave in. Maybe Hannah could help ease his mind. "I asked her about that guy you saw."

"And?"

"She hasn't replied yet. Do you think I should call?"

Hannah wrinkled her nose. "Are you okay? She could be chatting with Nolan or busy writing another novel. Who knows what she does with her free time? Also, what if she hasn't seen your text yet?"

Caleb frowned. "Am I going crazy? I'm more than a little unsettled, and I'm not sure why." Nova's shifty attitude earlier — like she was nervous about something when they were in his car waiting for Hannah — bothered him anew. Was she hiding something from him? The dreams he had been having about her drifted through his mind. Was Nova in any sort of trouble?

"You're not jealous, are you?" Hannah twirled the ends of her hair with her fingers, a smile slowly forming on her face. "You are, aren't you? Awwww... Caleb!"

"It's nothing to awwww about. Something's not right." Caleb grabbed his phone again. "This is stupid. I'll call." He gave Nova a call. It rang several times. She didn't respond. It rang again. Nothing. He stared at the phone.

"Well?" Hannah asked.

"She's not answering."

"Talk to her about it tomorrow, Caleb. I'm sure everything is fine." Hannah shifted in her seat, dropping her legs so her toes touched the floor. Genuine concern softened her expression. "I've never seen you act this way before. Had I known it would affect you this much, I wouldn't have told you about what I saw. I mean, if it makes you feel any better, it didn't seem like they were together. Nova seemed uncomfortable about—"

"I'm not jealous, Hannah." Caleb seethed. "Or at least I don't think I am." Was he? Was all of this caused by his lack of confidence after how his relationship with Olivia had ended? Caleb searched his heart. *Is that it, God? Why is this making me so anxious?* Not wanting to spend the rest of the night feeling the way he did, Caleb came to a decision. He rose to his feet. "I should go see her, make sure she's okay."

"Caleb, that's crazy. We were with her all afternoon. All you'll do is creep her out by showing up on her doorstep like this."

His sister's words made him hesitate. Hannah was right. He was acting irrational, but a surge of urgency had come over him, consuming him. He shook his head. "I'm going. Anyway, I want to spend more time with her. I'll pick up some flowers or something to make it a romantic surprise."

Hannah deadpanned. "You already brought her roses this morning."

"Chocolate then!" Caleb rushed to his bedroom to get ready to leave.

"This isn't you, Caleb!" Hannah called out. "You're supposed to be the sensible one in the family!"

Caleb hurried to get dressed and grab his wallet and car keys. He then hopped out of his bedroom as he tried to get his socks and shoes on. Hannah was still in the living room, shaking her head at him.

"You're acting like a stalker," Hannah said.

That made him stop in his tracks. Caleb gave it a moment's thought. To lighten the mood, he shrugged and winked at her. "Or maybe I'm just falling in love."

Despite her objections, at that, Hannah smiled and shook her head slowly. "You've gone on one date with her. Stop getting ahead of yourself." She rolled her eyes when he just responded to her with a long stare. "Who am I talking to? This is you. You can be such a dork sometimes. Just go. Hopefully, your instincts don't lead you astray this time."

Caleb grinned. "Pray for me."

"Oh, I will." She harrumphed. "Nova, too."

"Thanks!" Finally slipping his foot into his shoe, he rushed toward the door.

While driving in the car, Caleb took several breaths to calm his nerves. Hannah had been right to say this impulsive behavior was unlike him, but though he didn't know when or how, Nova had gotten under his skin in a way no woman ever had. The closer he got to her home, the more his gut told him something was amiss, and he prayed with all his heart he was wrong, because he would rather be perceived as a stalker than find her in any sort of danger.

His breath then hitched at the recollection of what he had flippantly told his sister. Sweat broke on Caleb's forehead. Was he falling in love with Nova? All of a sudden, it felt to Caleb like he was the one who was actually in danger.

twenty

THE ONE WHO CAME TO THE RESCUE

Nova shut her eyes upon seeing Caleb's message on her phone. Of course, Hannah would tell him about her run-in with Knox! She dropped herself on her bed, her feet dangling on the edge. She stared at the ceiling, with her hand gripping her phone against her chest. What should she say to Caleb? She tossed her phone on her bed and chose not to reply. Not yet.

Nova gritted her teeth. She had been typing a message to ask Caleb if she could call, so she could gush about how much she enjoyed the time spent with his family, but before she could ask, she had gotten his message asking about her encounter with Knox at church earlier.

She was nowhere near ready to have this conversation with Caleb. Everything about him was so pristine, so perfect. How would he take it should he realize just how troubled a past she had? Despite how much she wanted to continue talking to Caleb, she couldn't answer his question about Knox. Not yet. For now, she would just have to bear the hollowness of their empty home. What time were Ma and Nolan coming back from the Sinclairs anyway? She sighed. They doubtless wouldn't be back until past dinner.

To distract herself, Nova booted up her computer to continue work on the sequel to her first novel. She needed to lose herself in a story and not think about either Caleb or Knox. Within the next two hours, she kept writing, hoping to lose herself in a place where she, as the writer, was calling the shots. In a book, only her characters were vulnerable, never her.

When she hit a point in the story that still stumped her, Nova stopped. Once again, she checked the time. Eight o'clock.

Were Ma and Nolan still next door? Should she go check? She could use the company. Certain the Sinclairs wouldn't mind her going over there, Nova rose from her bed and checked her appearance in the mirror. She straightened her dress before descending the stairs. She opened the door and drew a quick intake of breath upon seeing Knox on their doorstep.

He grinned at the sight of her. "You do look lovely in that outfit."

"Knox? What are you—" She gripped the edge of their door, preparing herself to slam it in his face. "How long have you been standing there? You can't be here." Before her senses could kick in, he pushed her backward into the house and shut the door behind him. "What do you think you're doing?"

"Calm down, Nova. You know me. I won't hurt you."

"You already did once." With all her strength, Nova pushed Knox back. Thankfully, she succeeded, and his back hit the door with a thud. Gaining confidence, she planted her feet firm on the ground and lifted her fists into the air in a self-protective stance. "I won't let that happen again."

Flustered, it took a few seconds for Knox to regain both his balance and his senses. Once he noticed her raised fists, his eyes darkened. "How have we come to this, Nova? I didn't come to fight with you. All I want is a conversation. Can you at least give me that? Please."

Something about the desperation on his face lowered her defenses. He wasn't all that bad, was he? Had she overreacted back then? "If I give you that, will you leave me alone?"

Knox sighed. "Yes. Fine. Just at least hear me out."

"Okay then." Nova dropped her arms to her sides but tried to keep alert in case he suddenly tried something.

"So?" Knox swiped his arm in the air and gestured toward the living room. "Can we talk?"

"No. Not here. We'll talk in the front yard."

He threw his head back and clutched his hand against his chest. "Come on, Nova. Don't you trust me?"

"I obviously don't." She stood her ground, her jaw clenching as she flipped her head to the side. "It's that or you just go."

He smirked. "I'm not going without a fight, Nova." At her scowl, he rolled his eyes. "I don't mean that literally."

Nova pointed toward the door. "Let's go then. Let's talk. Outside."

Knox huffed, turned, and opened the door wide. He then slipped his hands in his pockets, leaned against the open door to allow space for Nova to walk by. "After you," he said.

"No." Nova shook her head. "You go first."

He eyed her for a second before shrugging and walking out the door. "You are hurting my feelings at this point."

"You'll live," Nova said under her breath before following him outside. Upon walking out, Knox took a seat on the stairs leading up to their front porch. Nova hesitated before sitting next to him. "Go ahead. Say what you want."

"I'm in love with you, Nova. I always have been."

"This again? No." That was the last thing she wanted him to say. "I can't handle this, Knox. It's been years. You have to accept I don't feel the same way about you." She motioned to stand up.

"Wait. Wait." He held her wrist gently and tugged at her to sit back down. "I know, okay?" He gulped. "Nova, please. Let me finish."

Nova lowered herself back down, but nothing he could say or do made her less tense around him.

"I was in a dark place back then. You know that. All I had was you, and I admit. I came on too strong, but that's only because I was afraid of losing you. I get it now. You want to stay friends. I'll accept that as long as I have you in my life, Nova. Please."

"Knox—" her words sounded breathless as she struggled to tell him what he needed to hear "—I am in a great place in my life. God has been restoring so much of what I've lost. It's Him you need in your life, not me."

"Then introduce God to me, Nova. I'll do anything you ask of me. We can be friends again, but don't kick me out of your life. You've always been so strong, so brave, and so wonderfully protective of the people you care about. Is it so bad that I would want to be one of those people?"

Something about the things he was saying appealed to a part of Nova that wanted to be in control, to be the one who was strong and able to protect those she loved, but the past years had already shown Nova it was better to give God all control. "Knox, if you really want to get to know God, I'm not the right person to lead you to Him. I'm about to visit the Sinclairs next door. Pastor Sam can talk with you and lead you to—"

"It has to be you, Nova. The only way I can trust someone to talk to me about some being I can't see is if it's you."

Nova's shoulders sagged as the disappointment weighed on her. This had nothing to do with Knox wanting to get to know God and everything to do with him wanting to be with her. "I can pray for you right now, Knox, and I can pray even after you leave, but I can't be that person for you. I'm not some hero who can save you, Knox. Only God can be that for you."

The moment she said that last sentence, his entire demeanor shifted. His form bulked up, his jaw clenched, his face tensed. His fingers closed against his palm to form tight fists. "You're making a mistake, Nova. No one can love you the way I love you."

"I'm sorry, Knox." The danger he exuded was palpable, so Nova leaped on her feet and backed away from him to get to the front yard, where she could yell and ask for help in case he tried anything. "Please go."

He just sat there, so Nova decided to walk away. "Fine. I'll be the one to leave." Craving safety coming from the presence of other people, Nova headed for the Sinclairs next door. As she was about to step off of their front yard into their neighbors' driveway, she breathed out a sigh of relief when she saw the front door of the Sinclairs swing open. Nolan stepped onto the porch soon after, but within seconds, he returned inside. Nova was about to rush toward her brother when she felt a large hand grab the back of her head, strong fingers coiling through her curls.

"Please don't go, Nova." One sudden movement and she had brawny arms wrapped around her waist, pulling her against him as Knox leaned forward to try to press his lips against hers. His grip on her hair burned her scalp. The moment his mouth touched hers, everything within Nova rushed into panic mode.

"Let go of me!" She threw her head back to avoid his lips. Her arms still free, she slapped him and clawed at him to break away from him. When all he did was stand there and take it while still keeping her hair and waist in his hold, Nova considered spear-handing his throat. She hung limply against his embrace to feign defeat, the anger within her simmering as she gave him another chance to do the right thing. "Knox, just go. Forget me."

"I can't." His voice broke as he leaned his forehead against hers and loosened his grip on her hair.

As she geared up to strike his Adam's apple, a male voice boomed from behind her. "Hey! Get away from her!"

Knox let go of her. A fiery glint flashed in his dark eyes. Disoriented, at first, Nova thought the voice had been Nolan's, and all her protective instincts flared. There was no way she would let Knox lay a hand on her brother, but it wasn't Nolan rushing toward them.

It was Caleb.

Before Nova's mind could fully process his presence, Caleb grabbed Knox's shoulder to turn him around. "What's going on here, man?"

Knox shoved him back. "None of your business." He cussed out a word that made Nova flinch. "Who even are you? Her boyfriend?"

"No." Caleb shook his head before glancing at her. "I care about her though, and I don't think she—"

"Screw you, man." Knox threw a sudden punch curving sideways, his fist flying in the air, landing above Caleb's left cheekbone, and knocking him to the ground.

Nova's entire body tensed at the sight, her hands balling into fists beside her and her pulse gaining speed.

Caleb scrambled back up as he brushed his thumb over the area on his face Knox had assaulted. His gaze swept past Knox and found hers. He gave her a nod, as if to assure her he was fine.

Knox scoffed at him. "What do you think you are? Some sort of hero?"

Caleb smirked. "I'm no hero," he said as he winked at Nova, "but she is."

Without a second thought, Nova sprung forward, pummeling Knox's lower torso from behind. When he stumbled forward, Caleb threw a punch to repay the favor Knox had given him earlier. The force was enough for Knox to lose balance and fall to the ground. Once there, Nova straddled his waist and lifted her fist in the air, ready to strike. All the helplessness she had felt as a little girl and as a grown woman exploded within her like a volcano, dormant for far too long. The sight of Knox beneath her made her rage burn like magma, coursing through her veins and stirring up her thirst for retaliation. Nova mustered all the strength she had, her knees retracting against his waist to keep him in place. With a broken yell, she plunged her fist down to land her first blow. Before the onslaught of all her pain could turn into an assault against Knox, a firm hand grabbed her arm and twisted it upward to take hold of her wrist.

Stunned, Nova looked up to find Caleb shaking his head at her.

Trembling, Nova tried to break away from his grip. "Let go of me."

Caleb held firm. "It's not worth it, Nova."

"You don't understand." Her voice broke as she shook her head. She twisted her arm to yank her wrist away from Caleb, to no avail. A tear ran down her cheek. She wanted to hurt Knox, hurt him like he had hurt her. "Caleb, let go of me."

Right then, Pastor Sam, Nolan, and Serene showed up. A quick scan of the scene told them all they needed to know. Nolan's face hardened. He marched forward, fists clenched and gearing up to join the fight, when Pastor Sam pulled him back.

"That's enough. This is no place for a brawl," their pastor said. "Aida is calling the cops as we speak."

Caleb's thumb brushed gently against the side of Nova's wrist. "Nova, you're okay now. We're okay. Let it go."

With his tender gaze on her, Nova somehow felt more vulnerable than she did hanging in Knox's arms only minutes ago. It was like Caleb was seeing right through her. She cracked. A tear trickled down her cheek, and then another. One by one, they came, cooling the fury that had exploded within her. Through eyes blurred by tears, she looked down at the only person who had ever dared lay a heavy hand on her. Only then did she notice the tears rushing down Knox's face, his cheek swollen from the sucker punch Caleb had thrown at him earlier. It was Knox who first broke into a sob before Nova followed.

Caleb tugged on her. Her knees weak, she hung onto him as she rose to her feet, sobs racking her body. Strong arms with a careful touch wrapped around her shoulders, encapsulating her as she sobbed into Caleb's chest. He didn't make any attempts to offer words of comfort. He just stood there. Like an immovable tower, a place of refuge sheltering her from her own pain, her own rage.

It felt like forever, but it couldn't have been more than several minutes before Nova's sobs subsided. She slowly pulled away from Caleb, blushing when she saw the spot on his shirt where her tears had soaked through.

Caleb pushed back her hair, his thumb wiping a stray tear from her face. He smiled, but his eyes held such sorrow. It broke her heart, especially knowing she might be the cause of it. She bit her lip upon seeing the red spot above his cheek and surrounding his left eye. She winced.

"That'll bruise," she croaked out.

He shrugged. "Bruises heal."

A police siren jolted her out of the momentary serenity of just being held by someone she trusted. Her eyes went on a frantic search for Knox, only to find him still crumpled on the ground in a fetal position, crying. Pastor Sam knelt beside him, praying over him. Nolan and Serene were walking toward the police officers, who had just gotten out of their cars. Meanwhile, Ma stood a few steps away from Nova, confusion in her eyes as she stared at Knox's sobbing form.

Caleb nudged her forward through the small of her back. Nova got the hint and approached her mother, holding Ma's hand and kissing her on the cheek. Mother and daughter embraced, drawing comfort from each other.

The next half hour consisted of some questioning and an arrest, which Knox submitted himself to without a fight. Just before the cops drove away, Knox dared a glance at Nova.

By some miracle, upon recognizing the desperation in his eyes, Nova's heart softened toward him. As the police car drove away, Nova said a prayer for Knox, hoping he would someday find himself on the path to salvation, because someone like him could also use some rescuing.

Once the adrenaline rush died down, the pain came. Caleb groaned at the ache on his face and his fist. The sound made Nova turn toward him and away from her mother. One quick look-over at him, and she winced.

"Let me take care of that," she said as she approached. "I'm so sorry, Caleb."

Sorry was the last thing he wanted to hear from her. Why was she apologizing? Even as she stared up at him and brushed her thumb against the edges of his bruise, the slight tremble in her smaller frame made Caleb clench his jaw.

Nova must have mistaken his reaction as a sign of his pain, because she gasped and pulled her hand away. She cringed. "I'm sor—"

"Stop apologizing," Caleb said, his voice an octave deeper than normal. "I'm fine, Nova. You should go rest. After that guy—" The anger that swept over him took him aback, making him tense up, especially as he saw the tremble in Nova's lips. "I'll go home. You need to go to bed, get some sleep."

Nova shook her head, her waves of black hair bouncing against her shoulders. "No way. We're going to get some ice on your face and your fist."

"Let's go inside." Clara squeezed herself between them and nudged both to follow her lead. "Nova's right, Caleb. We'll all regroup tomorrow morning to figure out what to do, but we need to have you looked at." She frowned as she checked his face. "That's going to leave a nasty bruise. Would you consider staying the night? We have an extra room you can sleep in."

Caleb glanced at Nova before responding. "I don't want to impose, Mrs. Stone. Our apartment isn't a long drive from here."

"Please. Call me Clara. It'll be easier for us to rest if we know you're okay, but I understand if you're more comfortable resting at home."

Before Caleb could respond, Nolan jogged over to them after having walked Serene and her parents to their home. Upon reaching them, he gave Caleb a hug. "Thanks for rescuing my sister."

At that, Caleb snickered as he gave Nova another glance, his heart moved by the paradox of her strength and fragility. "I'm not sure how accurate that is. There were parts of that encounter where she was the one rescuing me."

"Not surprised." Nolan shrugged. "Still, you were there for her. That matters."

Nova's silence drew Caleb's attention, his gaze lingering toward her delicate neck and how it moved as she swallowed. Then, he caught sight of the red handprint on her skin where her attacker grabbed hold of her earlier, and his ire rose again. Nova had been an object of fascination to him from the moment he had met her, but a prayer his father had once said on behalf of Hannah returned to Caleb, but this time, he said it on Nova's behalf — a prayer to serve and protect the women in their lives, to take care of them as best they could. Caleb wanted nothing more than to do that for Nova.

For the next half hour, Clara tried to make Caleb and Nova as comfortable as possible in their living room, bringing out ice packs for Caleb and providing them with two bowls of piping hot *arroz caldo*, chicken and rice porridge. Eventually, Nova convinced her mother to take a rest, assuring her they had it from here. Clara reluctantly gave in, bidding them good night as she climbed up the stairs.

Nova returned to her spot on the couch beside Caleb, curling one leg in front of him, so her ankle was positioned under the thigh of her other leg hanging from the edge the couch. She picked up the ice pack from the coffee table and pressed it against his right fist.

Caleb tried not to cringe at the dull ache as he pressed an ice pack on the corner of his left eye.

"I've never been punched in the face before." He grimaced. "I've also never punched anyone in the face. Books make it sound so easy. Then again, words can't ever prepare for you for how hard skull and bones actually are."

Despite how serious she had been since the cops had left, Nova cracked a smile. "You'll survive, Caleb. God made skulls hard for a reason." She lowered her gaze and brushed her fingers against his bruised knuckles. "Thank you for coming." Her smile turned bittersweet. "I tried my hardest to prepare myself for situations like this after graduating high school, but—" she gritted her teeth "—he was stronger. I wish for his own sake and mine, he'd forget me."

Yearning to know what this man's role was in her life, Caleb twisted his torso to face her. "Has this guy done anything like this before?"

She stared at his knuckles for a few seconds before nodding. The story unfolded of how Knox had wanted their friendship to turn into something more, but she hadn't. At the point when Nova told Caleb about Knox backhanding her, righteous indignation once again filled Caleb, his fingers twitching beneath her grasp.

At his motion, Nova retracted the ice pack from his knuckles. "Did I press too hard?"

"No." His jaw tightened. "I'm just furious he did that to you, Nova."

Her eyes moistened before she bowed her head. "So was I." She put the ice pack back on the table and turned his hand to brush her fingers on his palm before pressing her own palm against his, highlighting how small her hand was compared to his. "Playing his guitar calloused my father's hands the same way his musical ambitions calloused his heart. He never raised a hand against me, but he did so with Nate and Ma. I swore, from a young age, I would never let him do that to Nolan. Or to me. And he never did. So, when Knox hit me, I couldn't forgive him. It didn't matter what we had gone through together. I didn't want him in my life." Nova peered at Caleb through her long lashes. "You'll never hit me, right, Caleb?"

The question sounded so foreign to Caleb, but she had asked it, sounding like she was on the verge of tears. Caleb intertwined his fingers with hers, holding on to her as he shook his head, fully confident in his ability to say, "Never."

If it were up to him, no man would ever be able to lay a violent hand on Nova again, but it wasn't up to him. Even if every masculine instinct within him pushed Caleb to promise Nova he would always be there to protect her, that wasn't his promise to make. Not yet.

So, later that evening, Caleb bid Nova goodbye, returned to his apartment, and asked God if he was the right man for her. Before he drifted off to sleep, Caleb received peace from Above regarding how to progress in his relationship with Super Nova.

twenty-one

THE **O**NE
WHO **C**AME
TO HEAL

Nova thanked God for Caleb's presence when they both took leave from work on Monday morning, so she could meet with a lawyer to get legal counsel and a restraining order against Knox. To have Caleb there through such a traumatic moment in her life was a source of both comfort and embarrassment to her. To process the conflicting emotions, as he drove her back home from the courthouse, Nova found herself retreating to her shell. Caleb, however, had already somehow developed a knack out of coaxing her out of it.

"I have to show up at work tomorrow with a black eye." Caleb snickered as he spun the steering wheel to turn a corner. "There will doubtless be a lot of questions about why my face is black and blue, and I have no clue what to say. Any ideas?"

"Tell them the truth." Nova shrugged. "I think it's better we stay in the light. After all, we haven't done anything wrong. Why hide?" The irony of the question wasn't lost on her. Why was she constantly hiding?

Caleb gave her a quick glance before returning his focus to the road. "Are you sure? Just like that? Tell them the truth? You know what office gossip can be like, and by tomorrow, I'm pretty confident I'll be your agent. If they find out we're dating and that

I had a fight with your stalker—" he shrugged "—let's just say it's easy for people to make up stories in their head about things they know nothing about. I want to make sure you're up for all that, Nova. There's always the option of me staying silent. We don't have to explain ourselves to anyone."

It took a few seconds for Nova to process what he was implying, and a lump formed in her throat as she stared at him long and hard. How had she ended up dating a man like him? It was like his every instinct inclined to protect her, look out for her, do everything in his power to make her feel comfortable and safe. The fact he was still around after what had happened last night astounded her. So far, Caleb had proved himself even better than she had imagined him to be.

One side of Caleb's lips curved up when he noticed her staring. He grinned and flicked his brows at her. "Like what you see?"

Heat rose to her cheeks, but she kept her stare on him anyway as she mirrored his grin. She had never imagined him to be so cheeky. "You really are something, Caleb."

"Something good, I hope."

"As if you can be anything but amazing." The tension in her shoulders dissipated, and she leaned back in her seat, allowing herself to relax and assure herself everything would turn out fine.

Her answer, however, didn't appear to please Caleb, because his expression darkened, his brows knitted together, and his grin disappeared.

Nova opened her mouth to ask what she had said wrong, but her tension returned as quickly as it had gone, and she wasn't sure she wanted to know the reason behind Caleb's shift in demeanor. He was reminding her too much of how her father had been kissing her mother one moment, then poising to hit her the next. He gave her flashbacks of how Nate had protected her one moment, and ran away the next, of how Knox had once watched people with her one moment, and morphed into the kind of person she had to watch out for the next. Were all men like this? Like there's always a layer of anger beneath their skin, waiting to expose itself once provoked?

Nova shut her eyes to try to ignore Caleb's simmering broodiness. She approached God with no words to ask of Him other than a heart's sincere request for some semblance of peace. By the time she opened her eyes, they were already in her neighborhood. The familiarity of the Sinclair residence next to theirs comforted her.

Caleb pulled over in their driveway. The darkness had left his expression, and in its place was this pained gaze.

Neither of them budged for the next half-minute as Nova scrambled for something to say. She had no reason to apologize, because she had said nothing wrong. Beside her, Caleb seemed like he had gone off to a world of his own while driving, and she sat there, stuck with him, waiting for him to come out of it.

Finally, he did.

"I don't want to mislead you, Nova," he said.

His words were a hammer to Nova's chest. The lump in her throat grew as in her mind's eye, she watched all her dreams about a future with Caleb shatter. If Caleb was about to tell her what she feared he would — that he didn't want to be with her — it would hurt far more than Knox's knuckles against her face. Her fingers fumbled for the buckle of her seatbelt, so she could get out of there before she broke down crying, but Caleb grabbed her hand and gripped it hard. His eyes glazed over. His Adam's apple moved as he gulped. The sight of it reminded Nova of what she had been planning to do to Knox the night before — spear hand his throat. She would never want to have a reason to hurt Caleb. Her defenses fell away, and all she could wish for at that point was to find out what was going on in his head.

"Caleb?"

He swallowed back the tears before they fell from his eyes. "Sorry. I'm overwhelmed by everything that's been happening, that's all." Caleb let go of her hand, unbuckled his seatbelt and angled himself in his seat to look her in the eye. "I don't want to encourage you to have this idealized version of me in your head, Nova. I'm too human, and it's too much pressure. This — you and I — it won't work unless you know me. The real me. Weaknesses and all."

Nova winced and shifted in her seat. "What are you saying, Caleb? I mean, I want to get to know you, and I'm aware you're not perfect, but if you don't want to date me anymore, I—"

"No." Panic crossed his face as he lifted a hand and waved it in the space between them. "That's not what I'm saying at all." He rubbed his neck with his palm and blew out a sigh before composing himself and once again looking her straight in the eye. "Nova, you can't begin to imagine how serious I am about this relationship — how serious I want to be." He flinched. "I hope me saying that doesn't scare you away."

Nova shook her head. "Not at all."

"Good, because I know I can come off intense. My family says it's because I'm so sure of what I want, and make no mistake about it. I do want to be with you."

Despite his assurance, Nova's breath was still stuck in her throat. Where was he going with this?

"I'm overwhelmed, because all of this is a lot to take in. We go to the same church, we went to the same high school, we're about to work a lot closer together with your book. All of this can get really messy really quick, if we're not careful, Nova."

"Right." Nova couldn't come up with more to say. She feared her heart would thump its way out of her chest. "So, where does this leave us?"

"I'm not a casual dater. If I'm pursuing someone, it's because I see her as someone I might marry."

That threw Nova in for a loop. Wait. What? Marry? She was nowhere near wanting to marry anybody. Even him.

Caleb chuckled. "From the look on your face, marriage is the last thing on your mind right now. Of course, it is. We barely know each other." His shoulders sagged. "I realized that last night. There's still so much we need to learn about each other. Nova, as much as I want to rush into a relationship with you, it's best if we take our time, slow down a bit. I don't want to make the same mistakes with you that I made with Olivia, not only to protect your heart but also mine." He lowered his gaze and a warm red tinted his cheekbones, almost as if he was ashamed of something.

Nova bit her lip before taking a breath and asking him a question she desperately needed an answer to. "What happened with you and Olivia?"

"That's a long story." Caleb winced. "You sure you're up for it?"

Nova pointed her thumb outside his car and toward the house. "Should we go inside for this? Be warned, though. Ma won't let you leave the house without eating lunch with us. Possibly even dinner."

"Sounds like your mom." Caleb smiled.

The fondness in his tone at the mention of her mother stirred Nova's soul. How was she to keep from idealizing him when he kept on proving himself ideal? She unbuckled her seatbelt and sat still as Caleb jogged around the hood to open the door for her. The smile on his handsome face made her heart ache. Was it possible for her to stop putting him on a pedestal?

They headed inside and made themselves comfortable in the living room, and finally, Nova found out what had happened between Caleb and the girl she had envied so much, growing up. By the end of it, Nova understood his need for them to take their time.

"I was so sure Olivia was the one for me, but I got way ahead of myself." Caleb grimaced. "Obviously, despite how convinced I was that God wanted us to be together, it didn't turn out that way."

Nova gave him a bittersweet smile. "So, what does that mean for us? Where do we go from here?"

In response, Caleb laid out for her the path he believed they would be wise to take. As he did, Nova found herself more drawn to him, as she recognized in him someone she could trust with her heart, someone whose lead she could follow.

By the end of the day, despite all his attempts to remind her he was a human as flawed as she was, Caleb had only managed to convince Nova it was impossible for her not to fall in love with him. So, alone in her bedroom that evening, Nova whispered a prayer for God to help her guard her heart, because Caleb was right. They couldn't let themselves fall in love with each other just yet. Not until they could both give God space to heal their hearts.

Along with her yearning for Caleb and all the bitterness, anger, and hurt she still held against the men in her life, Nova surrendered her heart to the Lord once again, trusting that in all of this, God would be the One Who would heal her, defend her, and never forsake her.

The clock ticked twelve o'clock the next day, and the moment it did, Caleb stood from his chair, straightened his clothes, picked up a thick manila envelope, and walked out of his office. His assistant flinched at the sight of him.

Caleb grinned. "Are you not happy to see me, Molly?"

"Who would be happy to see you all bruised up? What happened? It's so unlike you to get into fights."

"Some fights are worth getting into. This—" he pointed at his black eye "—was over someone worth fighting for."

"Does she happen to be a stunning superhero?"

Caleb laughed. "Maybe. Any messages for me?"

"Just one from Mr. Holt. He sent his latest manuscript over. I've printed it out and told him you'll get back to him as soon as possible."

"Right. I'll get to that as soon as I'm back." He pointed toward the exit. "I'm going out for lunch. By the time I return, I'll have a new client."

Molly rolled her eyes, but the affection on her face was unmistakable. "Make sure you don't stumble into another cause worth fighting for," she said as he started to walk away.

"Can't make any promises, Molly." He turned his head to face her and shrug. "Where superheroes are, there be villains also."

Molly shook her head, but the smile remained on her face.

Confident Molly would eventually be rooting for Nova, Caleb strode toward the elevator and exited at the floor where the marketing department was. Curious gazes followed him as he made his way to Nova's cubicle. Upon arriving there, it didn't surprise him to find Vienna and another guy with her.

"Dude—" the guy cocked his head back "—what happened to your eye?"

"Got into a fight." Caleb extended his hand towards him. "You must be Miles."

"That, I am." He shook Caleb's hand. "You're welcome, Mr. Grant."

Caleb grinned. "You're everything Nova said you would be. Thank you, Mr. Bailey, for paving the way for me to meet Nova and for making it possible for me to discover her brilliant novel."

An arrogant grin appeared on Miles's face as he flicked his brows at Nova and Vienna. "See? What did I tell you? The man recognizes true talent."

"Hey." Vienna scowled. "I helped too!"

"I should thank both of you then, but—" Caleb gestured toward Nova "—I'm not this lovely author's agent yet, so I'm taking her out to lunch to convince her to let me sign her on as a client."

A timid smile appeared on her pretty face as Nova picked up her leather bag from her desk. Before she could hook it over her shoulder, Caleb tugged on the bag's strap as an offer to carry it for her. Without hesitation, Nova handed it over to him.

Miles narrowed his eyes at them "Are you sure this lunch is strictly professional?"

Vienna's jaw dropped. "Miles!"

He shrugged. "It's the question on everyone's minds, Vienna. Can't blame me for asking."

Caleb and Nova exchanged glances, a knowing smile on both their lips.

"We're getting to know each other," Nova said.

Miles shook his head and crossed his arms over his chest. "I hear wedding bells already."

"You're unbelievable," Vienna said. "Why are you making this so awkward?"

"I think that's our cue to go." Caleb pointed ahead as a gesture for Nova and him to move on, but something about the smile on Nova's face made him flat out want to agree with Miles. Still, he had said what he had said to Nova the day before. There was no taking it back. They were going to take things slow.

"Hey, wait." Miles called out to them before they could get away. "If you become her agent, will you let us read the end of the novel? Because she refuses to give us the ending, and that cliffhanger should be illegal."

Caleb tapped Nova's shoulder. "That's for my client to decide."

"You'll be the first to get a copy during my launch party, Miles!" Nova grinned. "You too, Vienna."

"I'm fine with that." Vienna relented before waving at them. "Enjoy, you two. And congratulations!"

Miles, on the other hand, wasn't having any of it. "This is injustice, Nova! Injustice!"

Caleb laughed as he and Nova made their way to the elevator. There was a lightness to her step that hadn't been there before. As much as they tried to keep their lunch as professional as possible, they had already built a rapport between them — something caused by the openness they both had with each other over the course of one weekend.

As much as he tried to keep his heart steady, Caleb returned to his office not only as Nova's new agent, but as a man asking God once again to guide his steps, because the more he spent time with Nova, the more he was falling for her.

Still, they had a long path ahead of them and a lot of things to work on. Caleb's gut was telling him they were doing the right thing. So, just as he had suggested to Nova, at the end of their work day, he picked her up from the marketing department and drove all the way to her neighborhood. There, they climbed onto the front porch of Nova's next-door neighbor and rang the doorbell.

For the next hour and a half, Caleb sought the guidance of their pastor regarding his past with Olivia, the present dreams he had been having, and his budding desire to spend a future with Nova. Meanwhile, Nova spent time with Mama Aida to process all the trauma she had gone through with her father, her brother, and her friend.

It was the first step they took on the road to healing and their way of remaining under a spiritual covering as they prayed for a future together. Though Caleb never admitted it out loud to Nova, that day was the first day he stopped seeing her as the fascinating superhero at the park and recognized that he had to surrender his own ideals about her, as well.

So, along with his attraction for Nova and all the self-doubt, uncertainty, and fear he had accumulated from his relationship with Olivia, Caleb surrendered his heart to the Lord once again, trusting that should Caleb fail in any way, God would be the One Who would heal and protect his Super Nova.

twenty-two

THE ONE WHO FAILED HER

The unfortunate news swept away Caleb's delight like winds of doom edging away the months of cloud nine he had enjoyed since Nova came into his life. He pulled over in the driveway of the Stone household and retrieved the birthday cake from the passenger seat. Since they were both September celebrants — Nova on the third and Caleb on the thirtieth — they had decided to have a joint celebration at the Stones' residence. But the last thing Caleb felt like doing was celebrate. How could he, when he had failed so miserably to deliver the promises he had made his girlfriend?

Caleb dragged his feet toward the house. Warmth enveloped him as he stepped onto the front porch as memories circled his mind of all the time he spent in that home over the past few months. Images of Nova jotting down notes on her novel and Clara cooking up scrumptious dinners came to mind. He had been working with Nova to make sure her novel was the best it could be, and now, on a day of celebration, he had to be the bearer of bad news. His heart ached for his girlfriend. She had been working so hard. How could he tell her the book deal they had tried so hard to secure had fallen through?

He heaved a breath before walking inside the house and straight to the kitchen.

"Finally!" Hannah tapped on the counter. "Place it here."

Caleb placed the cake on top, and Hannah lost no time in removing the box containing it.

"Perfect." She grinned.

"It smells good in here," Caleb said, trying to sound cheery.

"Caleb." Clara turned her head from whatever dish she was cooking and smiled at him. "Everyone will arrive soon. We were worried you would end up being late. Nolan and Serene should be here any time now."

Caleb's brow quirked up. "They're coming?" It had only been a few weeks since they had left for university for the fall semester.

"Nolan insisted even if Nova said he didn't have to." Clara shrugged.

"He probably just misses you and Nova."

A bittersweet smile appeared on Clara's face. "We miss him, too. It's good that Nova has you. It would have been much harder for her without you here."

At least I'm good for something. Caleb gritted his teeth while trying to keep a smile plastered on his face. Hannah was already eyeing him like she was suspecting something. His sister knew him all too well. Caleb cleared his throat. "Where's Nova?"

Hannah pointed up before her eyes widened. "My casserole!" She rushed toward the oven to check on her dish.

"Do you mind checking on Nova?" Clara asked as she sprinkled salt onto her dish. "She went up a while ago to get something from her room and never returned."

Caleb hesitated. He had never been inside Nova's bedroom before.

Clara's eyes flickered upon noticing he was still standing there. She smiled. "It's the last door to the right."

Caleb spun on his heel and made his way up the stairs and across a short hallway to find Nova's door wide open. He knocked on it, anyway. "Nova?"

She answered with a loud groan.

Curious, Caleb peeked in, and the sight of her induced a chuckle. "What is all this?"

Lying diagonally on her bed, Nova had her bare feet propped up on top of her bed's headboard. Her head hung by the neck from the edge of her bed, her dark curls touching the carpeted floor beneath. In her left hand was a bunch of index cards, with the top card full of her scribbles. She tapped her temple with the pen in her right hand. Crumpled paper, sticky notes, and colorful index cards laid scattered on the floor, surrounding her head like a messy halo. She giggled as he approached. "You look funny upside down. Happy birthday, Caleb."

"Happy birthday to you, too," he said. "What are you doing?"

"Ugh!" Nova dropped her pen and index cards on the floor, before she clasped her forehead with both hands. As she shook her head, her curls swept the carpet. "I came up here to get my cardigan, but then I got this amazing idea for how to start book two of Dr. Edge. I wrote it down, so I wouldn't forget, but then another idea came, so I wrote that down. And then another. And then another. Why do great ideas come at the strangest times? Now, my brain has hit a flow, and this story is begging to be written, but there's a party I have to go to."

"You mean our birthday party?"

Nova flashed him a full smile. "Do you think anyone will notice if I skip it?"

"What do you think?" He sat on the edge of the bed and flicked her chin with his finger. "None of that explains why you're upside down."

"To keep the ideas in my head, of course. Wouldn't want them to drain away."

Caleb smirked. "Of course. Makes total sense."

She jolted up to a sitting position in the middle of her bed. "Yeah. The ideas are gone now. You distracted me. I'll have to find a way to get them all back later." She turned and crawled on the bed so she could sit on the edge beside him. "Bummer. Guess I need to go to our party now."

Caleb nudged her. "We could just skip the whole thing and have a fancy dinner somewhere."

"I already made lasagna. It's your favorite."

"No way we're going anywhere then."

"I figured." Nova sighed.

A pause made Caleb consider if it would be a good time to tell her the bad news, but Nova beat him to the punch with news of her own.

"Knox called me from jail," she said.

"What?" His entire form tensed at the thought of this man breathing even a single word to his girlfriend. "Are you okay?" When would that man ever leave her alone? Even through his six-month jail sentence, he was still harassing Nova? "What did he say?"

She must have heard the edge in his voice, because Nova reached for his hand and laid it palm-up on his leg before pressing her palm against it. "He apologized and promised this will be the last I'll ever hear from him."

Caleb clenched his jaw. "Do you believe him?"

"I think so. Pastor Sam has been visiting him, introducing him to God. For his own sake, I hope he's sincere." Nova took a deep breath as she intertwined her fingers with his and leaned her head on his shoulder. "He deserves a second chance."

Caleb didn't quite know what to make of that. "You mean you're open to being his friend again?"

"No. I've forgiven him, but I think he's better off without me in his life."

"So, what did you tell him?"

"I told him to take whatever Pastor Sam says seriously and to pursue a relationship with God. It'll change his life like it changed mine. He promised he would. I hope he means it."

Caleb's grip on her hand tightened. His stomach turned at the idea of this man ever being anywhere near Nova. Leaning his head against the top of Nova's, all Caleb could think to do was pray. "God, heal this man. May he find what he needs in You instead of continuously seeking Nova to fill the space in his heart only You can satisfy. Continue to heal Nova, as well." He lifted her hand and pressed his lips against the back of it. "Someday, she will look back at everything she had gone through and not a hint of trauma will remain. All she will see is how You have turned it all for good. Thank you, Lord."

"Amen," Nova whispered in agreement.

They stayed there for another minute or two, snuggled against each other — a perfect fit, Caleb thought. It would have been a perfect moment had he not caught sight of all her notes on the floor, reminding him of the bad news he had to break to her. Should he tell her after the party and end the night on a sad note or tell her now and hope the party could make up for it? He could also wait until she finds out at work tomorrow. After a moment's consideration, the answer was clear to Caleb. "Nova, I have something to tell you."

"Hmm?"

Her light, nonchalant tone made him hesitate, but Caleb took a breath and spilled it out, anyway. "The publishing house retracted their offer for Edge of Darkness."

"Oh." The dismay in her tone was unmistakable.

"I got the call just as I was picking up the cake from the store."

"Did they say why?"

Caleb shrugged. "The only reason they gave was they're heading for a different direction with their fiction. They say they love the novel and believe in its potential, which is why they offered the book deal in the first place, but a shift in focus within the company makes it impossible for them to sign you on right now."

Nova lifted her head from his shoulder. "That's disappointing."

"I'm sorry, Nova. It was a good deal, and I know how much you wanted this."

"Nothing to be sorry about." Nova heaved a sigh. "Don't be too hard on yourself, Caleb."

"I'm not."

She raised a brow at him, a smirk forming on her face.

"Okay. A little." He rolled his eyes. "But only because I hate disappointing you."

Nova let go of his hand and cupped his face between her palms. That dimpled smile of hers was his undoing. "I know you, Caleb Grant. You are someone who is single-minded in purpose, and I have no doubt if you decide to get me a book deal, you'll exhaust all options to make sure I get one. I believe in you. With all my heart, I believe I have the best agent in the world, and nothing you say can convince me otherwise. And I'm not just saying that because we're dating. I honestly thank God for you every day, and I trust that if this book deal fell through, it's because He has greater plans. Whatever those plans are, you'll find a way to follow it."

With every word from her lips, Caleb's heart swelled. He squared his shoulders and chuckled over the way twirls of her messy mass of hair framed her face. He tucked some of it behind her ear to get a better view of her glistening brown eyes and sweet smile. How could she receive the kind of news he had given her and recover in a heartbeat? Was it all the years of disappointment that had formed this resilience in her? Or was it her trust in their Savior?

"You're unbelievable," he said, and out of the abundance of his heart, his mouth spoke, "I love you, Nova."

Her lips parted to draw in a short intake of breath.

Caleb caught his breath. It was the first time he had ever said those three words to her. "Nova…"

Her gaze softened, and her smile returned. "I love you too, Caleb."

Caleb brushed his thumb over her cheekbone. "I'll get you that book deal."

"No doubt here." Nova lifted her hands and rested them on the back of his neck.

All of Caleb desired to kiss her, but he summoned his self-control to keep himself from doing so. After all, they were in her bedroom, and that alone put them both in a compromising situation. Instead, he brushed a thumb over her lips, hoping to let her know how much he wanted to kiss her.

Nova laughed. "Someday soon."

He smiled. "Not until we get a book deal."

Her brows lifted in surprise as she threw her head back. "We better get one soon then."

"Oh, we will." Caleb nodded, grabbed hold of her wrist, stood up, and tugged on her to follow him. "Come on. All the guests are probably downstairs already."

"Yeah." She rose from the bed and gave him a quick peck on the cheek before rushing ahead of him to pull him out of the room. "Let's get out of here before we do something we regret."

As Nova skipped out of her bedroom and Caleb trailed behind her, his knee almost buckled beneath him, because the realization hit Caleb full force. This was a different Nova in front of him. She was no longer this timid young woman, running away from the world. The woman before him was no longer afraid to be seen, and Caleb could only thank God for allowing her to literally leap into his life.

Once, when he was young, his father had sat him and his brothers down to tell them how to treat their sister right. Marcus Grant had told them women were stronger than men in ways they would someday fully appreciate. For the first time, Caleb understood what his father had said back then, because he saw in Nova a strength he didn't have. Everything she had been through had developed a resilience in Nova's heart, soul, and spirit, and that was beautiful to Caleb — beautiful enough for him to be more earnest in praying to God for the right time to ask her to spend a lifetime with him.

Twenty-three

THE ONE
WHO GOT
A DEAL

The white catsuit hugged the contours of Nova's body like a glove. Vienna cinched the silver utility belt around her waist before Nova picked up her studded silver mask from the edge of the granite tiled sink. She laid the mask over the bridge of her nose. Behind her, Vienna fumbled with Nova's curls to tie up the string holding the mask in place. Once finished, Vienna grabbed the royal blue cape from Nova's duffel bag on the ground and laid it on Nova's shoulders. Nova pulled its strings forward and tied it up right above the middle of her collarbones to keep the cape in place.

Nova spun around to face her friend. She tugged on her outfit to secure its place along the contours of her body, the pure white lycra clinging to her skin. "The last time I wore this outfit, I was mortified." Her heartbeat's pace increased. "It feels more comfortable now."

"Maybe because you're a lot more comfortable in your own skin than you were before." Vienna shrugged. "Can't understand why you'd be anything but confident in this outfit when you look absolutely gorgeous in it. Caleb will fall in love with you all over again."

Nova turned to her side to peruse her reflection in the full-length mirror of the ladies' bathroom on their floor of Frontier Press. She smiled at her appearance. "Everything beautiful in its time," she whispered.

"What?" Vienna asked.

"God makes everything beautiful in its time," Nova said.

Vienna wrinkled her nose. "Hmm?"

"I can't believe there was a point in my life when all I could think about was exacting revenge on all who did me wrong, and now, I recognize the beauty in all of it."

"That's great." Vienna leaned forward against the sink, facing the mirror, and retrieved lipstick from her purse. "You never struck me as the vengeful type, though. I see it more in the characters you create. Dr. Edge, especially."

Nova sighed. "Dr. Edge was born from a season of pain and anger, a time when I blamed God for all the hurt in my heart."

"Thought you said you based Dr. Edge on Caleb." Vienna dabbed her lipstick on.

Nova laughed. "And Caleb strikes you as the vengeful type?"

"Good point." She smacked her lips.

"Caleb represented the noble parts of Dr. Edge, his redeeming qualities."

"I love that your muse for your stories eventually ended up as not only your agent but your boyfriend!" Vienna shook her head and let out a long sigh as her shoulders sagged. "God definitely seems to like both of you."

Nova's ears perked up at the mention of God. Vienna often listened to her talk about God, but it was the first time she had heard her friend reference her faith. "Pretty sure He likes you too, Vienna."

The lovely brunette placed her lipstick back in her purse. "Don't know about that, but I do know it's an injustice that God still hasn't made a way for you to get a book deal. Publishers are crazy for not getting in on this."

Nova couldn't deny the weight Vienna's words threw at her heart. She tightened her jaw. Caleb had been working so hard to get her a deal, even as he motivated her to finish the succeeding books in Dr. Edge's story. She was almost done with book three, and Caleb still hadn't secured a publisher for her. "Caleb hasn't said anything, but I know he's beating himself up over this."

"Well, he did promise you he would get a deal."

"To be fair to him, he almost did. Several times. Not his fault something always happens to cause the deals to fall through."

Vienna faced Nova and tugged at the ends of a few strands of her hair. "So, where's God in all that?" She said the words in a soft voice as if she was asking for herself, and not for Nova's situation. "Isn't God supposed to be some sort of Father Who likes to bless His children?"

Nova reached out for her friend's hand and squeezed. "He is. Sometimes, His blessings look nothing like we think they should. There's a story in the Bible where this guy, Joseph, was betrayed by his own flesh and blood. They sold him to slavery, where he suffered injustice after injustice, but he endured and overcame. God elevated his status and put him in a position where he could've paid his family evil for evil, but he didn't. He forgave them, because he recognized God's hand in everything he had gone through. Something good will come out of all this, Vienna. You'll see."

Vienna stared at her for a few seconds as she processed what had just been said. "We'll see." She shrugged and flicked her brows up and down. "So, you still haven't told us the plan. Why exactly are you in costume? I mean, sure. It's yours and Caleb's birthday celebration. Is there a specific reason you're dressed as Agent Snow?"

Nova lifted one shoulder. "I wanted to surprise him, to remind him of how we met and how, with or without a book deal, God brought us together through books and stories. Hopefully, Caleb will see how beautiful our story has been, is, and will be."

"Well, sure then." Vienna linked arms with her. "What a blessed man Caleb Grant is."

Someone knocked on the door.

"Are you ladies still in there?" Miles's voice boomed from the other side. "Molly messaged me already. Their meeting is almost over. Caleb will return to his office soon. Also, I can't keep carrying this balloon around."

Nova and Vienna exchanged glances and giggles.

"Let's go before Miles starts pounding on the door." Nova grabbed the duffel bag from the floor before they both marched forward and swung the door open.

"Nova baby," Miles said, "what a blast from the past. Super Nova is back."

Nova rolled her eyes. "Don't call me that, Miles." She took the balloon from him before handing him the duffel bag. "To my cubicle, please?" She then squirmed. "What do you think? Do I look okay?"

"Brilliant." Miles nodded. "Like a character who jumped out of your books. Speaking of which, when will I get my hands on book three?"

"When it's done." Nova smiled.

Miles let out a sigh of relief. "So, you're still writing it! Scared me when that last publisher fell through. Thought you might have stopped writing, which would be awful, because the story can't end that way."

Vienna elbowed him.

"What? Don't tell me you're satisfied to have it end with book two. That was a cruel cliffhanger."

"Of course I want another book, but you know—" Vienna nudged Nova forward "—she has to go encourage her agent-slash-boyfriend. He's taking all these rejections harder than she is."

"What a blessed man Caleb Grant is."

"That's what I said!" Vienna exclaimed.

Nova chuckled. "I'll leave you two to yourselves. I'm going to his office."

"We'll be waiting for the cake!" Miles yelled.

Nova rushed ahead, leaving her friends behind. When the elevator took forever to get to her floor, she took two flights of stairs up to his office, hoping to get there before him.

"Nova!" His assistant, Molly, greeted her with a big smile. "He's still not back from the meeting. It's been going on all morning, but he should be back in time for lunch."

Nova breathed a sigh of relief. "That's perfect." She was about to turn on her heel to get to Caleb's office.

"I never understood what's with the balloons." Molly pointed at the balloon in Nova's hand.

Nova looked up at the red helium balloon. She grinned. "It was Miles's idea. Something about superheroes being able to fly. He thought it might help agents remember me."

"Sure helped one agent remember you." Molly grinned.

Before Nova could respond, a glimpse of blond hair caught her eye.

"Nova!"

She winced. Caleb. Too late to hide in his office. She turned to her side. "Sur—"

"You stunning gazelle!"

Nova gasped when Caleb wrapped his arms around her waist, swooped her up, and spun her around. She laid her palms against his shoulders to keep herself steady. Laughter bubbled from her stomach as she tried to make sense of his exuberance.

"What's going on?" she asked. "Did you just call me a gazelle?"

Finally, Caleb set her down on the floor and cupped her face between his palms. "We did it, Nova!"

"Did what?"

His eyes cleared and, as if for the first time, Caleb noticed what she was wearing. "Nova, you—" He drew a breath. "Why are you wearing this?" He looked at the balloon. "What's going on?"

"Surprise!" Nova threw her arms in the air before dropping it to her side. She frowned. "You don't like it?"

"Are you joking? Nova, I love it. You're magnificent." He stepped back to get a better view of her before shaking his head. "This is mind-blowing, you have no idea."

Nova's pulse raced. Breathless, she pried him to tell her the reason for his joy. "Caleb, what happened?"

Strong hands took hold of hers. The handsome smile on his face reminded her of all the reasons she loved him. The anticipation grew within her as he led her inside his office. He left the door half-closed. Once they were hidden from prying eyes, he brushed his thumb along the line of her jaw before tucking her hair behind her ear.

"Let me see you," he said.

Those four words were thunder in her chest and a hurricane in her brain. What was Caleb saying? Did he not see her?

Caleb smirked and tapped his forefinger on the mask covering half her face. "Let me see you, Nova."

"Oh." Nova reached behind her head and under her hair to untie the string holding her mask in place.

Caleb took it from her and dropped it on the floor. He laid one hand on her waist and another on the side of her neck. He then pressed his lips to hers.

At first, his kiss was a storm of sensation within her, something so unexpected she couldn't have prepared for it. But, as his lips kneaded against hers, gentle and sweet, somehow, the passion turned into peace. Nova eased into his arms, seen, safe, and protected. The tension left her body as she responded to him, riding the winds and waves of sensation with him, following his lead, until he finally pulled away from her with a gasp.

Caleb backed a step away from her. He swallowed hard, his eyes fixed on her lips. His ragged breathing and pained gaze made him appear wounded. As if making an internal decision, he bobbed his head in one curt nod, squared his shoulders, and clenched his fist. A picture of determination as he backed another step away from her.

Nova brushed her fingers against her lips as her mind raced to figure out what had just happened. She gripped the edge of his desk to steady herself. Finally, her senses caught up with her. "Does that mean—"

Caleb nodded. "We have a book deal, Nova."

The sense of elation that swept over her was unlike anything she had ever experienced. Her mouth scrambled to speak out the questions rushing through her mind. "What? How? With whom?"

"Let's sit down before I do something I'll regret." Caleb pulled up a seat, gulped as he glanced at her lips, and made his way behind his desk.

Nova smiled as she made herself comfortable in the cushioned chair across the desk from him. The distance between them made her ache for his touch, but it was better this way. "So? Tell me all about it."

Caleb grinned. "Ethan Caine finally read your novel."

He proceeded to tell her all about a new imprint and a promising publishing deal, but Nova kept getting distracted by an inner conversation she was having with God. Mixed with all the gratitude and praise she was lifting to the Almighty was one question unveiling her longing: *Lord, when is this man going to marry me?*

twenty-four

THE ONE WHO (FINALLY) PROPOSED

After the Sunday service, the Grant household's backyard garden was brimming with church people who had come to celebrate not only Caleb and Nova's joint birthday party but also the upcoming launch of Nova's debut novel.

Edge of Darkness was the first book in the superhero saga of Dr. Edge, and the buzz surrounding the novel had far exceeded their expectations. As the first major book release of *Galactic*, the brand new speculative fiction imprint of Frontier Press, the pressure for Nova's novel to deliver stellar results had been immense. But on that day, the pressure had rolled off Caleb's shoulders. Under Ethan Caine's direct supervision, they had spent an entire year preparing Nova's books for the world to see. Through the whirlwind of it all, Caleb had prepared for this day and for the future he longed to spend with Nova.

Caleb stood behind the glass doors leading to the backyard. He found something deeply satisfying about seeing Nova hug his ex-girlfriend, Olivia. They chatted like they were old friends. The image was, to Caleb, a reminder of God's plan trumping his own.

The idea of being with anyone other than Nova was unfathomable to him. He reached inside his pocket and ran his thumb along the velvet box inside.

Before a proposal, however, an unexpected reckoning.

Someone cleared his throat behind him to get his attention. Caleb spun around. Pastor Sam nodded at him. Caleb nodded back before following his pastor through the entryway and outside into the front yard. Across their steel gate, Knox Cartier stood, leaning against a motorcycle.

Despite their pastor's assurances that Knox was a changed man, Caleb still bristled in Knox's presence, so he stopped in the middle of the front yard and gritted his teeth. Knox couldn't even look him in the eye.

Pastor Sam laid a hand on Caleb's shoulder. "He just wants to have a word with you, Caleb."

Despite the assurance, Caleb clenched his jaw and steeled himself for confrontation before opening the gate and facing Knox, who immediately extended his hand toward Caleb. It took a moment before Caleb got himself to shake the man's hand.

"What can I do for you, Mr. Cartier?" Caleb asked.

"Please." Knox shuffled on his feet as he rubbed the dark stubble on his jaw. "Call me Knox."

"Sure. Knox." What did this man want? Didn't he promise Nova she would never hear from him again?

"Thank you for agreeing to speak with me."

God, where is this going? Caleb sighed. *Help me see this man beyond what he had done to Nova.*

Through Caleb's silence, Knox looked past him toward Pastor Sam before lowering his gaze, his stare fixed on the ground. "I understand this visit is unexpected and uncalled for," Knox said, "but after being released from jail, I traveled the world for the past two years. I kept in touch with Pastor Sam and also made sure to find a community of believers wherever I went. Two weeks ago, I came back to spend time with my mother. Mama Aida has been reaching out to her while I was away, and—" Delight sparked in Knox's eyes, but he quickly reeled back his excitement. "Anyway, I digress. I've been meeting with Pastor Sam since I got back, and we've been discussing the possibility of me attending church at Connect. After all, he is my spiritual father. Pastor Sam and I wanted to make sure you and Nova would be okay with that. Whatever you decide, I will respect it. I was just hoping there could be a way for me to attend this church without causing you or Nova any trouble."

Caleb raced to process everything Knox had said. While his spirit rejoiced at the knowledge of this man's salvation, his soul still raged against Knox. He knew what the right thing to do was, but he still couldn't stand the idea of Knox being anywhere near Nova.

"I know this is abrupt." Knox looked at their house. "You seem to have an event going on, and I—"

"I'm about to ask her to marry me." Caleb stood to his full height, prepared to handle whatever Knox's reaction would be.

Knox didn't even flinch at the news. A smile spread across his face as he nodded. "That's amazing, man. Nova deserves the best, and you've always been the kind of man she has always dreamed of. Someone good. Someone who will treat her right. Congratulations to you both. I mean that."

Caleb narrowed his eyes at Knox, not sure what to make of him. His brain was screaming for him to make Knox go away, but a tug within him was compelling him to give this man a second chance. It's what Jesus would've done — what He had already done at the cross.

Caleb took a deep breath and made a decision about what to do with the man in front of him. As he walked back into the house, Caleb prayed to God he hadn't made a mistake, because if he had, Nova might have second thoughts about saying yes to marry him.

The last person Nova would expect to see in the Grants' backyard was Knox Cartier, and yet, there he was beside Pastor Sam, like a ghost from her past coming to haunt her. Their gazes locked for one second, but Knox immediately looked away and hugged Mama Aida, who welcomed him. Why was he here?

Despite the forgiveness she had already released to him, a tremble still traveled across Nova's body as Pastor Sam introduced Knox to people she loved and cared about.

"Nova, what is he doing here?" Ma held Nova's elbow.

Nova shrugged. "I don't know, Ma."

"Where's Caleb?"

"He went inside a while ago. He said he'd be back soon." Nova pried her eyes away from Knox and faced her mother. "I'll go inside and check on him." She hesitated. Knox was still standing beside Pastor Sam, too close to the backyard entrance. To her relief, a figure appeared behind the glass doors separating the house and the backyard. The door slid open and out came...

"Nolan!" Ma gasped. Delight sparked in her eyes, pride evident in her tone. "He's here!"

Nolan stepped into the backyard, with a guitar case slung over his shoulder and Serene trailing behind him. At the sight of Knox, his countenance darkened. Upon seeing him, Pastor Sam and Mama Aida immediately walked past Knox to welcome the couple. Their pastor said something to Nolan and Serene. Nolan cast a glance at Knox. He nodded at Pastor Sam before taking his guitar out of its case.

Nova pressed her palms against her dress. "What is going on?" Her phone vibrated inside the small leather purse hanging on her shoulder. She fished it out and found a message from Caleb.

Caleb: I let Knox in. Pastor Sam is vouching for him. Trust me, okay? He won't go anywhere near you.

Nova gripped the phone between her hands and shut her eyes as she calmed her nerves. Why would Caleb do this? *God, help me. You are my refuge.* A soft breeze caressed her skin, and somehow, with it, came a supernatural assurance as she reminded herself of all the healing God had already done in her life since she had last seen Knox. Her heart softened for her former friend. *God, heal him as You have healed me.* Nova opened her eyes and smiled.

"Are you okay, iha?" Ma ran her palm up and down Nova's spine. "We should ask somebody to get him to leave."

"No, Ma." Nova took her mother's hand and squeezed. "He's with Pastor Sam. They wouldn't let him come here if he's still dangerous."

Ma didn't seem convinced.

"Caleb texted me just to assure me Knox won't try anything."

"Where is Caleb?"

"Good question." She texted him.

Nova: Where are you?

Before she could get a response from him, Nolan suddenly clapped his hands together. "If I can get everyone's attention, please! I am Nolan Stone and this is Serene Sinclair. You all know us as *Red & Ice,* and we would like to wish my beautiful and talented sister a happy birthday and congratulations on her book release!"

Everyone clapped their hands as they all drew closer to Nolan, who was now strumming on his guitar. Nova scoped the crowd to find her boyfriend, but Caleb was still nowhere to be found. Ma squashed her idea of going in the house to search for him when she pulled Nova into the middle of the gathering crowd.

Nolan grinned at her. "This is a song entitled, *Supernova*, which I dedicate to you."

Nova pressed a palm against her chest to express her appreciation.

Her brother winked at her and scanned the crowd. "Everyone ready?!"

Several hoots and cheers of agreement echoed from their guests.

Nolan and Serene sang the first line in perfect harmony.

Clothed in white, gliding in the skies.

Pastor Sam and Mama Aida sang the second line with them.

An entire universe hidden behind her eyes.

With each line, others started joining in, and all Nova could do was drop her jaw and laugh at what was happening, even as she kept wishing Caleb could be there. After all, it was his birthday celebration too!

By the time they hit the chorus, everyone was already singing this song Nova had never even heard of before.

Waiting for the heavens to open,
so I can see her burst of light.
Lost in a galaxy of mystery,
dreaming of stars each night.
I never expected a Supernova
to completely change my life.
So I'm praying she will say yes
when I ask her to become my wife.

Nova's smile faded when they all sang out that last line. What? That didn't make any sense. A hush followed. Heat rose to Nova's cheeks when she realized all eyes were on her. Nolan was grinning at her as he stopped playing the guitar, and the gathered crowd parted to make way for Caleb to walk past them.

Nova's mouth hung open at the sight of him. He approached her in a black bodysuit with a white stripe running from his left shoulder to his left leg. Dark blue boots covered his feet and a black plastic mask with blue lining covered the upper half of his face. In his right hand was a red helium balloon. Over his right chest was a blue helix — Dr. Edge's symbol.

Like a character who jumped out of her books, as Miles would say. Her imagination coming to life.

Nolan started playing his guitar again as Caleb approached Nova. Caleb sang the lines of the chorus. Nova giggled, because even if she didn't know the song, he still sounded out of tune to her. Good thing Nolan knew how to transpose to whatever key Caleb had just invented.

The love of her life stepped right in front of her as he spoke out instead of singing the last two lines. "I never expected a Supernova to completely change my life, so I'm praying she will say yes when I ask her to become my wife."

He lifted his palm and revealed a black velvet box tied up by the string of the balloon hovering over them. Caleb untied the string and released the balloon into the air before opening the box to reveal a diamond ring.

Caleb knelt on the ground and lifted the box in the air. "Make my dreams come true, Super Nova. Marry me."

Choked up and overwhelmed with gratitude, despite all the people surrounding her, Nova had eyes only for Caleb. He was God's answer to her prayers. To this man whom God used to coax her out of her hiding, restore her wonder, and heal her heart, the only answer Nova could give was, "Yes!"

twenty-five

THE ONE
WHO VOWED TO
LOVE & PROTECT

A rustic and whimsical aesthetic transformed the woodsy setting into a scene right out of a fairy tale. Lanterns lined the aisle in the middle of the wedding chairs, seating their family and friends. Countless decorative lights strung around bushes or hung in the nearby trees, illuminating the generous space. The backdrop of the sunset behind them gave the cozy and casual wedding a more intimate atmosphere, reminiscent of home and family. Balloons of different metallic colors covered the long aisle separating Caleb from the floral arch where, any minute now, Nova would walk through.

The pianist played Nova's favorite love song right after the last of the flower girls finished her walk down the aisle. The sweet acoustic harmony might as well have had the intensity of a full orchestra by the way Caleb's heart drummed against his chest as he awaited the arrival of his bride.

Caleb's breath hitched at the first glimpse of Nova walking toward the arch, with Nolan by her side. Once, in a busy park, Caleb first noticed Nova as a vision in white, dressed as a superhero running from him. Now, she was still a vision in white in a stunning lace dress, holding a bouquet of royal blue tulips. Not only was Nova no longer running from him, she was coming to him.

A fierce sense of loyalty, commitment, and love swept over Caleb as Nova marched her way down the aisle toward him. Mesmerized, Caleb couldn't have prepared himself for what was next, though he probably should have predicted it based on how full of surprises his bride could be.

A quarter of the way down the aisle, Nova and Nolan stopped walking.

Caleb threw his head back in surprise. What were they up to?

Nova winked at him before throwing her bouquet over to her maid-of-honor, Hannah. Nolan bent forward and clasped his hands together, palms up, his arms forming a U. Nova lifted the skirt of her wedding gown to reveal white sneakers beneath it. She stepped on her brother's palms and used it to propel herself toward a nearby empty chair. Her one foot hit the back of the chair and then the chair in front of it before she landed her foot on its seat and leaped forward to stand in front of Caleb.

"Sweet and spicy parkour," Caleb whispered beneath his breath before he laughed at her. "What was that?"

"Like a gazelle, right?" Nova smiled at him.

His smile widened. "Beautiful."

Caleb offered his hand to Nova and led her to the altar. There, he vowed to love her and protect her from this day forward until death do they part, and this time, it felt like everything he was doing had all been going according to God's perfect plan.

- TWO MONTHS LATER; NOVA, 26 -

The ocean kissed the brilliant powder white sand before pulling away, shy but steady and strong. A soft breeze cooled Nova's skin as she fanned her face with an *abaniko*, the hand fan she had bought at the market the day before. The hot, tropical afternoon sun blazed against her as she rushed to get back to the resort hotel.

What were the words she wanted to say to Caleb again? She had asked for the translation from the hotel receptionist before strolling along the beach, hoping to take advantage of an overcast sky earlier hiding the sun. Nova enunciated the Filipino words: "*Boon-tees ah-koh. Buntis ako.*" She shrugged. Sounded right to her. Caleb wouldn't even know if she was pronouncing it correctly.

Nova hurried her steps, the sand beneath her feet still getting between her toes and all over her flip-flops. She was about to turn a corner to get back to the hotel when a sight stopped her in her tracks.

A mother and her son were walking along the beach, hands clasped together. The boy skipped on the water, his bare feet causing splashes that got his mother's dress wet. The woman only laughed in response.

Nostalgia swept over Nova as she choked back the tears when memories of Nate rushed over her. Even after spending her entire honeymoon with Caleb in the Philippines, she still sometimes pinched herself to convince herself it was all real. She was walking in the country where Nate had grown up not knowing anything about their father, who had gotten Ma pregnant while he was here on military service. It had been four years later that he had returned on vacation to discover his son's existence. Nova stared at the boy and his mother. Was that what Ma and Nate were like long ago? Had they ever taken strolls along the beach? What would have happened if Dad had just left them alone and not taken them back to America with him?

Nova laid a hand on her stomach. It was best for her to think of the future and not the past.

"Here you are."

Nova turned to find her husband walking toward her.

"I woke up from my nap, and my wife was gone," he said.

"Oh no." She grinned. "Have you found her yet?"

"Right where I expected her to be. Out here, soaking in all the beauty around her." Caleb held her by the waist and pecked her on the lips. "Where have you been?"

"I wanted to take a walk while it was still overcast, but the sun is out now, so I was rushing back, but—" She sighed and pointed at the strangers she had been watching.

Caleb followed the direction of her gaze. He creased his brows. "I don't get it. You were watching the kid and his mother?"

Nova shrugged. "They caught my attention."

Caleb nodded. "It's a sign."

"A sign of what?"

"We should get back to the hotel, so we can make a mother out of you." He flicked his brows at her.

Nova rolled her eyes. "Are you ready to be a father?"

Caleb swung his head to the side. "Come on. You know I am."

"All according to plan, huh?"

"God's plan, not mine."

"How are you so confident?"

"I just know."

"Fine then." Nova huffed. "*Buntis ako.*"

"Huh?"

Nova laughed, held his hand, and tugged him toward the hotel. "You can ask the receptionist what it means. Let's get out of the sun."

Caleb didn't budge, so his grip on her hand made her bounce back to him. "Nova, you just said you're pregnant."

"Wait. What? You understood me?"

Caleb shrugged. "We've been here for weeks. I've been reading up on the language. Am I right?"

"We should see a doctor to make sure, but you'll be a father soon, Caleb."

It took a second for it to register, and when it did, Nova would have paid everything she had to capture that moment, so she could relive it over and over again just to see the delight on his face.

Held in his arms, cherished and protected, Nova had no doubt Caleb would make a good father to their children someday. They would never have to experience what she and her brothers had gone through growing up.

Seven months later, Nate and Claudia Grant were born. As Nova held their son in her hands and Caleb held their daughter, Nova remembered the prayer she had often prayed as a little girl. She had constantly longed for a complete and happy family.

After all these years, God answered her prayer.

THE END

author's note

Thank you for reading **The One Who Wrote Away**!

I wrote this story during a period of longing, of vulnerability, as a single woman. Though my upbringing couldn't have been any more different than Nova's, I related so much to her fears and questions regarding marriage and regarding the male influences in her life.

While writing this, I was going through a period of asking God about the ways He designed men and women and how we are to interact in a Godly way in such a broken world.

My own personal romance is yet to be written — as is my life story — but I feel like a lot of it is already reflected in this story.

It is my prayer that you discover a few answers within these pages regarding issues on how God created men and women. If you were unable to find answers, maybe it will at least lead you to ask God the right questions.

May you always be blessed!

-JOANNA-

Caleb Grant - main male protagonist
Nova Stone - main female protagonist

EMPLOYEES AT FRONTIER PRESS
Ethan Caine - CEO, Caine Corp; Caleb's boss
Molly Reed - Caleb's assistant
Vienna Boulevard - Nova's friend and co-worker
Miles Bailey - Nova's friend and co-worker
Steve Chen - Nova's boss

CALEB'S FAMILY
Marcus Grant - Caleb's father
Naomi Grant - Caleb's mother
Isaac Grant - Caleb's older brother
Kelly Grant - Caleb's sister-in-law; Isaac's wife
Joshua Grant - Caleb's twin
Hannah Grant - Caleb's younger sister
Samuel & Deborah Grant - twins; Caleb's younger siblings
Kenneth Grant - Caleb's nephew; Isaac & Kelly's son
Jael Grant - Caleb's niece; Isaac & Kelly's daughter

NOVA'S FAMILY
Damien Stone - Nova's father
Clara Stone - Nova's mother
Nate Stone - Nova's older brother
Nolan Stone - Nova's younger brother

OTHERS
Olivia Meyer - Caleb's ex-girlfriend
Knox Cartier - Nova's high school best friend
Serene Sinclair - Nolan's childhood best friend and current girlfriend
Jeremy Sinclair - Serene's younger brother
Samuel Sinclair- Pastor at Connect Church; Serene & Jeremy's father
Aida Sinclair - Samuel's wife; Serene & Jeremy's mother
Max Owens - Jeremy's best friend
Gable - Nova's stuffed bunny
Rhoda Petersen - Lady at Connect Church; Remember her.
Rachel Petersen - Rhoda's daughter; Sigh.

THE PRODIGAL ONES COLLECTION

THE ONE
WHO WROTE
THIS BOOK

Joanna Alonzo is an author of Christian fiction novels with grit, grace, and wonder. She has a Bachelor's Degree in Information Technology from St. Louis University, but her creative leanings drew her away from software development to a career in faith and uncertainty. Her homebase is La Trinidad Valley in the Philippines, but she wanders around too much to have a permanent residence. She is a fascinated apprentice to the Greatest Storyteller of all and loves to highlight His supernatural grace in her stories. She loves having coffee chats with people, but isn't a fan of them hugging her too much.